B. G.

PLAYING BY HEART

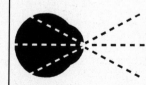

This Large Print Book carries the
Seal of Approval of N.A.V.H.

PLAYING BY HEART

ANNE MATEER

THORNDIKE PRESS
A part of Gale, Cengage Learning

GALE
CENGAGE Learning·

Farmington Hills, Mich • San Francisco • New York • Waterville, Maine
Meriden, Conn • Mason, Ohio • Chicago

GALE
CENGAGE Learning·

LIBRARY OF CONGRESS CATALOGING-IN-PUBLICATION DATA

Mateer, Anne.
    Playing by heart / by Anne Mateer. — Large print edition.
        pages ; cm. — (Thorndike Press large print Christian historical fiction)
    ISBN 978-1-4104-7635-7 (hardcover) — ISBN 1-4104-7635-9 (hardcover)
    1. Large type books. I. Title.
PS3613.A824P57 2015
813'.6—dc23   2014043989

Published in 2015 by arrangement with Bethany House Publishers, a division of Baker Publishing Group

Printed in Mexico
1 2 3 4 5 6 7 19 18 17 16 15

To all the teachers in our family:

Grandmother Palmer, Mom,
Dad, Debra, Dawn, Kris,
and our future coach, Aaron

And to my amazing pianist, Nathan

I stand in awe of the gift
God has given you.

1

Lula

"Mr. —" I glanced down at my seating chart, heart drumming in my ears. My third week in front of a college classroom filled with male students. Three weeks of looking past their disdain. Three weeks holding my ground by sheer force of will.

I could do this. For myself. For my father.

"Mr. Graham, could you please tell us about the concept of linear combination?"

Mr. Graham stretched out his legs and glanced at his classmates on either side. His lips twisted into a smirk as he twirled his pencil through his fingers. "I could explain it, but are you certain *you* grasp its complexities?"

I sucked in a breath, my back snapping as straight as a loblolly pine, my cheeks stinging hot. Not a new slur, to be sure, but no student had yet dared be insolent to my face.

The air in the classroom stilled, anticipation hanging as heavy as a chartreuse sky over the Oklahoma plains in springtime. My body tensed, waiting to see if others would add their opinions. I didn't know how to answer. I'd worked hard to get to this place, harder than I'd ever worked in my life. I couldn't crumble now.

I pressed a hand to my churning stomach. The committee had chosen me, Miss Lula Bowman, as the recipient of the Donally Mathematics Award. I received tuition to pursue my graduate degree as well as a stipend for teaching a first-year mathematics course. I'd weathered stronger gales than Mr. Graham to reach this place.

Arching my eyebrows, I tried to peer down my nose at the boy-man, wishing I had a pair of spectacles to complete the look. "I'm perfectly capable of understanding it, thank you. Let's hope you have the same capacity."

Mr. Graham's disdain didn't slacken. Instead, his mouth curved into a slow smile as his eyes raked down the length of me. "You aren't so bad looking, Miss Bowman. Couldn't you find a man that would have you?"

My lungs expanded as far as my corset would allow, hands fisting and loosening with each angry breath. I pulled up to my full height — wishing it were more than five feet two inches — and tipped my chin toward the ceiling, hoping to add a bit more stature. "I don't know why you are attending college, Mr. Graham, but I assume the others are here to learn. If you impede that process, I will take up your behavior with the dean. Are we clear?"

But even as the words left my mouth, I trembled, knowing I had no real recourse. To admit I couldn't manage the class would be the same as admitting failure. No, I had to handle Mr. Graham on my own, using the same granite resolve I had with my older brothers and sisters when they'd insisted college was a waste of time and money.

"I will thank you to respect my position as a scholar even if you can't reconcile it with my gender, Mr. Graham. Women are capable of more accomplishments than a pretty song on the piano or a tasty meal to fill your belly. You'd do well to remember that."

The pine table, littered with scribbled pages and mathematics journals, wavered. The pencil dropped from my fingers, rolled off the edge, and clattered to the floor. I rubbed my eyes and sucked in the still, hot air of an

Indian summer, temperatures far too warm for the last week of September. I reached for a book and fanned it in front of my face as I considered once more my latest calculations, the ones that refused to be solved.

A line of moisture rolled down the back of my neck, plastering an escaped strand of hair to my skin. I set it free, then blew out a long breath, attempting to make my own bit of breeze.

I groaned into the silence, replaying my altercation with Mr. Graham earlier in the day. He'd been quiet during the rest of the class, but I suspected he'd continue to be trouble, and he knew I knew it.

My elbows thumped to the table. I cradled my head in my hands and stared again at the equation that mocked me while voices buzzed through the hallway. A door closed in the distance. The clacking of shoes against the wooden floor grew louder. I sat up straight. The door opened.

Professor Clayton's white head appeared first, and then the rest of the rumpled man emerged. The corners of my mouth pulled upward in amusement. Ever since Mrs. Clayton's passing two years ago, the professor didn't seem to notice the niceties of life, only the unflinching surety of numbers.

"Ah, Miss Bowman. I'd hoped to find you

here." He switched a clutch of papers from one arm to the other as he surveyed the jumble of materials in front of me. I reached across the table and cleared a corner. He let his burden slap to the surface, then riffled through the top few pages until he pulled one free from the stack. His deep blue eyes brightened. "And how is the first female recipient of the Donally Mathematics Award faring this day?"

The male students of our college don't think a female intellect suitable to the rigors of mathematics. But I couldn't tell Professor Clayton that.

"Quite well, thank you, sir."

One white eyebrow quirked. "I've heard something to the contrary, my dear." He waited a moment. I didn't confirm or deny it. Only held his gaze until he sighed. "But then I knew I could count on you to prove the Donally committee wasn't mistaken in their choice."

"Yes, sir," I whispered, staring at the table, at the page with the unfinished equation. After six years of alternating work and college classes, I could finally do both at the same time, in the same place, thanks to the award. I refused to let swaggering young men of eighteen or nineteen ruin all I'd earned.

Professor Clayton peered at the paper in front of me. "Trouble with that one?"

I nodded, shame spreading heat into my cheeks.

"Work the problem again, Miss Bowman. You almost have the correct answer." He crossed the room to his desk.

I twisted in my chair. "But how can I fix it when I can't figure out where I've gone wrong?"

He blinked at me as if I'd asked him a question about the latest fashions, not mathematics. I started to repeat myself, but his hand rose to stop my words. "When all else fails, start again at the beginning." He returned to shuffling papers.

I stared at the page, at the scrawled numbers that refused to cooperate. Could Mr. Graham be right? What if I didn't have it in me to understand?

No. If I gave in, if I quit, I'd prove my daddy's belief in me wrong. And prove the naysayers right. The ones who said "Fruity Lu" Bowman would never amount to more than a flibbertigibbet, a pretty little hummingbird who could never alight on one thing for more than a moment.

My jaw tightened. I would not return to that reputation. Ever. I would finish what I'd started, no matter how difficult the task.

Picking up my pencil from the floor, I flipped the paper over and copied the equation once more. Daddy and Professor Clayton believed in my ability to succeed in academia, so I did, too.

A grueling twenty minutes later, I handed my page to Professor Clayton. He grinned, set it aside.

Outwardly, I stood unfazed, fingers loosely clasped, but inside I rejoiced.

"Go on with you now," Professor Clayton said gently, jerking his head toward the door. "We've both plenty to do again tomorrow."

I glanced at the clock on the wall. Nearly five. Mrs. McInnish would scold if I came late to the supper table once more this week. I gathered a mathematics journal with my textbooks before darting to the door. Then I stopped. Turned. Professor Clayton's head bent low, drawing his neat script closer to his aging eyes. I scurried back and planted a kiss on his cheek.

He looked up, eyes wide with surprise, then returned to his work. Out on the dusty street, I no longer noticed the oppressive heat. Professor Clayton's approval had turned the world as fresh and new as spring.

"Miss Bowman? That you?" The lilt of a

Scottish accent carried through the screen door as I raced up the steps.

"It is, Mrs. McInnish. I'll wash up and be right there!" I swooped up the stairs to my room, tossed my books on the bed, and splashed warm water over my face and neck before straightening the collar of my plain shirtwaist. The looking glass revealed a messy topknot, but I had no time to set my hair to rights. Back down the stairs I ran. I slid into my chair at the dining table just as Mrs. McInnish swept through the kitchen door with a bowl of green beans. I glanced at the three other boarders as I spread my napkin in my lap.

Mrs. McInnish said a blessing, and we all began to spoon food onto our plates. Conversation bubbled like soup on a hot stove: Miss Thompson regaling us with stories about her music students, Miss Readdy complaining about the girl she'd hired to help at the millinery, and Miss Frank giggling over the romantic gestures of her latest beau. I forked food into my mouth and kept silent. I'd learned quickly that none of these girls were interested in the world of mathematics.

My room at Mrs. McInnish's served its purpose, but not in the company it afforded. Long ago I'd decided I had no time for young women engaged in less than serious pursuits. Which meant, of course, that I had few female friends. Or friends of any gender, for that matter. I dabbed at the corner of my mouth with my napkin, anxious to be away from the table and engrossed again in mathematical theories and practical problems. Numbers remained constant in a way other things did not.

The telephone rang. Mrs. McInnish frowned and hopped up from her seat, wondering aloud who would interrupt supper. A moment later, she returned. "Someone wanting to speak with you, Miss Bowman."

All eyes turned to me. My stomach sank toward the floor. "Are you certain they asked for me?"

"Certain as the day is long. Hurry up now. Susie said the call's come through from Dunn. That's to the west, isn't it?"

Dunn, Oklahoma. My heart flopped in my chest and my legs turned to lead.

I hadn't heard from my family in months. Only my sister Jewel's occasional newsy letters filled the gap created when Daddy's stroke left him unable to write. And come to think of it, I hadn't had one of those letters since late August. My breath caught in my chest. Had something happened to Daddy?

Mrs. McInnish pulled at my chair. I forced myself to stand, to jerk my way into the kitchen, where the telephone box hung on the wall. I pressed the receiver to my ear and spoke into the mouthpiece protruding like a nose beneath the two bells that looked like eyes. "This is Miss Bowman."

"Lula." My name came as quiet as a breath across the line. "Lula, I need you."

"Jewel? Is that you?"

The rhythm of crying. My fingers gripped the earpiece more tightly. "What is it, Jewel?"

"Davy's gone."

My whole body tensed. Davy? Her husband?

"What do you mean, gone?"

She hiccuped a sob. "The funeral's Saturday."

Davy Wyatt, always so full of life and laughter, dead? How could it be?

"I need you, Lula. The kids need you. Please come home."

Fear rose in my throat, threatening to choke me. All my life, I'd been in the way. The littlest sister. The baby. And yet it was Jewel who took me in when Mama passed, who helped me afford that first year of col-

16

lege. In spite of her infernal matchmaking schemes, I knew she loved me. And now she needed me. She *needed* me. "Of course I'll come."

"Tomorrow?" She sounded so frail, so fragile.

I swallowed hard, praying for strength. "Tonight."

"Thank you." The line went silent, at least until Susie, the operator, squawked in my ear. I hung up, stumbled into the dining room, and fell back into my chair.

"What is it?" Miss Frank leaned closer, her face as pale as mine felt.

"My sister's husband has died. I have to go to her." New strength surged through my limbs. I rose. "I have to catch the train. Tonight."

Questions followed me up the stairs, but I had no answers. I brushed aside my satchel, filled a suitcase with a few clothes, then scrawled a quick note to Professor Clayton, telling him I'd return by the beginning of next week. I knew he'd understand. I only hoped the college administration would be as obliging.

2

Chet

"Ma? You ready to go?" My words echoed through our tiny clapboard home. One large room and a kitchen downstairs, two tiny bedrooms and a water closet upstairs. The click of a door opening on the second floor answered.

"I'll be there when I'm ready." The thunk of wood connecting with wood, shutting Ma back inside her room.

I knew better than to hurry her, even though I was sure she'd complain when we arrived late to the Wednesday night prayer meeting. For the hundredth time, I coached myself to hold my tongue and accept her as she was, not as I wished she'd be.

My brother was always so much better at that than I was.

"I'll be outside," I called to Ma, shoving my bowler on my head, then jogging down the porch steps, reminding myself yet again that God had called me to take care of Ma. He'd chosen me to stay and Clay to go. No sense rehashing a situation that couldn't be changed. Ma needed me. My students and my basketball players needed me, too.

I rubbed a hand across the back of my neck. Already damp. The weather was far too hot for a late September evening. We needed autumn to blow in. Maybe cooler weather would ease the foulness of Ma's temper.

Or not.

Shoving my hands into my pockets, I crossed the yard and kicked the tires of my two-year-old Tin Lizzie, the roadster version, with a buggy-like bench seat, spoked wheels, electric headlamps, and crank-up leather top. And my favorite part — the electric starter. I buffed a spot from the radiator hood with my sleeve, wishing the church sat two miles from our house instead of two blocks. Foolish to drive such a short distance, even in the heat.

Ma bustled out the door and down the steps. "Stop dawdling. We need to go."

My mouth opened and closed. I found a smile, remembering the way Clay's easy grin would diffuse the sting of Ma's tongue. I fell into step beside her, offering my arm for support.

19

"Coach Vaughn!" I turned to see Reed Clifton — *Blaze* to his teammates and classmates — wave from down the street.

"Just a minute, Ma. I need to speak with Blaze."

Her lips pursed as her hand slipped from my arm. My star basketball player loped toward us. I prayed his father hadn't been on a rampage against schooling again.

Blaze's eyes cut to Ma. "Ma'am."

She nodded, then turned away, giving us the illusion of privacy.

Blaze leaned in and lowered his voice. "Just wanted to make sure you heard about Miss Delancey, Coach."

I cringed. Just the mention of the woman's name made me want to don a tin cap and dive to the duckboards of a trench in France with Clay and the others. I shook off the willies. Come to think of it, she hadn't pestered me for the past few days. "What about her?"

Blaze threw me a cocky grin. "She's eloped."

"Eloped?" I hooted. "And who is the lucky groom?"

Blaze's shoulders bounced with silent laughter. "My uncle Sal."

"You're kidding." I grinned. Until the next thought hit. Then I groaned. "I guess that means a new music teacher."

Please, God, let her be as old as Ma.

Maybe Principal Gray would see fit to hire a woman devoted to her profession instead of a husband hunter. But I doubted it. Every new, young female he'd hired had been more interested in her own future than that of her students.

"Chet? We're already late!"

I glanced at Ma and nodded, then returned my attention to Blaze. "You want to walk with us to the prayer meeting?"

The boy sobered, then shrugged. "Sure, but I can't stay."

We started off again, Ma moving at a faster clip than normal, Blaze beside me, looking as if he wanted to speak but dared not. At least not until we reached the church building, its whiteness stark and bright against the browning landscape.

The congregation was milling about the yard, not inside the church. Escaping the heat? Or . . .

Tight faces. Hushed voices. My gut twisted. Ma let go of my arm and hurried toward a group of older women. I lingered with Blaze, neither of us able to find conversation.

Blaze cleared his throat and backed toward the street. "Guess I'd better get on home."

21

I nodded. He broke into a run, eager to escape whatever anguish had settled over those gathered here. Something was wrong. Very wrong.

Ma returned to me, eyes wide. She clutched at my arm. "It's Davy Wyatt. Nicked in the barber shop last weekend and succumbed to blood poisoning. Left his poor wife with those four little children."

I winced, my hand involuntarily rising to my neck. If a nick of the barber's blade could end a life, what chance did Clay have in the path of bullets and poison gas? My gaze cut to Ma, wondering if she thought the same thing.

Her features twisted, exposing both fear and pain. I'd prayed for years she could leave the past behind.

I softened my voice. "Let's go home, Ma."

She chewed her bottom lip, then shook her head. "I need to go to her, Chet. Make sure she's all right."

"Go to whom?" I'd met Davy Wyatt — the affable guy who ran the livery stable — a couple times, but we'd had little contact since I'd purchased my Ford. Ma wasn't overly acquainted with the Wyatts, either, as far as I knew.

"Jewel Wyatt. We roll bandages together at the Red Cross."

■ ■ ■ ■

Pastor Reynolds grimaced and settled his hand on Mrs. Wayfair's shoulder as she bumbled to the conclusion of the second verse of the closing hymn at Davy Wyatt's funeral on Saturday afternoon. She ended with what I assumed she meant to be a triumphant chord. If only her fingers had hit the right notes.

Ma's head shook with displeasure. "You'd think she could get it right for once," she whispered. I nodded, observing Mrs. Wayfair's preening, as if she'd just played a perfect concerto. I'd been glad to wish Miss Delancey good riddance, but I already missed the way she made the piano music wrap around our congregational voices. Whether on my phonograph or in person, I did enjoy good music. It was the one thing Ma and I had in common.

Mrs. Wyatt rose from her seat on the front pew, her gaze fixed on the window that overlooked the cemetery. She swayed. The young woman beside her, also clad in black, leapt to her feet and steadied Mrs. Wyatt. Together, they approached the pine box. Mrs. Wyatt pressed her hand against the unfinished wood, over the place where her husband's heart rested. Then she turned and hurried up the aisle, the same hand now pressed to her mouth.

The rest of the family stood and filed past the coffin with solemn faces before escorting the Wyatt children outside.

Four men came forward and carried Davy Wyatt out the side door to his final resting place beside the church. I glanced at Ma, wondering if the scene brought back memories of her grief. Of *our* grief.

Low murmurings accompanied the rustle of women's skirts. I helped Ma to her feet, eager to escape the closeness of the large crowd. But before I could guide us toward the exit, a hand pressed against my arm. A lace-gloved hand.

Careful to keep a neutral look on my face, I raised my head.

Wide blue eyes stared into mine. Yellow curls peeking out around a pale face. "Mr. Vaughn! What a pleasure to see you." She blinked twice. "You do remember me, do you not?"

I took a step into the emptying aisle. Her hand fell from my sleeve. "Of course, Miss Morrison." I tipped my head in acknowledgment, not wanting to offend the banker's daughter. Then I let my gaze roam over the congregation of mourners. "But if you will excuse me, I believe I'm needed — over there."

I gave a quick smile to diffuse her sputtering before I escorted Ma outside. I meant to join the men who stood in clumps, hands in their pockets, asking two-word questions and receiving one-word answers, but my focus snagged on Davy Wyatt's widow. She stood apart from the mourners, her face chalky above the collar of her dark dress. Two little girls flitted around her skirt while a smaller child lay limp against her shoulder. Her grief seemed to draw a circle around her, preventing others from penetrating the space.

All except Ma. She bustled right up to the widow and laid a hand on her arm.

Mrs. Wyatt's face brightened a bit at the touch. They spoke out of my hearing. Then Ma reached for the sleeping child and nudged the widow toward the men shoveling dirt into a gaping hole amid a cluster of gravestones behind the wrought-iron fence. The gate creaked loudly under the woman's hand. She stopped, looked back. Ma nodded again.

I didn't want to watch her plodding steps through the cemetery as she attempted to avoid the resting places of those gone far longer than her husband. But I couldn't seem to turn away. Pastor Reynolds and her relatives followed at a distance for the short graveside good-bye. When Mrs. Wyatt knelt at the new grave, I lowered my chin, not wanting to witness the private moment with her husband. Had Ma ever wished she could visit Pa's grave in the sad aftermath? I couldn't imagine it possible, but then I'd never been able to make sense of the female mind.

I hung back with the other men as Mrs. Wyatt returned through the creaking gate. A man dressed in an army coat and breeches, complete with canvas leggings and a Montana-peak campaign hat in his hand, approached and took the sleeping child from Ma.

A blur bolted from the graveyard. Two ladies shrieked and jumped back.

"JC? JC, come back!" A feminine voice rose above the hum of the crowd.

I eyed the road open before the boy, a lonely stretch leading as far as he could run. I stepped into his path. The boy slammed into me, stumbled backward. I caught his arms, held him upright. "Whoa, there! Moving pretty fast, aren't you?"

He wriggled and twisted, trying to escape my hold. I bent down, one knee in the dirt, peering up at the child's tear-streaked face.

"I've got you, son. Let me help."

JC stilled, red-rimmed eyes finally meeting mine. "You cain't help. Cain't nobody help. 'Cept God. And He let my daddy die."

The childhood ache of missing Pa hollowed my stomach. "You're Davy Wyatt's boy, aren't you?"

He nodded and looked to the angry faces of those standing just beyond us, those ready to snatch him up and scold him for running.

"You're right. Nobody can bring back your father. But I can listen if you want to talk."

His eyes pinched almost shut as his arms tensed beneath my hands. "Talk about what?"

Two men I'd met on Wednesday night tried to pry JC from my grasp. I refused to let go. This boy needed to know someone understood his situation, understood how he felt. "Whatever you want. Your pa. God. Life and death."

Mrs. Wyatt pushed through her relatives, huffing and puffing, hat askew, dust clinging to wetness that streaked her cheeks. JC wrenched himself from one of the men who'd grabbed his arm and threw himself into his mother's embrace. Mrs. Wyatt knelt in front of him and pushed back his damp hair.

"Don't run from me, JC. Please." She pressed a kiss to his forehead. When she stood, her gloved hand closed around his small fingers. She studied me for a moment. "I'm so sorry —"

I waved off her apology. Her expression softened. "Thank you. Mr. Vaughn, isn't it?"

"Yes, ma'am."

A tiny smile curved her wide mouth. "I might have known Louise would have such a compassionate son."

I glanced at Ma. She looked away. Maybe I didn't know my mother as well as I'd imagined.

3

Lula

The surge of energy that got me on the train Wednesday night carried me through Thursday, Friday, Saturday. The minutes blurred into hours, my hands never stopping, my mind never settling. Not until the last mourners left Jewel's house. The last unrelated mourners.

If only Mama were here. But she rested near the new mound of Oklahoma soil that covered Davy. And we didn't have Daddy's guidance, either. He resided in a bed in my brother Don's home, two hours north, half of his once-strong body rendered useless by a stroke. I pushed the image from my mind, unable to deal with my grief over Daddy on a day already filled to the brim with sorrow.

My two brothers, two sisters, and I remained. Three of my siblings were old enough to be my parent. Jewel and I were closest in age, but even then, almost ten years separated us.

"Why don't you and the children go on to bed." My eldest sister, Janice, threw the statement at me.

Long before her suggestion, I knew they didn't want me in their powwow. Even though I was twenty-five years old, they still considered me a child. I wanted to sass back that I could stay awake with the grown-ups, but then I figured seeing the children to bed would be more pleasurable than the ensuing discussion. Besides, Jewel looked done in. I'd hate for her to worry over one more thing.

I managed a sad smile for Jewel as I shooed the children up the stairs.

All but ten-year-old JC. Him I had to drag.

We reached the bedroom my nieces and nephews would share until I returned to the university. JC sulked in the corner. I pushed up the sleeves of my dress, anxious for any relief from the warm night, before gathering the children's nightclothes.

Two-year-old Russell wiggled and laughed until I lifted him into his crib. Then he stared over the railing with solemn eyes, thumb jammed between his full lips.

Eight-year-old Trula's hair hung in limp strands around her face as I unbuttoned her dress. Had it been only this morning I'd pulled the rags from her locks and arranged the curls of gold down her back? She tugged the thin white nightdress over her head and crawled into bed.

Four-year-old Inez whimpered, climbed up beside her sister, sighed, then stilled. I brushed my hand over the child's damp face.

JC remained huddled in the corner, arms crossed over his narrow chest, face twisted into a scowl. But I recognized the pain beneath the anger. I motioned him to me. He shook his head. "C'mon," I whispered. "You need sleep, too."

His head shook again, more violently this time.

I crouched down beside him. "I understand, JC, I really do."

The corners of his mouth quivered, and tears filled eyes the color of the walnut gramophone casing downstairs. So much of Davy in those eyes. I almost couldn't bear to look. I pulled him to my chest.

"What will happen to us, Aunt Lula?" The muffled question soft and wet against my dress.

"Jesus sees, JC. And you have your mama still." I stroked back his dark hair, kissed his sweaty forehead. "Cry now, if you want. No one can see you here."

His body slacked, letting go of its grief in the circle of my arms. I stroked his hair, rocked us back and forth, and begged God to help my nephew untangle the mass of confusion and sorrow I knew stirred inside him. Slowly, his breathing evened, anguish surrendering to the oblivion of sleep. I hefted him onto the bed beside the girls, who curled into each other like two puppies. In the crib, Russell lay splayed on his back, arms and legs akimbo.

I envied Russell, unaware of the meaning of all the commotion. I imagined JC did, too. Russell wouldn't remember his father. Not losing him. Not having him around in the first place. Unlike JC, who would miss Davy every day of his life.

While the others talked, I packed my suitcase. Then I crept down the stairs and perched on the next-to-bottom step. The glow of electric light from the parlor splashed the hall floor and exposed my worn shoes while the voices scraped against the rawness of my heart.

"Lula's the obvious choice," Janice said. "She's the only one who doesn't have other responsibilities."

My back jerked straight, shoulder blades pinching. No responsibilities? I had a class to teach. My own studies to complete. But to them, no husband and no children equaled no life. Anger burned hot and fast, like a prairie fire, almost lifting me to my feet. But I kept my back end firmly attached to the step.

"Will she do it?" My other brother, Ben. Older than Jewel but younger than Don and Janice. I imagined him tapping his foot, looking at his pocket watch, eager for the train to take him back to his Texas home.

"She'll have to." Don's deep voice, followed by his heavy tread. "Jewel can't deal with all this alone. Especially not if her boy is determined to be reckless."

My chest tightened. Did they not remember what it was like to lose a parent? Or maybe it felt different as an adult. I didn't know. I only knew I still ached for Mama. Already grieved for Daddy. Understood JC.

"But Lula —"

"Hush, Jewel." Don again. The sofa creaked, as if protesting another occupant. "Lula is the least encumbered. We'll just tell her this is the way it is. It'll be best for her anyway. Keep her from chasing Daddy's fantasy." He snorted, then laughed. "A woman PhD."

My lips pressed into each other, and my heart picked up speed. They might not esteem my college degree or understand my need for graduate work, but they couldn't dictate my life. I wouldn't let them. Daddy wouldn't let them.

No, I couldn't count on Daddy. Not in his current state. I'd have to fight for myself. Jewel was a grown woman. She'd be fine on her own.

Strong, even strides carried me into the front room. Every head turned in my direction.

"Here's Fruity Lu now." Ben rubbed his hands together and grinned. My fists clenched at my sides as my jaw tightened. His face blurred as anger roiled through me like storm clouds across the Oklahoma sky.

"Now, Ben." Don reached my side and slid his arm around my shoulders. He led me to the sofa, sat me next to Jewel. Jewel dabbed her eyes with a soiled handkerchief and managed a weak smile. Compassion softened my frustration. I reached for her hand.

Janice cleared her throat. "Lula, you'll have to stay here and help Jewel."

"I can't." I looked into the face of each of my siblings, Jewel last. "You know I love you, Jewel, but I have a scholarship for my graduate studies and a job teaching at the university. The term is well underway. I have obligations to fulfill."

Voices burst forth all at once, words jumping over one another, fighting to be heard.

"Graduate work? A college degree was bad enough." Janice.

"You need a husband, not more schooling." Don.

"I always told Mama she'd spoiled you selfish." Ben.

While the others glared, my gaze rested on Jewel, usually more my champion than anyone else. Jewel let go of my grasp and stared at her hands. The handkerchief twisted between them now. She understood, didn't she? My heart clenched.

Janice huffed. "I'd take you all to my house, Jewel, but I have no room. You know that."

Jewel nodded, balling the handkerchief into her left hand. "I know."

Don cleared his throat. "Audra and I are taking care of Pop. It's all we can handle on top of the ranch and our own kids."

Jewel nodded again, stared out the window.

Don and Janice looked at Ben. His focus darted between them. "Don't look at me! I only have two rooms over the mercantile. I can't handle a woman and four children!" He flipped open his gold pocket watch. "I have to go or I'll miss my train."

He threw me a wicked grin. "Of course, Fruity Lu wouldn't have stuck it out anyway. You know how she is. First this, then that. It'd be like leaving Jewel with yet another child."

I lunged toward him. Don stepped in front of me, held me back. Ben chuckled, plunked an awkward kiss on Jewel's cheek, and patted her shoulder before he dashed away.

I dropped back down on the sofa beside Jewel. Good riddance. Ben, of all my siblings, goaded me with his never-forgotten taunt of "Fruity Lu" and his self-importance. I'd show him — and the others, too — that I wasn't that girl anymore. I didn't give up. I didn't quit. And no matter what any of them wanted, after church tomorrow I'd return to the university and the degree that would lay Fruity Lu to rest forever.

4

Chet

Ma leaned her shoulder against mine as the congregation struggled to sing on Sunday morning. "Even God must be plugging His ears," she whispered.

I covered my mouth and coughed down a laugh. I didn't appreciate Mrs. Wayfair's piano playing, but I did enjoy the unusual camaraderie it sparked between Ma and me. I'd come to think of it as a gift, especially since we'd come home from Davy Wyatt's funeral to find a letter from Clay. He'd be shipping out soon, wished we could be in New York to see him off. While he hadn't meant to, his news had brought an awkward silence between Ma and me. Both of us missing Clay. Neither of us able to share our feelings with the other.

The painful hymn ended. Pastor Reynolds rose to preach, but I couldn't focus on his words. I thought of Clay, on leave in New

York City. What was it like? Would I ever see it? Maybe after Clay returned from the war, I'd get to have my adventure. Until then, I had work God had given me here. I blew out a long breath and glanced at Ma. Her mouth dipped in a frown. Not at the sermon, just in its usual repose.

Clay and I had hoped when I took the job at Dunn High School three years ago that relieving her of the need to work would lighten her spirits. But it hadn't happened. In fact, she seemed to sink more deeply into her own woes. When America went to war, she joined the Red Cross and tended her victory garden. Lots of activity — but none of the peace of spirit we'd hoped she'd find.

Help her, Lord. Help her to find what she needs in You. Help her overcome the shame of the past and fear for the future. Help her to see Your hand in her life right now.

The words I prayed slammed into my chest like a basketball I hadn't seen coming. Had I looked for God's hand in my life right now? Was I wallowing in the past? Anxious about the future?

I wished I could answer no, but I knew that wasn't true. I shifted in my seat, remembering how many times lately I'd envied Clay, wished it had been my name on that draft letter.

Forgive me, Lord.

Ma elbowed me. Pastor Reynolds had dismissed the service.

Before Ma could scold me for my inattention, Mrs. Adams steered her toward some other Red Cross ladies. I ducked my head as Miss Morrison passed by, only to look up and see Janet Green, the telephone operator, wiggling her fingers at me with a shy grin.

I lifted my hand but turned away as quickly as I could. Tried to look occupied. I skimmed the crowd, looking for . . .

My gaze stopped on a face that caused a glimmer of recognition. A young woman — older than my high school students but younger than most of the congregation. A shapely form. A slender neck. Defined, classic features. She ought to be dressed in bright colors. Instead, her coal-colored dress spoke of suffering.

The funeral.

That's where I'd seen her.

She'd walked with Mrs. Wyatt to the coffin, held her steady.

She bore some resemblance to the widow, with her dark hair and creamy complexion. Was she a relative? Niece? Sister? Friend? She stepped even with my pew, affording me a closer view of ivory skin, dark eyes, pert nose. I rose. She turned and reached behind her. JC appeared at her side.

He spied me. I smiled and nodded, wondering if I could wrangle an introduction to his companion. But they slipped past me without a word.

What had I been thinking, anyway? With the distraction of Miss Delancey out of the way, I had no desire to add another.

Outside, I greeted Mr. Glasscock from the dry goods store and Mr. Leland, who taught with me at the high school. But my eyes kept wandering back to the pleasing face sheltered beneath a wide-brimmed hat. Her lashes lowered as she chatted with several longtime Dunn residents. Then she hefted one of the little Wyatt girls into her arms. I inched closer even as I told myself to steer clear. Then Mrs. Wyatt was there, though I hadn't seen her earlier.

She leaned toward the younger woman. "Did you hear that, Lula? The high school needs a music teacher. You could stay with me and do that."

The woman — Lula — shook her head, her full lips pulled tight.

"But you'd be perfect in that job." Mrs. Wyatt's wan complexion brightened a bit. She shifted the little boy draped across her arms. Then she *looked* at Lula. Pursed lips.

Raised eyebrows. Widened eyes.

The look that said, *I know best what you should be about.*

A look I'd seen too many times in my life.

Ma appeared beside me. "If we don't hurry, our dinner will be burnt."

I offered my arm and a smile, remembering my resolution to be more patient, more kind. More attuned to what God had asked me to do here. But I couldn't help wishing to see Mrs. Wyatt's friend once more before we left. I twisted around. Mrs. Wyatt and her brood were coming in our direction. I slowed our pace, heart pulsing in my ears. Then a man in uniform jogged up from the opposite direction. The one from the funeral.

Tall and stiff, he yanked his wide-brimmed campaign hat from his head. Mrs. Wyatt gestured to Lula, who nodded, then looped her arm through the soldier's. Their unusual brigade retreated in the opposite direction.

The next three days, I walked to school instead of drove, relishing the smell of leaves crushed underfoot. Some would call it the smell of death. But not me. Autumn propelled us closer to winter. To basketball season.

I'd taken to sitting on the bleachers in the

gymnasium before school, early morning sunlight casting gray squares across the rectangular floor. I wished the school board could provide a better facility for basketball. We needed space between the walls and the out-of-bounds lines. More seating for spectators. When this building was built about three years ago, few schools played basketball as anything more than a physical education activity. Now we traded games with the high schools in the towns around us. If we ever hoped to boast a winning program, we needed a proper place to play.

But the nation was at war. There could be no extraneous construction. Materials, money, and manpower were committed toward making the world safe for democracy, not bolstering athletics programs.

Leaning forward, elbows on knees, hands clasped, head bowed, I begged God for inspiration. He directed the path of my life. Of that I was sure. So was there some greater purpose for me here in Dunn? Something bigger than myself or my mother?

Ma would have said God had more important things to think of — like those in harm's way in Europe. But I couldn't shake the feeling that He cared about kids like Blaze, too. Kids seeking to find where they fit in life, a reason for their existence.

Not that that reason was basketball, of course. Or any athletic endeavor. But so much could be taught — and learned — through the discipline of the game. I glanced at my wristwatch. Still a few minutes before classes commenced. Maybe I should chat with Principal Gray. We hadn't had a private conversation for a couple of weeks.

No one was sitting behind the reception desk, so I proceeded straight toward the principal's office and poked my head in.

Principal Gray grinned. "Come on in, Chet." We shook hands, then he clapped me on the back. "How are your classes going?"

I slid into the chair opposite his wide desk, then leaned back and rested my left foot on my right knee. "Still trying to settle the kids down after a summer running free."

"Thankfully, we have this blast of cooler air today. I always found it easier to teach without sweat rolling down my face."

"Or my back." A companionable silence settled between us. I liked that about Ronald Gray. He didn't need to hear his own voice. He listened. Much like Mr. Slicer had in my boyhood days, Principal Gray filled a fatherly role in my life.

"I guess you heard I have to find a new music teacher."

I grinned. "So Blaze said. Any candidates?"

"Not officially, though I heard a rumor of a possible applicant." Principal Gray wiggled his eyebrows at me.

My gut twisted.

"Don't worry, son. No one has designs on you at the moment."

"Right." I couldn't keep the cynicism from coating my response. He didn't see the artillery pointed in my direction every week at church. Perhaps I ought to switch to the Methodist congregation, where he attended. Maybe the women were more settled there.

Principal Gray chuckled. "I wouldn't be too concerned. From what I've heard, you've become quite an expert at dodging women with matrimonial intentions."

I shuddered at the remembrance of the previous music teacher's thrice daily jaunts from the music room at the west end of the basement to my east-side, second-floor math classroom. Much like Fanny Albright's visits to my basketball practices last season. Or Janet Conway, the domestic science teacher before Bitsy Greenwood, who arrived with hot cookies during lunch hour and always served me first. Those actions couldn't be disguised as anything but *inter-*

est. Interest I did my best to kindly discourage.

Principal Gray leaned forward, a bit of a twinkle in his aging eyes. "One day you'll see a woman you won't want to run from."

I started to protest, then remembered a pair of intriguing dark eyes and thought better of it. Thankfully, Principal Gray had moved on.

"What are the prospects for our Bulldogs basketball team this year?"

The tension of matrimonial talk ebbed into the comfort of athletics. "We should be in good shape. Blaze is back, along with Clem, Virgil, and Glen. Four strong seniors and some underclassmen who came along nicely last year. Of course, it would help to have a legitimate gymnasium instead of that cracker box out there." I nodded toward the rear of the building.

Principal Gray sighed, rubbed his forehead. "Oklahoma University's gymnasium isn't much better than ours. And with the war effort . . ."

"I know. Yet some of the surrounding high schools have managed to get nicer facilities."

He nodded. "If we could just come up with a way to persuade the school board —"

I leaned forward, a spark of an idea gaining flame. "What if we asked to use the town hall? Some schools do. Much more floor space in there."

"It's worth a try. I don't think there'd be much issue with the boys, but I don't know how people will feel about the girls playing in such a public venue."

I thought of Blaze's girlfriend, Nannie Byrd, and her teammates. Those girls had spunk. And my friend Giles, their coach, would be up for any challenge.

"I feel sure we could persuade them once they agreed to a venue change for the boys. But we need another incentive. Football is still the bigger draw as far as spectators."

What would bring people to a game in a time of war? Spontaneous energy pulled me to my feet. I paced the small space as my thoughts ran in circles, honing in on a proposition that would multiply our chances of gaining the town hall for our games as well as increase support for the basketball program.

I looked down. A flyer on the corner of the desk caught my eye.

If you can't enlist — invest
Buy a Liberty Bond
Defend your country with your dollars

46

I snatched it up, held it out toward Principal Gray. "Liberty bonds. A patriotic community initiative, spearheaded by the boys' basketball team. Nickels turned to dollars. Dollars that will defend our country."

"What?"

An excitement I hadn't felt since Clay boarded the train for camp and left me behind stirred my blood. "The new war bond campaign began two days ago. What if we convinced the town to let us use the hall without charge and donated the admission nickels toward buying liberty bonds at the end of the season? The town hall holds more people, so more money would be raised. Our team would become allies with those serving in France."

I couldn't stand still. Already I pictured the community's support. "The war bonds could be held in trust for the school district to use when they mature. Thirty years, well out of range for when we'd need a new gymnasium, but it might give them an incentive to at least consider a new gymnasium when the war ends, knowing they have this bit of savings for the future."

It could work. For our team. For our school. And if we had success on the court, it could be the reason God wanted me here in Dunn. Or at least redeem me in the eyes

47

of my mother. Maybe even justify Blaze's time and effort in his father's estimation.

Principal Gray tented his hands and tapped them against his mouth. "It could work. It could actually work."

I'd already leapt beyond the venue, beyond the money. Now I pictured Blaze's skill and leadership, the teamwork of the seniors and the burgeoning talent of the underclassmen. If I could inspire them with the idea, sell it as their contribution to their country and to future generations in Dunn, Oklahoma, perhaps we could do more.

I knew the schools we'd play. We'd be evenly matched — in fact, I believed we could beat several of them. It could be our own challenge to ourselves: raise funds for the war, for our school, and leave a legacy of the first basketball team in Dunn to log more wins than losses.

"It's a gamble whether the school board will agree to any of it, but nothing lost by trying." Principal Gray was focusing on a point far away. His thinking look. Then his eyes returned to me. "If you want to propose this, I'll support you. But you'll have to take the lead."

I dropped into the chair I'd abandoned, suddenly spent. "Absolutely. I'll enlist Brian Giles' help, as well."

Before Principal Gray could answer, female chatter drifted in from the reception area. I eased from my seat and escaped the gathering in the outer office with nothing more than a tip of my hat.

5

Lula

I couldn't shake Jewel's great sorrow. Not in my classroom at the university. Nor at Mrs. McInnish's boardinghouse. Nor while trying to solve a difficult equation or explain a basic concept. Jewel stared back at me from the faces of my students. Her crying echoed in my head as my pencil scratched across the page.

"Your mind is elsewhere, my girl." Professor Clayton peered down at my paper. I followed his gaze. The square root of six is three? For heaven's sake! I pushed an eraser over my error. Calculated again. 2.44948974278.

"These have been some rough days, Miss Bowman." His face drooped with understanding. "Why don't you put your work away for now? Go home early. Get some rest."

He was right. I'd been pushing myself,

trying to banish Jewel's need from my head and my heart. But I was tired. So tired. I gathered my things. "I'll be ready to finish this tomorrow. I promise."

He smiled at me as if he didn't quite believe my words. To be honest, I didn't believe them, either. If only I could know how Jewel and the kids were getting along. Maybe I could go to Dunn on the weekends. Give her a break from the children, the housework. But to arrive late Friday night and leave again on Sunday wouldn't do much to help her. Or me.

What if I paid someone to help her? I chewed my lip and toyed with that idea. It would require economy on my part. A cheaper boardinghouse. Turning my dresses, resewing them with the faded fabric to the inside, instead of buying new ones. Surely I could find enough extra in my pay to relieve her of the need to find work, at least for a little while. Not that she'd find much in the way of employment. Not in a small town like Dunn. Not with her eighth-grade education. Maybe in nearby Lawton?

Trudging into Mrs. McInnish's, I sought out the newspaper to put my plan in motion. But Mrs. McInnish handed me a letter instead.

Miss Lula Bowman was penned across the

outside in Jewel's elegant hand. I tore it open, eager for news to relieve my anxiety, more determined than before to enclose a generous gift in my reply.

The front door slammed shut behind Miss Frank and Miss Thompson, their laughing chatter filling every crevice of the room. I angled my knees toward the wall, hoping they'd read my need to remain undisturbed. As they climbed the stairs and their voices faded, my eyes drank in Jewel's words.

Dearest sister,
I hope this finds you well and happy. In spite of the reason for your visit, know that your presence here is greatly missed. The girls still can talk of nothing but Aunt Lula. You truly stole their hearts during your short stay. JC spends much of his free time at the livery stable. Mr. Timmons has kindly allowed him to help with the horses, but I fear that he needs more of me than I can give right now.

My heart clenched. Jewel, the one who'd set aside her own grief over Mama to help me through mine, shouldn't have that guilt. Of course, back then she'd had Davy to help shoulder her burden. Now she had no one. I cringed.

Send someone to help her. Please, God? Someone besides me.

I devoured Jewel's words about Daddy, but she had nothing new to report. He remained the same. Stricken in body, active in mind. I should have made time to go see him. Don would have driven me to Chickasha. But the thought of Don and Audra hounding me to stay with Jewel had overpowered my need to see my father. My champion. Or maybe it gave me the excuse to remember Daddy as he'd been before the stroke.

I returned to Jewel's letter. Janice's daughter, my twenty-year-old niece, had given birth to a son. Nothing from Ben in Texas, of course.

And then there is my own news, Lula. The news I suspected when you all were here but didn't know for certain. The sweet, sad secret I've told no one but you, even now.

I closed my eyes, but only for a moment.

I'm going to have a baby, Lula. In March. Davy's final gift, the last tangible reminder of our love.

My cheeks flamed, then my heart swam in

my stomach. Losing Davy with four children to raise had been bad enough. But another child on the way? How would she manage alone?

Dread settled on my shoulders. My throat tightened.

Please, Lula, can't you come and stay?

A vise squeezed my heart. I wanted to oblige. I did. But if I went — if I quit school — I'd forfeit too much. My scholarship. My education. My employment. Daddy's hope that one of his children would get a PhD. If I left here, I'd be Fruity Lu once again, giving up before I reached the end, getting distracted by other things. Couldn't Jewel of all people see that?

I blew out a hard breath, but it didn't relieve the pinch in my chest. I'd have to find a way to send Jewel money. My brothers and sisters might still think me a child, but I'd been taking care of myself for years. I could sacrifice my own comfort for Jewel and her children.

I rose, determined to stow the letter in my trunk upstairs and get on with finding a new, cheaper place to live.

"Everything all right?" Mrs. McInnish

opened the front door to let in the evening air.

"Yes, Mrs. McInnish. Just fine."

"Your sister, then? She's well?" Concern laced the words, threatening to break my resolve.

"Fine. However, I —" If I said the words out loud, committed myself to my plan, then the roiling guilt inside would calm, right? "I'll be looking for a new place to live. Less expensive, so I can help my sister's family."

Her eyes saddened. "I'm sorry to hear that, Miss Bowman. You're a good boarder. You'll have any reference you need from me. But are you certain . . ."

I sucked in a deep breath. "I'm certain. My sister has four children to support." I sat hard on the sofa. Five, now.

Mrs. McInnish plopped down beside me. "What's the matter, dear?"

"She's — she's going to have another baby. In March. She . . . she needs —"

Mrs. McInnish's hand closed around mine. "She's going to need more than money, I fear. She'll need someone to stay with her."

Her words haunted me through the commotion of supper and in the quiet of my bedroom. I paced the narrow space beside my iron bedstead, Jewel's letter crumpled in my hand. I couldn't go back. I couldn't. If I did, I'd remain Fruity Lu for the rest of my days. The child who nearly caught the house on fire after leaving a lamp burning in the kitchen, who contaminated the well with a shovelful of manure. The girl with half-finished paintings littering the attic, scads of piano music disintegrating in a box in the cellar, a string of broken hearts behind her. The girl who threw away the prestigious Donally Award.

The bedsprings creaked as I lowered onto the edge of the mattress, head hanging. Mrs. McInnish was right. Someone needed to be with Jewel, and it seemed God was calling me.

My hands shook. I clenched them still.

"You and Jewel help each other," Mama had told me just before she passed away. Jewel had heartily obeyed, helping me through my last year of high school and my college applications. To go would be to honor Mama and repay Jewel. To stay here would be to please Daddy and to take a stand for every woman who desired to further her education. My heart pulled and stretched, breath-prayers rising to heaven in desperation.

The next morning, I sought out Professor Clayton, told him everything. I expected him to jump into the silence when I stopped, remind me of my commitments, urge me to stay. But he didn't speak. I bit my lower lip as his chin tilted toward his shoulder and his gaze slipped from mine.

"What?" I whispered. But my heart already knew.

"When I lost Elvira, it was my one regret. Putting this life" — he swept his arm to encompass the office — "before her. Don't make the same mistake, Miss Bowman."

"But the Donally —"

"You do what needs to be done and leave the rest in God's hands. And mine." He patted my shoulders, compassion in his eyes. "I'll do all I can to sway the committee to put your scholarship on hold, but you must go to your sister."

"Lula?" Jewel stood on the porch of her house Saturday morning, hair unbrushed, skin sallow, arms tight across her middle, as if holding herself together. My chest ached at the sight.

It hadn't been easy to resign from my

position and pack my trunk. My heart felt shredded, like a piece of silk beneath unwieldy scissors. But seeing my sister now, I knew I'd chosen correctly.

Her tired eyes strayed to the valise in my hand, then jumped back to my face. Relief spread over her features as she hurried down the steps and met me in the yard. She threw her arms around me, pulled me close.

"I knew you'd come." Her whisper in my ear birthed tears in my eyes. I shook them away, unwilling to let her see. She pulled back, smiled. But the corner of her mouth trembled. "I'm sorry I didn't tell y'all earlier. I thought —" She sighed and rubbed a finger across her forehead. "I guess I thought I could handle all of it alone. But I can't."

We made our way arm in arm up the steps. Inside, Trula and Inez dropped their dolls and ran to me, pressing their small bodies into mine, gazing up at me with rapturous faces. Russell toddled in a circle around his sisters, clapping his pudgy hands. My eyes skimmed over the room. No JC. I raised an eyebrow at Jewel. She winced and sat in the wide leather armchair near the piano — Davy's chair — hands writhing in her lap. "Girls, take your brother outside and push him on the swing."

They protested a moment but then did as she bade.

"He's always at the livery."

I nodded. "It reminds him of his daddy."

Jewel sighed. "I suppose so. Mr. Timmons has been gracious to let him run about the place pretending he's useful, as Davy used to. But one day JC'll have to understand that he has no right to be there anymore."

"You sold it?"

Jewel nodded. "But Davy owed more money than I'd thought. There wasn't much left to live on. Janice and Don are coming today to discuss 'my financial situation.' " She hesitated. "They don't know about the baby yet."

I blew out a long breath. My hand grazed the top of the piano. Dust came away on my fingers. I tried to rub them clean on the floor as I knelt next to the chair Jewel occupied, but they came away dirtier than before. Already things were further out of hand than I'd imagined.

I clasped Jewel's hand in my clean one. "We'll figure things out. Together."

She nodded, then leaned her head back and closed her eyes — almost as if Davy's chair were his arms wrapped around her once more.

Don settled at the dining room table less than an hour later. "I don't have time to dawdle, so let's get right to it." I set a glass of cold water in front of him. He drank half in one gulp.

Janice pressed her cheek to Jewel's, then mine. "We didn't expect you here," she told me.

I just smiled. Let her wonder. For now.

Don pulled some papers from a leather bag and spread them out on the table. "From what I see, Jewel, if you sell the motorcar and the house, you and the children ought to be able to sustain yourselves for a year or two."

Jewel stared at the table. Janice and Don stared at Jewel.

"What?" Don barked. "You didn't think you could simply go on as you are, did you?"

Jewel shook her head but didn't look up.

"Now, Don, this has all happened so fast. She needs time to adjust." Janice patted Jewel's hand. "We just want to help you find your feet again."

Jewel lifted her head slowly, as if it weighed a hundred pounds. Her desperate gaze traveled from my face to Janice's to Don's. Tears swam in her eyes, and she swallowed hard. "I need y'all to know I'm in the family way." Her cheeks glowed as red as ripe tomatoes. "Three months."

Don and Janice gaped at one another, their eyes blank. Then Janice turned to face me. Don turned, as well.

"That's . . . wonderful, dear. Why don't you let us chat with Lula for a few minutes?" Janice nodded to Don, then took my arm and guided me into the front yard.

Don paced back and forth, head wagging. "No more arguing, Lula. Even you must see now that you have to stay and help. I have no room for her, nor does Janice."

"Besides," Janice chimed in, "you're the only one who can handle her. I love her, but I have no patience with her."

I craned my neck toward the house, the one Davy had bought and assembled for Jewel the year after Mama died. Davy had been my sister's whole world. He'd petted and coddled and romanced her. He'd indulged her love of music and laughter. And he'd made sure Don and Janice and Ben didn't goad her into doing their bidding. Now she only had me.

But was that enough?

Jewel eased out on the porch, her face swathed in sorrow. She and her children needed my help. They needed to keep their home. They needed time to grieve, time to adjust, time to figure out what life looked like without Davy. I wouldn't let Janice and Don push her to do anything before she was ready. My resolve became as hard as the granite atop the Wichita Mountains. "I'll stay with her. At least until the baby comes. But we'll be living here. In their home."

Don crossed his arms and lowered his voice. "She can't afford to stay here, Fruity Lu."

I lifted my chin, pulled back my shoulders. My sister might have lost her husband, but I wouldn't let her lose the house, too. "I'll get a job."

Janice glanced at Don with an almost pleading look. He rubbed a hand over his bulging jaw. "Fine. I don't care what you do, just as long as someone keeps her out of the poorhouse. Now, if we have this settled, I need to get back to Audra and Pop."

Jewel walked down the steps. Don kissed her on the cheek before striding toward his automobile without another glance at me. My blood went hot, and my hands tingled. I stalked after my brother. "Just because I'm staying *now* doesn't mean I'm staying forever. Just you get that through your thick skull, Donald Bowman," I hissed, thrusting my hands onto my hips to punctuate my point.

Don patted my head. Chucked me under the chin. "Maybe while you're here Jewel can help you catch a husband. Then you won't have to go back to school again."

Janice swept up beside me, her hand on my back. "Don's right, dear. Daddy wasn't thinking straight when he encouraged you with all this college stuff. He was out of his mind with grief over Mama. It's time you got married, settled down. You've wasted your best years and oodles of money and time on that nonsense." She climbed into the seat beside Don.

I pressed my lips together, holding back the tears that threatened to rise. I thought I'd cried them all in the past three weeks, but apparently those were only the ones reserved for Jewel and her children. These were engraved with my name.

6

Chet

"Watch out!" Ma's hand gripped my arm. I glanced in her direction. Her eyes were closed, her shoulders tense. Our usual Saturday routine. I shook my head and continued motoring down Main Street. The bustle of town on Saturdays made Ma nervous — bicycles, motorbikes, automobiles, and horse-drawn wagons all vied for space along the newly paved road.

I, on the other hand, found downtown Dunn on a Saturday too tame for my taste. I wanted to be in the middle of this changing world, the energy of the crowd surging through my limbs like an electric current. I glanced at Ma again, eyes open now. A little more relaxed. Maybe if I'd opted for the touring car with a back seat instead of the roadster she'd have been more comfortable. But I couldn't remedy that now.

I eased my Tin Lizzie behind Mr. Glasscock's dry goods store and stilled the engine. "I'll meet you here in an hour. Is that enough time?"

Ma nodded as I helped her from the motorcar. She'd shop while I took care of a few errands and socialized a bit. After escorting Ma into the store, I stepped back onto the street, dodging in front of an automobile and then behind a wagon. I found myself walking in front of the post office and wondered if Clay had written.

The familiar ball of jealousy pulsed in my chest. Ma would have been happier for me to have been drafted instead of Clay. Me too, come to that. But though Clay knew Ma depended on him, his eyes had lit with a surge of pride when the notice to report had arrived, even as he'd apologized for leaving us. And in the end, I couldn't begrudge him the opportunity to restore our family honor. Not after all we'd endured.

I turned toward the street, as if somehow I would see Clay, in his khaki uniform, strolling down the sidewalk. A child flashed past me, shoes kicking up dust, shirttail flying in the wind. A horse shied. A motorcar jerked to a stop. The boy ran on, disappearing into the livery stable.

JC.

Shared experience pulled me in his direction. Would he remember our encounter at the funeral? Would he accept my offer of friendship? I knew what he felt. And I knew what it had meant to me to have Mr. Slicer to turn to.

But as I reached the other side of the street, Blaze climbed down from a wagon in front of the Feed and Seed. He stopped as if wanting to talk. I glanced toward the livery. JC could wait.

"Ready to play some ball, Blaze? Only three weeks now."

"Yes, sir. I'll be glad to be on the court instead of digging in the dirt." He glanced down at his overalls, speckled with sod.

"Long day already?"

He nodded. "Been at it since sunup."

"You finding time to get your schoolwork done, too?"

Blaze ducked his head. "I don't know, Coach. I'm trying. I really am. But . . ." He glanced at the wagon, and I read all his unspoken words. His pa worked him hard, leaving little time for pursuits of the mind.

I sighed. "Don't give up. You've got six weeks behind you already. Only a few more months to go. And this year, there'll be a diploma at the end."

Blaze stared past me. His jaw ticked. "You

66

might be seeing graduation, Coach Vaughn, but I'm not lookin' further than basketball season right now."

I clapped the lanky senior on the shoulder, noting that it seemed more solid than last year. He might not like helping his pa plant and harvest, but it strengthened him all the same. "I hear ya. It won't be long now."

Like Blaze, I yearned to be out on the court, teaching the boys teamwork and strategy, tenacity and focus and giving your all. But until November, I'd be content with my classroom full of students grappling with numbers.

"Don't worry. We'll get you through, just like we did last year."

He didn't respond. His focus had fixed on the opposite side of the street.

I glanced behind me, expecting to see Blaze's girlfriend, Nannie, and a cluster of her friends. They often arrested his attention in class. But my grin fell away as I saw he'd fixated instead on three men in uniform. My gut clenched. With Fort Sill nearby, soldiers weren't an unusual sight in Dunn, but I didn't want Blaze to get any ideas about enlisting before he finished school.

Blaze shifted his weight, cleared his throat. Apparently this wasn't a subject he wanted to address. He darted a glance back to the Feed and Seed, then to me. "Gotta go, Coach. Gotta get home before Pa thinks I'm slackin'."

I jerked my head toward the store. "Get your work done. I'll see you Monday."

As Blaze dashed away, Ma handed me a package — brown paper tied up with twine. "Was that Archie Clifton's boy?"

"Yes. Blaze Clifton. You remember."

"One of your ball players."

"And one of my students."

She snorted. "What kind of person calls their child Blaze?"

"It's his nickname, Ma. The kids at school call him that because he's fast. Reed's his given name."

She grunted. We reached the car in silence. Once I navigated us off Main Street, Ma seemed to relax.

"A cantankerous old cuss."

I jerked the wheel in surprise, then straightened us out again. "Who?"

"Archie Clifton."

My jaw tightened. I'd tussled with Blaze's ornery dirt farmer of a father over his son's need for a high school education since I'd started teaching at Dunn High School Blaze's freshman year. But our battle in August had been the worst yet. Mr. Clifton

68

had made it clear he valued his son for his physical labor, a hired hand without the necessity of letting go of a dollar. I'd purchased Blaze's court shoes for the coming season myself since his father refused to part with the money.

My hands gripped the steering wheel more tightly. "It's amazing that the boy's still in school, to be honest. But Blaze — Reed — will graduate this year." And no one would be able to take his education away from him.

"Then he'll go scratch out a living with Archie, I suppose."

"I doubt it." We rounded a corner. I waved at Mrs. Wayfair on her front porch, dreading the thought of her piano playing in the morning. Couldn't Pastor Reynolds find some way to gently relieve her of her service?

"Surely the boy won't go to college."

I pulled myself back to our conversation. "No. I imagine he'll join up."

Ma blew out a breath. "Maybe the teacher should take a lesson from his student."

Archie Clifton's determination to sabotage his son's education had nothing on Ma's resolute belief that both of her sons must engage the enemy and atone for their father's cowardice.

■ ■ ■ ■

"Do you think they've found a new pianist yet?" Ma asked as we walked to church the next morning. It was the first time she'd spoken to me since our conversation about Blaze enlisting. In spite of all my explanations, she still couldn't accept my reason to stay in Dunn rather than go to war. She didn't believe that Clay and I had forged our agreement because we loved her. Because we didn't want her to live alone, working herself into an early grave.

"I guess we'll see. I haven't heard of a new music teacher at school yet, though. Maybe Pastor Reynolds is waiting to get a two-for-one, like with Miss Delancey."

"Hmph. That girl knew the songs well enough, but her mind was never where it was supposed to be in God's house."

Or in the classroom. I grinned, in spite of myself. I'd had no idea Ma had seen through the woman as easily as I had.

We slipped into our usual pew. I looked at my wristwatch. Right on time. But Mrs. Wayfair wasn't at the piano. I twisted around. Pastor Reynolds stood at the door with Mrs. Wyatt and —

Lula. Yes, that was her name. One corner

of my mouth lifted.

Pastor Reynolds asked Lula something, and she shook her head, hard and fast, the ribbons on her hat whipping every which way. Mrs. Wyatt nudged her forward a step. Then Pastor Reynolds strode up the aisle and took his place on the platform in front of the church.

"I'm sorry to announce that Mrs. Wayfair, who so graciously took on the job of pianist when Miss Delancey . . . when we were in need, has had an accident and will not be able to continue in that capacity."

Murmurs rose, Ma and the other ladies conjecturing as to the nature of Mrs. Wayfair's injuries. Likely nothing too serious or Pastor Reynolds would have asked for prayer. I crooked my arm over the back of the pew and looked at Lula. Her eyes stretched wide, as if she were afraid. Or maybe feeling exposed.

Pastor Reynolds cleared his throat and clutched a hymnal to his chest. "Thankfully, the Lord provides. Jewel Wyatt's sister Lula has just moved back to Dunn temporarily and has agreed to accompany our singing." He motioned toward the back of the room. "Come on up. Don't be shy."

She frowned, then tucked her chin to her chest and scurried to the piano at the left of

71

the pulpit. Were her hands shaking as she turned the pages to the first hymn listed on the wooden board affixed to the front wall? She bent the hymnal's spine, set the open book on the music stand, and huffed out a breath.

Ma's elbow poked into my side. Was she already questioning the woman's ability? I concentrated on the slender fingers poised over the ivory keys. Almost anything would be preferable to what we'd endured since Miss Delancey's hasty exit.

The congregation stood and sang. Not a perfect accompaniment, but not bad, either. Her mistakes didn't seem to be inability. More like rust from disuse. I studied her profile as she played, then followed Ma outside after the service ended, waiting as she visited with one lady, then another. But my gaze strayed to the cemetery, where Lula was sitting beneath a tree with Mrs. Wyatt's younger children while Mrs. Wyatt and JC stood hand-in-hand at the new grave.

I tipped my bowler hat back a bit and sauntered in Lula's direction. To talk to JC, of course. All while keeping watch on Ma so I'd know when she wanted to leave.

The little Wyatt boy — the baby — sat in Lula's lap, his hands hidden in hers as she clapped. "Patty cake, patty cake, baker's man. Bake me a cake as fast as you can."

They continued through the rhyme, finally throwing the cake in the oven as Mrs. Wyatt and JC returned to them. Lula stood and brushed some dead grass from the back of her skirt. I tried to catch JC's eye to wrangle a formal introduction, but he turned away and kicked at the iron fence.

Mrs. Wyatt stood beside her now. "You did fine today, Lula. I knew you would."

Lula's eye caught mine for the briefest moment. Not even long enough for me to encourage her with a smile.

"Chet?" Ma's tinny voice.

I spun around. "Ready to go?"

"Yes. Oh, wait. Let me speak to Jewel a moment." Ma hurried past me. I wandered after her, not wanting to appear too eager. I reached Ma's side mid-conversation.

"Don't you think she should consider it, Louise?"

Ma pursed her lips, looked at Lula. "Might be best."

Consider what? Being the church pianist? I grinned, picturing this woman at the front of the sanctuary each week. Admiring God's stunning creations was a form of worship, wasn't it?

Lula frowned. "I don't —"

"Mr. Vaughn?" A timid voice. A tug at my

sleeve. JC looked up at me with solemn eyes. "I think that lady over there's trying to get your attention."

I followed his nod. Sarah Morrison batted her lashes in my direction. I groaned.

"Don'tcha wanna talk to her? She's real pretty."

I scratched the back of my head. How to explain the wiles of women to a boy? I leaned down, spoke behind my hand. "It's the pretty ones you have to worry about most."

7

Lula

The shadows under Jewel's eyes bothered me. I sent her to the front room to put up her feet while I warmed the dinner I'd cooked the night before. A scrawny chicken with potatoes mashed into a fluffy mound. At least I was helping — but Jewel needed so much more than my limited skills in the kitchen. For one, she needed me to help her family keep their home. In order to do that, I needed a job. Now. Accepting the position of church pianist might help out, but it wouldn't supply all our needs.

After Sunday dinner, we enjoyed the crisp afternoon air, sunlight falling like bright jewels through the baring branches of the large oak tree. All of us except JC. He asked permission to visit the horses at the livery. Jewel wanted to say no; I could read it in her eyes. But with a heavy sigh, she consented.

JC raced away. I didn't comment. Jewel didn't, either. Instead, we listened to the *clop-clop* of a horse walking over the hard-packed dirt road in front of the house. The squeals of neighborhood children nearby. The chirp of squirrels gathering their winter store of acorns and pecans.

Trula plopped down in Jewel's lap, where we were lounging beneath the oak in the backyard. "Sing me a song, Mama."

Jewel laughed, though I thought I heard her gulp down a sob at the end. "That was your daddy's talent, not mine."

I cocked my head and stared at my sister. She had a nice singing voice. I'd heard her hundreds of times, usually in tandem with —

Davy.

I closed my eyes, willed Trula to accept her mother's answer. But the child's bottom lip jutted out and the corners of her mouth trembled. "Please?"

Jewel's gaze met mine, her eyes liquid and anguished. "I'm sure Aunt Lula wouldn't mind."

"Me?"

Trula bounced into my lap and clapped her hands. "Please, Aunt Lula!"

Jewel cleared her throat. "She can sing *and* play the piano, Trula. Much better than your mama can."

Trula's eager eyes found mine. I knew I ought to smile, but couldn't. Jewel understood that I'd left behind things like music when I'd settled into academic pursuits. But for the second time in a matter of hours, she'd pushed me in the old direction. Mama had encouraged things like music and art — things Fruity Lu dabbled at. Things that had no place in the scholarly world Daddy encouraged.

Jewel rose from her place on the grass beside me. "Trula can show you where we keep the sheet music. I'll bring Inez and Russell inside."

I mashed my lips together and glared at Jewel's back. I hadn't made a fuss at church this morning, playing in public when I hadn't touched a piano in years, but now . . .

Trula pulled at my arm, forced me to my feet. Before I could protest, I was on the stool at the piano, Inez jumping up and down, arms flapping like a bird taking flight. "Sing, Auntie Lula! Play and sing!"

Jewel certainly knew how to make it so I couldn't refuse.

I snatched a hymnal from atop the stack of music, hoping it would keep my focus on God, not on my playing. The book opened easily. I set it in place and squinted at the notes, my heart fluttering the same as it had this morning in church. One tentative finger pressed a treble key — slowly, so that it made no sound — then harder, the hammer striking the taut strings beneath it. The tone sounded off, as if they hadn't had the instrument tuned in some time.

Inez plopped down near my feet and popped her thumb in her mouth, eyes wide.

I took a deep breath, let my fingers find their way once more. And as they had that morning, they remembered more than I'd imagined they would. Tremors of fear skittered from my fingers to my toes, but the enraptured looks on the faces of those listening terrified me even more.

I jerked my hands to my lap and clamped my lips shut, leaving the strains of the piano to die in the silence.

"See? You'd be a perfect music teacher!" Jewel's smile brightened.

"Music teacher?"

"I told you. The high school needs a music teacher because the other one" — she cut her eyes to her little girls — "E-L-O-P-E-D. As far as I know the position is still available."

I bit my lip, knowing how much Jewel wanted me to take up music again. But teaching it? That went far beyond accompanying hymns at one Sunday morning service. To teach music meant embracing it altogether. I could teach a far more important subject than music — I was *meant* to teach more than music. "I don't think that's a good idea. I'll just look —"

"Nonsense. You'll go right on down there tomorrow morning and apply. Tell Principal Gray you're my sister."

My frown grew deeper. I'd committed to keeping Jewel and her children in this house, the house Davy had constructed with his own hands, even if he did buy the kit from Aladdin. If I abandoned that goal now, Don and Janice would roll their eyes and mutter about the unreliability of Fruity Lu.

Teaching was by far my most profitable skill. So I'd present myself at the high school tomorrow. Talk with the principal. Ask for a job.

As anything but the music teacher.

Darkness fell, and JC still hadn't returned. I picked up a ball of yarn and a crochet hook.

"Go on to bed, Jewel. I'll wait up."

"He ought to be home by now." She stared out the window, arms folded across her chest as if to barricade her heart. "You'll come get me if he isn't back soon?"

"I promise." The hook missed the loop. I

let the short string unravel as Jewel plodded up the stairs.

Oh, JC. Can't you make things a mite easier on your mama?

Only crickets answered my unspoken plea. Or was it a prayer?

I hadn't prayed much lately. I'd sat in church every Sunday, heard the words. But very little had penetrated to my heart. Why was that? In my younger years, I'd often felt close to God. Even when Mama passed, I could sense Him there with me. Then something changed. I changed.

My gaze wandered to the piano, and my fingers twitched. I slipped them beneath my thighs and searched for something else to do.

Clear the supper dishes. Tidy up the kitchen. Turn out the lights. By the time I finished, JC would be home again. Or I'd slip out to find him. I shivered at the thought of the chill in the air and the blackness of the streets.

As I set the last dish in the cupboard, a bump sounded from the living room. I held my breath, tiptoed across the wide hall. Caught JC with one leg over the window sill, half his body inside, half outside. His head jerked in my direction, and he gasped. Then relief coursed through his brown eyes as he considered me in the half-light.

I decided it best not to scold. "Glad you're finally back. We missed you."

He shrugged, swung his other leg into the house, eased the window shut, then studied the floor. I wanted to sweep him into my arms and tell him to cry on my shoulder as I had the night we buried his father. But I sensed a difference in him now. A manly pride in place of little-boy grief. Was that why he didn't want to be at home? Did he not want to appear weak?

My insides crumpled like a sheet of paper in a fist. I had no idea how to inspire him to work out his sorrow in tandem with his family. Jewel had Davy when Mama died. Don and Janice had growing children to grant some reprieve from grieving their mother. And Ben, he'd spent only a day at home before returning to Texas. Daddy couldn't handle his own loss, let alone mine.

For a few months, I'd hidden my pain under a frenzy of laughter and music, of flirting and silliness, as if nothing had happened to my mother. Then one day Daddy noticed my math test. A perfect score.

"I was a schoolteacher when I met your mama, you know," he told me. I nodded, having heard the story a hundred times from Mama's lips. "But all my children took after her. 'I don't need more schooling,' they told me time and again. But you." His eyes lit with a pride I'd never seen him direct toward me. "You are my last chance. My only hope. You could make me proud."

I'd scrunched up my face in confusion. Wasn't he proud of Don and his ranch? Or Ben owning a store in Texas? And both Janice and Jewel had husbands who loved them and provided well for their families.

He looked at my test again. "Yes, you could be the one." He sat down beside me, outlined a plan for my education. Not just high school, but beyond.

"But Daddy, girls don't go to college!"

"The smart ones do. We'll make sure you're one of them. After college, a master's degree. Then a doctorate. The first woman PhD in the state of Oklahoma!"

I held my breath, not sure I wanted to follow his plan. Or did I? I searched his weathered, wrinkled face. He'd not paid much attention to the child of his old age. Until now.

That day, I quit music. And painting. And parties.

It took longer to leave off boys, but they soon made it clear they had no interest in a girl with ambitions such as mine.

I'd thrown myself into my education to

deal with the ache in my heart over Mama. What could distract JC from his grief? I squatted in front of my nephew, took his shoulders gently between my hands. "I know you miss your daddy. Your mama and sisters do, too. But they need you sometimes. And even if you don't think so, you need them, too."

He looked away. "You play piano better than Mrs. Wayfair."

I huffed out a long breath. "Do you really care about that, JC? Or is it just an opportunity to argue?"

"I care." His lips clamped shut.

I reached over, took his hand in mine. "Tell me why." The soft, coaxing tone I'd often heard in Mama's voice layered my own.

"Daddy liked good music. Especially at church."

I let the silence hold his words. They lingered between us, poking at the roots that tethered me to my carefully constructed plans. "Are you saying you'd like me to continue to play the piano at church?"

He nodded. "I heard Mama tell you Pastor Reynolds said you could."

"If I play the piano at church, will you promise to stay at home more and tell us — or at least me — when you feel sad or mad?"

His eyes narrowed, as if seeing through me to judge the sincerity of my proposition. Then his head dipped. Once.

With a heavy sigh, I guided him toward the stairs. "I'll talk to Pastor Reynolds tomorrow. Happy?"

His skinny arms snaked around my waist, and I hoped to heaven he wouldn't ask me to take the position of music teacher, as well. Because for him, I'd do almost anything.

8

Chet

"Leland and the others are heading to Dilly's Café for lunch. You coming, too?" Brian Giles, girls' basketball coach and German teacher, stood at my desk, the characteristic grin absent from his round face.

Something was wrong. I glanced at the papers I'd been correcting. They could wait. My friend could not. I tossed aside my pencil and grabbed my jacket from the back of my chair, shoving my arms into the sleeves as I followed him out of the building.

But at the top of the stone steps, he stopped. I ran into his back as I straightened my collar. "Why'd you —"

My gaze slammed into Lula, whose face intruded on my thoughts more often than I cared to admit. I swallowed hard, watching her watching us.

Her small booted foot rose to the first

step. Then the next. And the next. Bringing her nearer. Pumping my heart faster. I pushed Giles aside, reached for the door that had shut behind me, and held it open. She passed in front of me, a stiff smile on her face, the smell of lilacs and autumn air lingering after she'd entered the building.

Giles and I both stared through the small square of glass in the door. She looked back, hesitated, then walked toward the office, her skirt swaying.

Giles whistled, long and low. "She's a looker, for sure."

I nodded. What was she doing here? Elation and fear spun in my gut as I remembered Mrs. Wyatt's mention of the open position. "New music teacher?"

"Maybe." Giles slid a look at me. I didn't like what his grin implied. "Wonder if she's as eager for a husband as Miss Delancey was."

My jaw clenched as I followed my friend down the stairs and toward the café. Female teachers of a certain age generally had more on their minds than conveying information to their students. Would Lula be the same?

We took our usual table in the café, the one we claimed when we didn't have to supervise the students during the noon meal. In our fourth year of teaching together, these men and I had become friends. I could count on them. But as I took my seat, I realized the conversation was about her. About Lula.

"Do you think she might be Miss Delancey's — or should I say, Mrs. Clifton's — replacement?" Carl Whitson, the manual training teacher, asked.

I shrugged, looked around for our waitress. "Principal Gray mentioned he might have a candidate applying, but that was a while ago."

Giles' eyebrows danced up and down. "Maybe this one will let you do the pursuing."

I snorted, unfolded my napkin, and laid it across my lap. "I'm not pursuing anyone. You know that."

"Maybe Carl will get a chance with her, then."

Carl rolled his eyes while the others exchanged amused grins.

Leland smoothed thinning gray hair over his ears. "If I didn't have this band on my hand, I might pursue her myself."

Laughter all around. Harold Leland, Latin teacher, was sixty, if he was a day. Married for forty years. Father to six. Grandfather to . . . several.

Our waitress arrived at the table, diffusing

the talk of music teachers and matrimony. The conversation turned as we waited for our food.

"Guess they're still at it near Ypres," Carl said.

"Lots of artillery fire at Verdun, too." Joe DeMarco, football coach and history teacher.

"And looks like they finally have good weather instead of all that rain," Leland put in.

Each man contributed something to the talk of the war. Except Giles. He sat silent. Stared at his plate. Out the window. Into the opposite corner of the room.

His gaze stuck there. I twisted in my chair. A table of soldiers. I jerked back around. Surely Giles wasn't considering . . .

I snuffed out the thought. Giles had other things to think of right now. Like the upcoming basketball season. And his unspoken infatuation with the doe-eyed domestic science teacher.

But what if he hadn't been given a choice? Like Clay.

9

Lula

I mumbled thanks to the two men who held open the door into the high school — a round-faced man with a wide smile and a receding hairline, and Mr. Vaughn from church. His handsome face drew my attention, but I forced my eyes back to the hallway before me.

I'd spent the past eight years avoiding romantic entanglements. I wouldn't let his finely chiseled features trip me up now. Besides, I'd only be here a few months. Just until I got Jewel back on her feet.

I lifted my chin and lengthened my stride. Then I slowed. Stopped. Drew in a deep breath. Was I really about to offer to be a music teacher? If only this were a math problem to solve. An equation that needed the right numbers in the right places. I bit my lip, smoothed my skirt, switched my handbag from my left hand to my right. And then the answer fell into place with the ease of a first-year algebra problem.

An existing teacher could take over music, and I could teach an academic subject. Hope surged. That's how I'd approach it. Calm descended as I pulled open the door to the principal's office and announced my name and my interest in a teaching position.

The woman behind the desk smiled. "You've come at the perfect time. Principal Gray is eating lunch in his office today." I followed her to a closed door. She knocked, then pushed it open. I stepped boldly inside.

A middle-aged man stood, wiped his hands on a square of cloth, and swallowed before speaking. "Ronald Gray." He extended his hand, gave mine a firm shake. "How may I help you, Miss —" He gestured toward a chair. I sat.

"Bowman. Lula Bowman." I clutched my handbag in my lap, fingering the clasp. "I . . . moved to town recently and am in need of a job." No use playing up Jewel's sob story. Either I'd secure this position with my own experience or I would not.

The man smiled, then his bushy salt-and-pepper eyebrows inched toward his nose. "Are you Mrs. Wyatt's sister?"

I sighed. I might have known news of my

presence in Dunn would have spread. "Yes, sir."

He shook his head. "Such a sad situation. Davy will be missed in this town. He was a friend to all."

I nodded, a lump lodging in my throat. Davy had been coming around to see Jewel since I was just a bit older than Inez. He'd acted more a brother to me than my own. *"Hang on, Fruity Lu,"* he'd tell me. *"One day they'll all see that you and Jewel are the cream of the crop."* Then he'd wink and tug on my ear. He even slipped five whole dollars into my hand the night I announced I intended to go to college.

"So you're staying with your sister indefinitely?"

My eyes snapped to the principal's. "No, sir. Only until I resume my graduate studies in mathematics next fall."

My heart stuttered. What if they withdrew my scholarship? Would I be stuck in Dunn for the rest of my days? Forever known as Fruity Lu, who could never finish what she started?

Principal Gray tented his fingers in front of his mouth. "You've taught school before, I take it?"

"Yes, sir. I went to normal school first, got my teaching certificate, then taught until I had enough money to pursue my B.A. When funds ran out, I taught again. I graduated last spring. I received the Donally Mathematics Award — post-graduate tuition as well as a position teaching a first-year class at the university."

His eyebrows lifted. "And how was that going?"

"Fine." My gaze slid away from his, but I forced it to return. "Of course with my sister's situation . . ." I let the words trail to nothingness. It wouldn't do to pronounce Jewel's delicate condition to this man, even if it would soon become apparent to all.

"So you're seeking a position only until the end of the school year."

"Yes, sir." Would that prejudice him against me?

His smile put me at ease. "As a matter of fact, I do have an opening, Miss Bowman. I lost a teacher a few weeks ago. Our music teacher. The question is, do you know anything about music?"

My stomach knotted. I didn't want to lie. And I didn't want to lose any hope of employment. I had no other recourse that would support Jewel and her children and me as teaching would. "I did have some musical training in my youth, but I haven't pursued it in many years."

He nodded. Then he pulled a paper from a drawer in his desk and slid it across to me. "We keep to the same rules of conduct as most other schools. No loitering downtown, especially around soldiers. We expect you to be at home between eight p.m. and six a.m. unless you are attending a church or school function. No smoking. No dying your hair. Skirts no more than two inches above your ankle. No keeping company with men — including riding in a carriage or automobile with a man other than your father or brother. And of course I assume you understand that you are not to marry during the term. I can't afford to lose another teacher to matrimony this year."

I pulled back my shoulders and sat up straight as I read through the list. "Mr. Gray, I am fully dedicated to my profession as a teacher, be it in high school or college. I assure you there is no cause for concern over my personal habits. I do not keep late hours or keep company with men. Ever. And even if I were so inclined, I've come to Dunn on behalf of my sister. I won't have time for any other dalliances."

A grin stretched Principal Gray's face. "Wonderful! Then the job is yours."

He hopped from his seat and scanned the books on a nearby shelf. Then he pulled two from their places and extended them toward me. "You know how to teach, and you know something of music. These books will help you put them together."

My confidence deflated. I didn't want to teach music, but to turn down the job at this moment seemed foolhardy.

"Go on. Take them."

My hand closed over the spines. A gold-stamped title on a dark cover: *Music Teacher's Manual* by Julia E. Crane and a quarterly journal entitled *School Music.*

"Principal Gray, perhaps you have a more qualified music teacher already on staff? I'd be happy to switch places. I could teach math, science, English . . ."

Principal Gray chuckled. "I have no other options for a music teacher, Miss Bowman. God obviously sent you to fill this spot."

I lowered my eyes, seeking courage from somewhere near my feet. *Was* God leading me in this direction? "It's just that I'd prefer more of a challenge." I raised my gaze to his, hoped he'd read the desperation in my face. "I'm used to intellectual stimulation, not days of . . ." I lifted the books in my hand, as if they could better convey what I thought.

Mr. Gray's eyes seemed to twinkle as he rubbed his hand across his mouth. My shoulders tensed. Was he laughing at me?

"Please understand, Mr. Gray. I'm grateful for the offer of this position and of course I'm happy to take it if you have nothing else, but . . ."

"Actually, the position of music teacher does come with another responsibility."

"Yes?"

"I'm also losing a teacher to the army. I need someone to cover —"

A male teacher leaving? His responsibilities would be more desirable than music. Energy surged through me, straightening my spine, curling my lips into a rare smile. "I'll do it."

This time Principal Gray smiled unapologetically. "It's quite a challenge, Miss Bowman. Are you sure you're up to it?"

"Of course." I wet my lips. Something to stimulate my mind, to keep me anchored in academic pursuits. "I'll help wherever you need me."

He opened a bottom drawer in his desk and pulled out a pamphlet. My heart pulsed against my chest, so eager was I to wrap my hands around the challenge. I accepted the slim volume, looked down in giddy anticipation.

Spalding's Official Basket Ball Guide for Women, 1916–1917.

I blinked. The words remained the same, as did the ridiculous picture of two girls in bloomers facing each other on the front cover, one holding a ball, the other with her arms outstretched. My chin jerked up. "I don't understand."

Amusement danced across his face. Irritation coiled tight inside me. I'd presented an earnest request, and he made sport of me? This was the result of being a music teacher instead of a mistress of mathematics. I wanted to fling the pamphlet to the desk and stalk out the door. But I needed this job. So I set the pages down with slow deliberation, then removed my hands quickly, as if holding such a thing might bring physical contamination.

The smile slid from Mr. Gray's face. "Miss Bowman, I —" He sighed, rubbing his forehead. "I took your offer to help in any capacity needed as a genuine one."

I swallowed. "And I assure you, my intent was sincere."

He pushed the pamphlet in my direction. "As was mine. Besides teaching German, for which I have a retired teacher willing to take over the classes until I find a suitable replacement, Brian Giles coached the girls' basketball team. I must have someone to take over that responsibility. I'd already

96

determined it would be required of the new music teacher because, again, I have no other options."

"But I don't know anything about" — I flipped my hand toward the collection of pages — "games."

"You are a smart young woman, Miss Bowman. And if my guess is correct, a good teacher, too. That's all a coach is. A teacher of athletics instead of academics. I believe if you would study the game a bit, you'd find the intellectual depth you seek in the strategy involved. But beyond that, I simply need your help. Practices don't begin until November, an hour at the end of each school day. You'll be able to read up on the rules and drills and strategies before then. The games will commence in January and conclude in early March, so you see, your time coaching basketball will be more than manageable with your other duties. And if you need any help, I'm sure the boys' coach can give you some pointers."

I had come about the music post against my better judgment. Could I really take over something as silly as girls' basketball, as well?

"Miss Bowman." Principal Gray waited until I looked at him. His eyes took on a mischievous twinkle. "Did I mention the coach receives extra pay?"

If I hoped to save anything at all for my continued education, every extra cent would be beneficial. But to stand in front of this town — Fruity Lu in the ridiculous position of basketball coach?

Could I sacrifice my pride for the sake of my sister and her family? Principal Gray and I stared at each other in silence.

I took the pamphlet.

Principal Gray clapped his hands together. "Congratulations, Miss Bowman. I have no doubt you will give our music students and our female basketball players your very best. A man in my position can ask nothing more."

10

Chet

Giles leaned back in his chair and belched. I glanced at my wristwatch and pushed my chair from the table. "Time to head back, boys."

We each left money for our meal with a bit extra for our waitress.

As we neared the high school, Giles pulled me away from the group. "Hey, Vaughn, can I talk to you a minute?"

I slowed. "Sure."

"I've been thinking . . . I mean, I've considered . . ."

A bell clanged inside the building. Our conversation dropped. We picked up our pace. I charged inside, determined to reach my classroom before the final student did. I glanced over at Giles. His eyes went wide. "Look out!"

I slammed into something. Some*one*. A small cry. A tumble backward. Books falling, sliding. Instinctively, I reached out. I couldn't catch her arms. She sat. Hard.

My eyes focused.

Lula.

I stared at my feet, fighting a grin. Not the best introduction, but an official introduction all the same. Finally. "I'm so sorry, Miss . . . ?" I reached out a hand to help her up.

She blinked as if she were going to cry. That wouldn't do. Not at all.

"Let me help you." Squatting beside her, I took her elbow in one hand, reached my other arm around to cradle her back, then lifted her to her feet. Lighter than a sack of sugar. Would she prove as sweet?

Her pretty mouth pulled into a frown. Best try again. "Are you injured, Miss . . . ?"

"Bowman," she finally answered. "Miss Bowman."

Giles stepped between us. "The new music teacher, I presume?" He handed her the books that had skated across the floor.

She hesitated, then reached for them, moving one small pamphlet inside a larger volume. A blush stole up her thin neck and colored her cheeks.

She was even prettier when flustered. My heart surged forward in spite of my efforts to apply the brake. Last year had been a delicate dance, avoiding Miss Delancey's pursuit. And yet I couldn't ignore this woman. She seemed . . . vulnerable. Yet strong. Determined, but lost somehow, too.

"Do forgive us for not paying attention, Miss Bowman."

She nodded. "Yes. Yes, of course. Now if you'll excuse me?"

She took a step toward the front doors. I blocked her path.

Her eyes sparked. "Do you wish to knock me down again, or do you have another aim, Mr. Vaughn?"

"Ah. I see you already know my name. Chet Vaughn." I held out my hand. "My mother is friends with your — with Mrs. Wyatt."

She squinted.

"I talked with JC. At the funeral." My voice died away. *Great job, Vaughn. Bring up the funeral.*

"Nice to meet you. I have to go," she whispered.

I stepped aside, watched her leave the building.

Lula Bowman. The new music teacher. Would she remain as alluring after I got to know her better?

I was almost afraid to find out.

11

Lula

I couldn't exit the building fast enough. Escape Mr. Vaughn and his eyes as dark and soft as a barn cat I'd once called Midnight. Escape the kindness and curiosity in his soothing voice. Escape those sturdy shoulders, the solid build not often found in academic men.

A man like Mr. Vaughn would no sooner look at me with romantic intentions than, well, than that insolent boy Mr. Graham would.

I pressed the books to my chest as my feet carried me forward. No direction in mind, just escape. My breath caught as I remembered that I'd signed my name to a contract that forbade any entanglements of the heart.

With long, deep breaths, I took comfort in numbers. Recited mathematical formulas. Concocted arithmetic problems. Walked until my legs ached. Until I noticed a familiar steepled building rise up on my right.

I stopped, peeling the books from their place over my heart. JC had asked me to continue playing the piano at church, and Pastor Reynolds wanted me to, as well. I stared at the white spire poking into the blue sky. Had the Lord directed my steps to this place? Whether it was the Lord or my own two feet, I knew I was where I needed to be.

The heavy door squeaked as I pulled it open. I found Pastor Reynolds in his small office at the rear of the church, the afternoon sun slanting through a high window and surrounding him like a halo. I could find no reason to tiptoe around the issue. "Have you found a permanent pianist yet?"

He removed the spectacles from over his nose. "Why no, we haven't." He glanced out the door, as if fearing Mrs. Wayfair herself would suddenly appear before us. "I confess, I had hoped you'd decide to accept the job."

My face heated. Pastor Reynolds hadn't been in Dunn long enough to know of my reputation as Fruity Lu, who came and went on a whim. He only knew me as Jewel's sister, the one who'd come home to support her. "Can you tell me a bit of what would be expected as pianist?"

"Of course." He motioned me to a chair. I sat. He paced. "I would supply you with a list of hymns — three or four — a week in advance. You would simply provide the accompaniment to our worship services."

"That's all?"

"Yes. And for your time, we are able to offer a small stipend."

I sat up straighter, wet my lips. "A stipend?"

He smiled. "Mrs. Wayfair volunteers her . . . talents, but our usual practice is a paid pianist. We'd be happy to welcome you into the position, Miss Bowman."

A bit more money in addition to fulfilling my pact with JC. Maybe the Lord had led me here, after all.

Pastor Reynolds stopped pacing. "You are welcome to practice here at the church whenever you'd like."

My throat tightened. Yesterday, I'd not had time to coddle my fear of playing in public after so long an absence. But it would have to be faced now. I ought to practice, lest I be deemed as incompetent as my predecessor. And I'd rather do it here than at school. Or at Jewel's house.

"Thank you. I believe I will."

"I've already inserted the hymn numbers for next Sunday into the board." The kindness in his grin settled me a little. "I'll be writing out my sermon, but if you don't mind, I'll leave my office door cracked. I don't often get the pleasure of a melody to accompany my study."

He left me alone in the narrow sanctuary. I rubbed warmth into my hands, then plucked a hymnal from a table at the back before circling the upright mahogany piano at the front of the room. Its dark wood gleamed in the bath of sunlight through the window panes. The intricately carved panels above the keyboard drew my touch. This piano had been in the church since before I could remember, hauled over miles and miles of prairie, coming to rest in Oklahoma territory long before it officially became a state. I pulled out the matching round stool and sat, my feet resting near the brass pedals at the floor.

The spine of the hymnal cracked as I opened it. I ran through the first two songs listed, my fingers remembering enough to be more passable than Mrs. Wayfair. But as the notes swirled around me, I knew I wanted to be more than passable. I wanted to be a rousing success.

I took a deep breath and turned to the third song. I didn't recognize the title, and the tune didn't come easily to my hand.

Four flats in the key signature. I peered at the notes while my fingers slipped and faltered. After three times through, my mistakes grew fewer.

My taut muscles relaxed. I sought the words, trying to fit them to the music, but as soon as I did, my hands leapt back into my lap and the sound dissipated. I stared at the words. *Perish every fond ambition? All I've sought, and hoped, and known?*

I folded my arms across my chest, contending with the words on the page. I would never give up my ambition. I'd strive to prove myself worthy of Daddy's hopes. To show the people of Dunn that Fruity Lu was only a distant memory. Grown up.

The urge to pray pressed firmly against my chest. *I don't understand Your ways, Lord. Why now? Why this?* Mama would've said God could handle my questions and my doubts. But Mama wasn't here. And Daddy's voice rang loud in my ears. *"You can't rely on anyone but yourself."*

In that moment, I knew the blackness of my heart. But I couldn't bring myself to crack open the door and let in a sliver of light.

I sighed. In spite of my feelings or the words of the song, it would have to be played. Just as music would have to be taught and basketball coached. My chin lifted. If I had to do these things, I would do them to the best of my ability. Give no one cause to resurrect my past flightiness.

I began the hymn one last time, just to be sure of myself. Then a movement caught the corner of my eye. My fingers landed on discordant notes as the swish of a skirt accompanied the click of the closing door.

I stood, waiting. When the woman didn't return, I wondered if I'd really seen anyone at all.

I found Jewel in the front room of her home, Russell in her lap, turning the pages of a picture book. I cupped the boy's chin and rubbed noses with him. He giggled, raised his arms. I hoisted him to my hip and bounced until he cackled with laughter. The sound eased the boulder of uncertainty that threatened my breath. Then I looked at my sister. My vision blurred as sadness caved my chest. Her entire future had changed. Mine had only been deferred for a few months.

"Well?"

I focused on the far wall. "I've accepted the position of music teacher at the high school and pianist at the church."

"Oh, Lula!" Jewel hugged me quick and

tight. She sat again with a satisfied sigh. "Davy and I have long thought you worked too hard. You need some fun in your life. This is it!"

Russell squirmed out of my arms, grabbed a wooden car, and ran it across the floor. I chewed my thumbnail. "My position at the high school came with a secondary assignment."

"Oh?" Jewel glanced up. "A math class?"

"No." I imagined myself in a gymnasium with a group of girls looking to me for direction. How in the world had I let Mr. Gray talk me into this?

Oh, right. The money.

I tried to smile, but it wouldn't stick. "Apparently I'm to coach girls' basketball, as well."

"Oh my!" Jewel raised a hand to her cheek, as if she, too, realized the ridiculousness of the assignment. Neither of us had ever gone in for athletics. Nor had our brothers.

I dropped to the sofa beside my sister. She reached for my hand. Squeezed. Then an alarming glint appeared in her eyes. "This is perfect!"

"Perfect?" I squeaked. Perhaps the grief and the pregnancy had addled her brain.

"Yes!"

Russell tapped Jewel's knee. "Mama?"

Jewel lifted him onto her lap, but her gaze never left my face. "It's exactly the excuse to invite Bo to dinner."

"Bo?"

"You remember. Davy's friend from high school. Bo."

I lunged to my feet, crossed the room, and stared out the window at a swirl of red and orange leaves dancing in the breeze. "I don't think that's a good idea."

"Why not?"

"Because according to my contract, I'm not to keep company with men."

"Oh, pshaw. Bo isn't other men. He's my friend. And he can help you."

"I don't need any help." Well, actually I did. Desperately.

"Of course you do!" She stood behind me now, her hand on my shoulder. "What do you know about basketball?"

I groaned. Coaching basketball suddenly sounded easier than dodging my sister's matchmaking attempt.

"Exactly. It's the perfect way for you and Bo to get to know one another."

I'd hoped her broken heart would afford me some protection from her attempts to find me a husband. "I appreciate your . . . thoughtfulness. I really do. But I'm not interested in pursing a relationship with any man."

Jewel shifted Russell from one hip to the other. "Now, don't get all in a huff, Lula. You're a lovely young woman. Men will notice, when you let them." She leaned closer. "Men like Bo."

"I'm not here to catch a man."

"Are you sure? Because Bo's one of the best, right behind my Davy."

I whirled to face her. "It wouldn't matter if he were Major General Pershing himself. Please, Jewel. Leave it be." My teeth ground into one another. How many ways did I have to say it for her to understand?

Jewel softened. "All right, little sister. But I know there's a man out there who'll turn your world upside down. If Bo doesn't spark something in you, we'll find someone else. What about at school? Aren't there any single men there?"

Laughter spilled out before I could stop it. "I haven't even been there one day! How would I know?"

I thought of Chet Vaughn. His arresting eyes refused to vanish from my mind. But handsome faces could be avoided. Especially if his classroom sat miles from mine, like I hoped it did.

As if reading my thoughts, Jewel said,

"Doesn't Louise Vaughn's son teach at the high school? He's quite handsome, and JC seems to like him." She angled a glance in my direction. "I'll introduce you to him on Sunday."

Mortification singed my lungs. "Chet Vaughn would no more look at me than a . . . a . . . ." I couldn't think of anything ridiculous enough to finish the sentence.

Jewel's eyes twinkled. "So you didn't notice anyone. I see."

I stooped to pick up Russell's car and books and rubber ball. "It will take much more than a pleasing face to stir my affections. I'm happy on my own. And Principal Gray gave me a book of basketball rules to review, so I won't require Bo's help. If I get desperate, I'll ask the boys' coach."

"The boys' coach?" Jewel's face brightened like that of a child at the candy counter. She bumped her shoulder against mine. "Is he handsome? Is he married? We could invite *him* to dinner!"

I kissed my sister on the cheek and prayed that the boys' coach was a doddering old codger far beyond the reach of my sister's scheming.

12

Chet

The final bell of the day sounded. As I left the building, noticeably cooler air hit my face. I savored the change, thankful for the promise of winter's arrival. With winter came basketball. Before long my afternoons would be spent in the gymnasium, and my Friday nights, if I had my way with the school board, in the town hall.

Whistling, I turned toward home, eager to stretch my legs over the few short blocks.

"Chet!" Giles sprinted toward me, face red, breathing hard. When he stopped, he bent over, hands on his knees, gulping air. "I — need — to — tell — you. Tried — earlier — today." He finally straightened. "I've enlisted."

The words slammed into me, leaving me the breathless one.

"I report to camp in two weeks."

Bile rose in my throat. I swallowed it

down, reminding myself why I'd chosen to stay here. I couldn't leave Ma alone, even if she had declared she could take care of herself. And if I were completely honest, I knew my students needed me, too. At least Blaze did. No one else would push him to graduate.

No, unless Uncle Sam required my presence with a draft letter, I'd remain in Dunn, doing what God had asked me to do. But that didn't mean Giles had the same path to travel.

"That's great." My voice sounded flat in spite of my effort to be positive. "But isn't this kind of sudden?"

He shrugged, eyes faltering from mine. "Not really. I've been thinking about it for a while."

I shoved my hands into my pockets, knowing Giles was waiting for me to say more. But I couldn't muster any excitement. I rubbed a hand across my forehead, wishing I could erase my frustration. No matter what, Brian Giles was my friend. I'd support him, same as I did Clay.

"Just don't go getting yourself killed over there, all right?" I said.

He blinked, as if he hadn't considered that possibility.

I jerked my head in the direction of home.

"Come to supper. Ma'll never forgive me if I don't give her the chance to fatten you up before you go."

"Ma?" I walked through the front door, right into our main room. A shabby sofa. A pedestal table surrounded by three spindle-backed seats. And the gramophone.

No sign of my mother. I ran up the stairs, calling again. "Ma!" I stood on the second-floor landing and scratched my head. It wasn't like her to be out, let alone out at suppertime. Maybe she'd run out of flour or baking soda or some such thing and gone to borrow some from a neighbor.

Muffled voices drew me back downstairs to the kitchen. Ma was chatting with Giles as she tied on her apron. Then she shooed us into the front room. Two phonograph records later, we sat down to supper, Giles spilling his news, Ma flitting around the table like a schoolgirl instead of a middle-aged woman.

"Eat up, Brian. There's plenty more." She smoothed his hair, patted his cheek. He chewed and smiled. The same scene had been repeated with Clay a hundred times over. But never with me.

I shoveled black-eyed peas and ham into my mouth, sopped up the gravy with a square of corn bread. And changed the subject. "So what about your basketball team? What do you think will happen to them?"

Giles wiped a trail of butter from his chin. "I feel real bad about that, but I talked with Principal Gray right after I enlisted. He said not to worry. He'd find a replacement coach as well as a teacher to cover my classes."

I pushed my plate away. Principal Gray knew. Had he known when I'd spoken with him before? Of course he wouldn't have felt free to tell me even if he had. Suddenly all my plans for war bonds and a new gymnasium felt impossible. I'd pictured Giles and me making it happen together.

"You know, I'd counted on your help to recruit the school board's support for a new gym."

Ma picked up our empty plates. Giles thanked her. Once we heard the water flowing in the kitchen, he leaned back in his chair, hands behind his head. "What are you up to now, Vaughn?"

I lowered my voice. "I plan to bolster Dunn's contribution to the war effort and maybe secure us a new gymnasium when the fighting's over."

I'd stayed late at school for several days, putting the plan on paper. The more figures

I considered, the more convinced I was it could work.

His eyebrows arched. "You always did have ambition."

"If you're still here a week from Thursday, I'd love to have your support at the school board meeting."

"You got it." The legs of his chair thumped to the floor. "I don't leave until the following Saturday. But you don't need me. You'll have the school board seeing things your way in no time."

He had more confidence in my powers of persuasion than I did. I shook my head. "Even if I do, I'm going to miss having you on my team."

13

Lula

On the second day of my new job, I finished reading the book and the journal on teaching music. Julia Ettie Crane insisted students start with learning to read written music. I'd already surmised that the former teacher had subscribed to this theory. I had a phonograph in my classroom as well as a supply of classical recordings. She'd left a few popular songs, too. But I decided not to pay attention to those. Not if I intended for my students to take this class seriously. To take me seriously.

Teaching my students to recognize the arrangement of notes on the page was similar to teaching mathematical formulas. Not as enjoyable as working out equations, perhaps, but just as fundamental. If the students demonstrated some proficiency in reading music, we could move quickly to performing the more difficult pieces.

Once I felt the students knew the notes by sound and sight, I'd adopt the approach of Dr. Hollis Dann of Cornell University: that the aim of music in schools should be toward culture and refinement, cultivating music makers, not noise producers. We would be serious vocal musicians.

It helped some, settling my philosophy on the subject matter I would teach. And realizing that high school students were less likely to criticize a female teacher than their collegiate counterparts. Especially a female *music* teacher.

I arranged my scribbled lesson plans, then picked up the pamphlet on basketball and skimmed the pages once more. It was like trying to read Chinese. And I only had a couple weeks to figure it out.

With a sigh, I stuffed the pamphlet into my handbag. Maybe it would look different after another night's sleep.

Jewel's smile stretched wide when I found her in the living room that evening. But her eyes remained sad. "I fixed supper. We just need to heat it up when we're ready."

I dropped to the sofa beside her, unable to squelch a whimper.

"You aren't having trouble already, are you?" Her needles clacked faster, knitting

118

something small and soft.

"No. Everyone's been great. Really. Miss Greenwood —"

"Bitsy Greenwood? The domestic science teacher?"

I nodded. Did Jewel know every single person in town? "She even invited me to sit with the other lady teachers at noon."

"And did you think for some reason they wouldn't?"

Not exactly. Yet it had been so long since a woman had been my friend.

The front door opened and shut.

Jewel's knitting dropped to her lap. "JC? Is that you?"

A muffled reply.

"JC, come speak to your mother," I said in my best schoolteacher voice.

"Yes, ma'am." He slouched in the doorway, sliding his cap from his head. "I'm home, Mama."

I crossed the room and ran a hand through his feathery hair. He looked up at me with mournful eyes. "Can I go now?"

Jewel motioned for her son to join her. When he complied, she wrapped her arms around him. Her eyes glistened. "I miss your father, too."

My chest felt as if it would explode, bleed sorrow over the walls and floor. Then Jewel simply began knitting again. Needles steady in her hands.

"Mama?" Inez's bare feet slapped against the wood floor as the sun dipped below the horizon. "Mama, Uncle Bo's here."

I slipped the basketball pamphlet under the cushion of the sofa and tugged Russell into my lap as a buffer, all while my sister flew out of the room to welcome our unexpected guest.

On the other side of the room, JC slumped more deeply into the wide chair. Davy's chair. Eyebrows lowered, he peered up at Bo as Jewel, chattering like Trula after a day at school, drew him into the room. "Lula got the job as the new music teacher at the high school. Isn't that grand? And thank heaven she'll sit in for Mrs. Wayfair from now on at church, too."

"That is good news!" He sat down beside me, rather sheepishly, I thought. "I wish I could attend more often."

I scooted away from him, closer to the opposite edge of the sofa, as his gaze swung from me to Jewel. "Y'all are a sight prettier than my men over at Fort Sill." His mouth crooked into a lopsided grin. "And you smell nicer, too."

I wanted to sink into the floor, but at

Jewel's laughter — the first I'd heard since Davy died — my chagrin turned to gratitude. My eyes sought Bo's. His expression sobered for a brief moment before he looked away. Warmth spread up my neck. Russell clamored for Bo's attention. He lifted the child, then tossed him toward the ceiling. Russell's giggles put me back on firm footing, at least until JC skulked from the room.

Jewel frowned, looking from me to Bo and back again. She reached for her smallest son, ending the gaiety. "I'll put this little guy in bed and then retire myself. You'll see to the girls, won't you, Lula?"

My lips parted, but Jewel didn't give me time to reply. She turned to Bo. "You know, of course, that you are welcome here anytime."

Several emotions I couldn't identify swept across Bo's face. He stopped Jewel with a gentle touch on her arm. "If you need anything at all, Jewel, I'm here to help."

My sister studied the floor. When she raised her head, I glimpsed Mama in her steady gaze. My breath hitched. "Actually, there is a way you can help."

"Anything."

My sister glanced at me, wet her lips. "If you could sell Davy's automobile, I'd greatly appreciate it. I need the money to cover the doctor bill that's coming." Her cheeks paled but then colored as pink as a summer sunset.

Bo's eyebrows gathered above his generous nose. "A doctor bill? From Davy — ?"

"Excuse me." Jewel fled, leaving me alone with Bo and his bewilderment.

He pushed back his hair, drew in a breath. "I thought that was all taken care of."

My chin fell to my chest as heat rushed into my face. "She'll be fine in a few months."

Heavy silence. I peeked at his expression. He blinked, clearly mystified. I sought a more direct, though still delicate, explanation. "Nothing she hasn't experienced four times before." I prayed he'd take my meaning without any more specific words.

A few moments later, he grimaced. "Poor Davy."

Compassion and sorrow mingled in the man's voice. Poor Davy. Poor Jewel. Poor JC and Trula and Inez and Russell. And the new little one, too. With the load they had to carry, I had no right to feel as sorry for myself as I had lately.

Inez pattered back into the room, face streaked white, fingers dripping with thick liquid. "I need help."

I stooped in front of the child, my hands on her tiny waist. "Inez! What have you gotten into?"

"Making a cake. For Uncle Bo."

I darted to the kitchen at the back of the house. Flour dotted the walls, the range, the icebox. Four eggshells littered the small work table, a yolk dripping yellow onto the floor.

I covered my eyes and groaned.

"May I help?" Bo's voice in the doorway.

"No, thank you. I'll take care of it." I picked up a rag and ran it under the spigot that protruded over the white ironstone porcelain basin. "Like Jewel said, we appreciate your stopping by." I met his eye. "And I appreciate your offer of help to my sister."

He cleared his throat, his gaze sliding from mine. "There's nothing I wouldn't do for her."

Before I could decide what he meant, I found myself alone, scrubbing away Inez's attempt at hospitality.

"Overall, I am very pleased with your knowledge of written music notes and symbols. That will make our time together much more enjoyable." I walked the aisles of my classroom my first Friday on the job, setting each student's graded test on the table in front of him or her.

A freckle-faced girl grinned as she read the A+ at the top of her paper.

"I've been thinking about our performance programs for this school year. We have the Christmas concert, of course. And National Week of Song in February. Patriotic music is suggested for that. And we'll culminate the year with a cantata." My hands empty of papers, I returned to the front of the room, to my podium. "I'm considering a new composition, *Columbus,* by E. S. Hosmer. Again, I feel the patriotic theme to be in keeping with the times."

One of the boys in the back raised his hand. Charles, if I remembered correctly. Seventy-eight on his examination in music reading.

"Yes?"

Charles stood, eyes laughing. "When do we get to do the fun stuff?"

"I'm sorry. I don't believe I understand your meaning."

"You know, popular music. 'For Me and My Gal.' 'Sweet Little Buttercup.' 'They Go Wild, Simply Wild Over —' "

I held up my hand like a policeman directing traffic. "We won't be singing those types of songs. We are here to make music, not noise."

The collective groan undermined my point but firmed my resolve. They might not take this class seriously, but I did. "Our goal is to listen to and perform music that is worthwhile."

"Anything that gets my gal in my arms is worthwhile to me," quipped a boy to my right. "With Miss Delancey we did all kinds of fun stuff."

Laughter tittered across the room. I pressed my lips together, then rapped my knuckles against the desk. "We're not here to while away our time with nonsense. We are here to learn."

Chins tucked toward chests, alleviating the need for me to see disappointment in their eyes. Except for Charles, who cocked a grin in my direction.

My gaze locked on his.

He didn't waver.

Visions of Mr. Graham returned. My chin lifted. I might only stand in front of a music class in a high school, but I refused to be trifled with. I'd lived with that from my siblings for too many years. Daddy said education would change everything. I still believed him.

The boy's lazy smile grew. I spun around,

putting my back to my students as I shuffled through sheets of music. If that boy thought for one minute he could make me change my mind, he didn't know a piano from a trombone.

Slow, deep breaths calmed the banging in my chest and cleared my vision. The sheet music in my hand read "Amazing Grace" at the top. They ought to be familiar with this one. We could work on assigning parts.

I took my place at the piano and peered at the black notes on the white page until my eyes burned. Mama's twang rang loud in my ear, warbling her favorite hymn. When my students' voices joined in, tentatively at first, then breaking into full-out song, air returned to my lungs. My shoulders relaxed. And my hands settled into a sequence of notes I thought they'd long forgotten.

14

Chet

The coolness that had been so refreshing turned bitter on Sunday when a north wind barreled through town. So Ma and I motored to church instead of walking. Just after I got the motorcar parked, a knickers-clad figure hunched at the perimeter of the graveyard caught my attention.

"I'll be there in a minute," I whispered to Ma at the church door. Then I trotted toward JC. We stood side by side, both of us with coat collars flipped up over bare necks, shoulders rolled forward against the blast of early winter air.

"Getting late," I said. "You coming inside?"

He glanced toward the building, then shrugged. "Guess so."

"Come on, then." I started walking. He fell into step beside me. I expected we'd part ways at the top of the aisle, JC to sit on

127

the right side with his mother, me to the left with Ma. But he slid into the pew beside me. I glanced around, hoping Mrs. Wyatt wouldn't see it as betrayal, as Ma had when I'd shadowed Mr. Slicer after Pa died. When Mrs. Wyatt smiled at me, I relaxed.

In the preservice quiet, JC talked. I listened, just as Mr. Slicer had done for me. I nodded when he complained about school. Laughed at the story of the fish he caught on Saturday. Prayed when his eyes roamed in the direction of the cemetery. Then the music called us to worship.

Good music.

Music provided by Lula.

I closed my eyes. The melody relieved the weightiness in my soul.

Opening my eyes again, I glanced to my right, at Ma. She was warbling the words of the hymn, her expression sincere. I prayed for her again, that she would let go of the past — of the shame of my father's death — and live in the light of today. Of sons who loved her, not a husband who'd abandoned her.

Shifting my focus to JC, I followed his gaze to the piano. Did Lula see the boy's pain? Did she comfort him? I slid my arm around his shoulders. He looked up. Smiled.

And as with my commitment to Ma, I

knew my being here mattered to this child, whether he realized it or not.

The rustle of the congregation's sitting eclipsed the final note of the song. Miss Bowman scampered somewhere out of sight. Next to her sister, I supposed. I kept my eyes trained on Pastor Reynolds, but my mind wandered to brown eyes set in a milky complexion. A dainty nose with just the right slope at the tip. A mouth —

No, I couldn't think about that mouth.

JC squirmed beside me. A grieving boy, yes. But also her nephew. Could he help — ?

Cold shivered down my back. To use the boy in my matchmaking scheme seemed as chickenhearted as my father's sneaking out of Fort Riley, Kansas, after his regiment was ordered to Puerto Rico during the Spanish-American War.

I winced. At least JC's father hadn't committed a dishonorable act in his death. Davy's accident was tragedy, pure and simple. JC's memories would be of a man everyone liked, everyone mourned. Would that make it easier or harder to live without him?

Pastor Reynolds asked the congregation to bow their heads in prayer. My chin dropped to my chest. I hadn't heard a word the man said. When my head rose again, my eyes locked on Miss Bowman at the piano, her graceful fingers gliding over the keys. What a gift to be able to make music instead of just imbibe it.

Ma touched my arm as Pastor Reynolds dismissed the congregation. "I need to speak with Mrs. Reynolds about this week's Red Cross meeting."

I nodded, turned to JC. "Did you enjoy the service, son?"

He looked up at me with solemn eyes. "Yes. It's better with Aunt Lula playing the piano." He crooked his finger, beckoning me closer. "Mrs. Wayfair hurt my ears."

I chuckled, slapped the boy on the back, and guided him out of the pew. Davy Wyatt could be proud that his son had an ear for good music. And I could praise God for yet another common interest with the boy to build a friendship upon. "How about you and I go get a soda next Saturday?"

"Oh boy! Could we?"

I nodded. "We'll ask your ma."

JC pulled me toward Mrs. Wyatt and Miss Bowman, my mouth suddenly dry as I searched for a way to open a conversation with Lula. But as we neared, Lula's delicate jaw tightened.

I slackened my steps, angled myself away

from her conversation with her sister, not eager to intrude. Yet Mrs. Wyatt's words carried clearly.

"But Lula, I specifically asked him so y'all could spend some time together." I didn't have to see Mrs. Wyatt's face to gather she disapproved.

"I told you, I don't want to spend time with him." Words solid as stone.

Mrs. Wyatt huffed. "If you don't spend time with a man, you won't find one to marry."

"How many times do I have to tell you?" she hissed. "I'm not marrying anyone."

I couldn't help but glance at them now. Not marrying anyone? A woman like Lula? It didn't make sense.

Mrs. Wyatt's hand swatted the air. "Oh, pshaw. You say that, but no girl means it."

Lula swung her gaze away from her sister, slamming it into me.

I took a step back, my collar suddenly tight. Her revelation should have set me to singing *hallelujah.* But for some reason it didn't. I felt something more akin to disappointment.

With a quick smile at JC, I patted my pockets and headed to the front of the church as if I'd forgotten something. I wished I could tell her I knew how much energy it took to fight the plans someone else had for your life.

Thursday evening, I copied figures onto one more piece of paper, blew on the ink to dry it, then set the page in the stack with the others. Numbers added, checked, and rechecked. I laced my fingers behind my head and leaned back in my chair, imagining a modern gymnasium, built to encompass a basketball court as well as bleachers along the sides. Either the school board would catch my vision, or they would not. I wasn't asking for a new gymnasium right away. And who could reject a plan that would ensure the people of Dunn did their part in funding the war?

Ma bustled into the front room and sat near the window, her basket of mending near her feet. I slapped my hands to my thighs and stood.

"I'll be home by nine o'clock, I imagine." I swept the stack of papers into my hand.

She looked up, squinted. "Where're you going?"

"The school board meeting about the basketball program, remember?" I'd told her I'd be attending, though I hadn't explained the details. Not yet. Not until I'd secured approval.

Her mouth twisted into a scowl. "You play little boy games while your brother does a man's work." She reached into the pocket of the apron still covering her clothes and yanked out an envelope. "Clay's last letter from the home shores." She looked down and started reading aloud.

" 'Tomorrow we sail for France. But don't fret, Ma. I'll make you proud. You have a son helping to make the world safe for democracy.' " She folded the sheet, slipped it back into the envelope. "Nothing you do here can compare to the honor he'll bring to our family over there."

I rubbed the back of my neck, ill-tempered responses battering my brain like whizbangs. But I kept my mouth shut tight, forcing my mind back to the day Ma sat with the telegram in her hand, tears streaming down her face. What mother should have to tell her young sons that their father had been shot for desertion? What wife should have to endure that mortification? Remembering helped me find the grace to forgive her harsh words.

The screen door creaked open. Giles crossed the room, greeted Ma. She smiled and patted his cheek. I looked away.

"Ready?" Giles asked.

"Ready as I'll ever be." I picked up my hat.

Giles chuckled. "Don't worry. You have a way of making people come to see things your way."

Right. Nothing I've ever said has made Ma come around to my way of thinking. Now, Clay, on the other hand, had a golden tongue. I grinned, wondering what disagreeable army tasks it had saved him from so far. I missed seeing him talk himself out of every jam.

"Let's go." Papers in hand, I trotted down the front steps. Giles' shoes slapped the ground behind me. Once we put some distance between us and the house, I slowed. "Thanks for coming with me tonight. I know it isn't important in the light of world events, but —"

"Hey now! Basketball means a lot to these kids. As does contributing to the war effort. And isn't that what we're fighting for? The right to decide our own destiny?"

I shrugged. In a sense, I guessed he was right. But even with my plan to purchase liberty bonds, it did seem like a paltry task compared to Clay's — and now Giles' — sacrifice. Maybe Ma was right. Maybe I was hiding. A coward like my father.

Squares of light cut into the darkness,

angling upon the sidewalk as we neared the high school. I breathed a quick prayer. I'd been willing to go to war, but I believed God had told me to stay here, to care for those who depended on me. I prayed He'd be with me as I dug my own sort of trench, ducked my head, and held my ground.

The school board discussed other business first. My foot tapped against the hard floor as I read through my notes again, rehearsing the arguments in my head. Then Giles' elbow bumped my ribs. When he had my attention, he nodded toward the front.

"Now we'll hear new business from Mr. Vaughn. Something about the basketball program, I believe?" Mr. Tanger's bushy eyebrows lowered, as if he'd already decided against my proposition.

I stood, cleared my throat, and handed the fact sheets to Giles. He distributed them to the school board members, his usual optimism giving him an air of nonchalance.

"I've come tonight not only on behalf of the Dunn Bulldogs basketball program but also on behalf of our community's desire to participate in the Great War being waged in Europe."

School board members snapped to attention at the mention of the war. Now to procure their full support.

"Our town has embraced the young game of basketball, as have our students. But we have a problem. Our gymnasium."

"Which was built just three years ago, as I will remind you, Mr. Vaughn." The gravelly voice belonged to one of the older members of the school board.

"Yes, sir. As I was saying, when the gymnasium was constructed, the game of basketball wasn't on anyone's mind at all. When drawing out the court later, we were forced to put the out-of-bounds lines almost at each wall, with room for only one stand of seating along the end, behind the basket. Not the ideal spot for spectating."

"So you want a new gymnasium — is that your request?" Mr. Tanger asked, jumping in.

"You know all unnecessary construction has been suspended due to the war," drawled Mr. Morrison, the portly director of the only bank in town. If only he were as predisposed to like me as his daughter seemed to be.

"Now, Charles, hear the man out." This from Pastor Reynolds. "Go on, Chet." He smiled his encouragement.

"I'm not asking for a new gym. Not right this minute. I am asking that you consider a change of venue, which would be of twofold benefit.

"I would like to move our basketball games to the town hall for the time being. This would allow more court space. And we could seat more spectators, as well. This change of venue would not only boost our basketball team's ability to focus on the competition instead of the walls, it would allow more students and parents to enjoy the games."

"I thought you said this would benefit the war effort," Mr. Tanger said.

"Yes, sir. My idea is to charge a nickel for admission — two pennies for students — and use the money to buy liberty bonds. These could be held in trust, perhaps by Mr. Morrison's bank, to donate to the school district at maturation."

Mr. Morrison leaned forward. "I'm not even sure we should indulge our young people with this foolishness at a time when we are at war."

A murmur swept across the panel of men.

Mr. Tanger's head wagged. "You aren't proposing we send the girls to play in the town hall, too, are you? Such a public display would be . . . would be —"

"The girls already play their games in public, Mr. Tanger. At our gymnasium. They are modestly attired and kept to a minimal amount of exertion, so I don't see a problem with letting them play games at the town hall. And Mr. Morrison, I believe, sir, that games such as basketball have much to teach our students — about teamwork and discipline — that will serve them well not only in life but should they so choose, also in defending freedom."

A couple of heads nodded. Others shook. Two men leaned in to whisper to a neighbor. Eyebrows angled toward noses. Mouths dipped into frowns.

I was losing them. I could feel it.

My gaze met Principal Gray's. His chin fell toward his chest, then rose in a slow motion. I could almost hear him say, *Go on, son, you're doing fine.* I took a deep breath and plunged forward.

"If you'll look at the paper you've received, you'll see my projections as far as attendance and income for games played in the gym at school and at the town hall. By using the town hall, we would raise a significant percentage more to be used to purchase liberty bonds.

"My boys have not had much success on the court so far. I admit that. But with four seniors this year, I think we can win some games. Maybe even win more than we lose.

A successful season would be a good thing for our school, our town, and our country. In return for our effort, I ask only that you commit to building a new gymnasium as the first project once the war in Europe has been won."

I had their full attention now.

Mr. Tanger's eyes narrowed. "Don't see why we should tie one thing to another."

Excitement climbed into my chest, my throat, my words.

"Mr. Tanger, are you a man of faith?"

"Well now. I believe I am. I'm a good churchgoer, aren't I, Pastor Reynolds?"

Several coughed down laughter.

"I have faith in my boys, Mr. Tanger. Faith in the ones fighting in France and faith in the ones that play ball on a court. I have faith that by moving venues we can raise a good bit of money to help our country and our school and bring a sense of pride to Dunn and to Oklahoma."

The room went silent. If nothing else, I'd shocked them into consideration of my proposal.

"We need to confer on the matter, Mr. Vaughn," Mr. Morrison twanged.

They gathered at one side of the room, speaking quietly. Giles pumped my hand. Principal Gray regarded me with proud eyes. No matter what the school board decided about this season or our new gymnasium, I'd given my all to make it happen. I only hoped it was enough.

A few minutes later, they returned to their seats.

Mr. Tanger's stare pinned me in place. "Make arrangements for your games at the town hall, Mr. Vaughn. The girls' games, too. And if your team can manage to win every single game, we'll build you that gym just as soon as victory in Europe is achieved."

Every. Single. Game? Surely they were joking. All I'd proposed was a winning season, something we'd never yet achieved. There was no way I could guarantee my team would be undefeated. And yet Mr. Tanger's stony smirk confirmed the challenge. I swallowed hard. Nodded.

The boys and I needed to start practicing as soon as possible.

15

Lula

I pulled the pamphlet of basketball rules from the bottom drawer of my desk in the music classroom. I turned the slim volume over in my hands, granite tenacity rising to the surface. I'd defied most of my family. Pursued a college degree. Won the Donally Award. I would conquer basketball.

I opened to the first article again: "Basket Ball for Women," by C. Ward Crampton, M.C.

> The teacher's purpose is to use the game to inculcate a habit of hygienic living, to provide organic exercise, to develop motor skill and to stimulate the social-athletic qualities of courtesy, fairness and co-operation.

I believed in those things. Well, I certainly believed in courtesy, fairness, and co-operation. It was the next line of text that turned me cold: *The girls wish to play a game to have a good time and to be on the winning side.*

My stomach lurched. I knew the girls expected me to coach them, but I hadn't actually considered the possibility that they'd want to *win.* How could I help them win a game that appeared no easier to understand than Egyptian hieroglyphics?

I closed the cover, closed my eyes. I'd have to seek help from the boys' coach.

On Wednesday, I rapped on my lectern, hushing the whispered conversations of my final class of the day. Seven girls gazed up at me. But in the back row, I saw the top of a head instead of a pair of eyes. I peered down the aisle. Nannie Byrd's hands framed her oval face, restricting her downward view to the book open on the table in front of her. The girl in the next seat elbowed Nannie. Nannie shook her head and continued to stare at the book.

My clipped steps echoed through the room. I hoped the noise would catch her attention, but she didn't flinch. I flipped the book shut. *Plane Geometry.*

Nannie's head jerked my direction. Tears darkened her deep-set eyes and red splotched over her round cheeks.

I slid the book into my hand, leaned near Nannie's ear. "See me after class, please." Then I returned to the front of the room. "Now, let's work on that Christmas medley once more. We only have a few more weeks until our concert."

Everyone cooperated nicely, but by the time I dismissed class and my students dashed for the door, my neck ached from the tension. How should I handle Nannie's infraction? No, I couldn't think of it as an infraction. Not after witnessing the naked anguish in her eyes.

Nannie fidgeted in her seat in the back, no doubt bracing herself for a lecture.

I took the chair next to her, then slid the confiscated book back in front of her. "Want to talk about it?"

She shook her head. Then she nodded. "I've always been good at math, until this year. Now I can't seem to understand any of it." A wail punctuated the end of her sentence. She buried her head in her arms and wet the book with her tears.

I winced, remembering days long ago when the slightest disappointment sent me into a crying jag. But Nannie didn't appear to fit the mold of Fruity Lu. I'd observed her as one who laughed easily and had many friends, but with the confidence to be herself and work hard at her studies.

Nannie lifted her head, wiped her face. "I'm sorry, Miss Bowman. It's just that Blaze needs this so much."

"Blaze?" I couldn't recall any such student from my classes.

"Reed Clifton." She hiccuped. Covered her mouth. Swallowed hard. "I help him in math — and other subjects." One shoulder lifted and fell. "He's not so smart with books, but he's great on the basketball court."

My eyebrows lifted. Did she tutor him on her own initiative or had someone assigned her to the task? "I don't think you need to worry about anyone but yourself. Now —"

"But Miss Bowman! Blaze and I are —" Her faced turned scarlet.

I crossed my arms. If she finished the sentence with "in love," I'd tell her a thing or two about boys and love and high school.

Her eyes challenged mine, as if she knew what words stood ready on my tongue. "He's my best friend. And I'm his." Her tone softened, but her look did not. "I help him with his schoolwork. He helps me with basketball."

"So you're on the basketball team?"

She nodded. "Do you like basketball, Miss

Bowman? I think it's fun. But of course, Coach Giles has gone off to the army now. We'll have a new coach, so I guess things will be different."

Should I tell her? Perhaps she and I could assist each other in overcoming our deficits. My mouth tightened. "You know, I'm more than a music teacher, Nannie."

Her eyebrows lowered in confusion.

"I'm also trained in mathematics."

My words transformed her back into the winsome girl I'd known for the past month. "Oh! Can you help me?"

I nodded, tamping down the excitement that leapt from my toes to my chest to my face. No need to get silly over mathematics. "I can help you. But I have a favor to ask in return."

Her expression turned serious. "I'll do what I can, Miss Bowman, but I don't play the piano very well."

Laughter spilled out, surprising even me. "I don't need you to play the piano, Nannie. I need to you to help me with —" I took a deep breath — "with basketball."

"I don't understand."

My fingers brushed the cover of the book in front of her. "Principal Gray asked me to coach the girls' basketball team."

Her mouth rounded into an O. "But you

don't know anything about basketball. Is that it?"

My voice lowered to barely a whisper. "I've never even seen a game played."

Nannie frowned, and my heart sank to my knees. What if she resented the fact that someone who knew nothing about the game had been assigned to coach? What if she wanted to quit the team? I held my breath, praying she'd understand my situation as I understood hers.

Then the easy grin returned to her face. "The girls will think it's grand to have you as our coach. But I don't know how much I can help you. Blaze teaches me to shoot the ball better, but I don't know anything about strategy. You should ask Coach Vaughn —"

Coach Vaughn? My heart jumped into my throat. He was the boys' basketball coach?

"Oh, I'd rather not." Even as the hasty words fled my mouth, I knew I had little choice. Well, except for Bo. Why did both men who knew about basketball also kindle my sister's matchmaking fire?

"But you'll still help me understand geometry, right?" Nannie chewed her lip.

"Of course. We can get started right now if you'd like."

"Thank you!" She threw her arms around my neck. "Coach Vaughn's completely given up on me and math these days."

I shut my eyes for a brief moment. "So Mr. Vaughn is your math teacher?"

"Yes."

I pressed my fingertips into my forehead. So much for thinking I'd be able to avoid his friendly eyes and knee-weakening smile. Maybe the man would enlist, like the girls' basketball coach. Until then, I had to find a way to deal with him — as a fellow coach and as Nannie's math teacher.

Just like when I looked at a group of numbers to be added, I suddenly knew the answer. I'd trade Coach Vaughn's help with basketball for my tutoring of Nannie. A simple exchange of information and expertise. Surely a man like Chet Vaughn could see value in that. I only hoped he'd understand it was a reciprocal agreement, for I'd seen what owing a handsome man did to a girl. And I had no intention of letting my feelings — or my future — run away from me.

16

Chet

I picked up a wadded sheet of paper from the floor of my classroom and shot it toward the wastebin.

Two points.

Four more days until the first basketball practice of the season, until I could savor the musty smell of the gym, the pound of the ball on the wood floor, the echo of my whistle against the close walls.

I straightened the desks in my room while whistling the popular tune "All the World Will Be Jealous of Me."

Could Lula's nimble fingers bring the song to life on the piano? Did she possess a pleasing voice to accompany the instrument? I smiled. Better than Mrs. Wayfair or even Miss Delancey, I'd wager.

Get your head in the game, Chet. I needed to throw off my infatuation with Lula. Especially considering the new pressure of an undefeated season. We'd secured the town hall. We'd play our best. We'd raise money for the war effort. But in the end, we carried no guarantee of a new gymnasium, even when the building restrictions were lifted. Not unless we managed to win every game we played.

I gathered papers and clipped them together, tried to find the jaunty tune again, but failed. Blaze plopped into a desk, head down.

"You need something?" I continued my work, knowing if I made too much of his presence, he'd not say a word.

He glanced sideways. "I'm having trouble again. And not just in math, either."

Jaw clenched, arm tight, I scrubbed away the equations that covered the blackboard at the front of the room. He and I had come to an impasse with numbers lately, none of my explanations sparking understanding. In fact, if I were honest, several of my students were struggling. Most in geometry. Never before had I encountered such difficulty in a class grasping the angles of polygons. Just triangles put together. How hard was that? But for whatever reason, this group of kids didn't get it. I needed a new way to explain things. But how?

"Nannie can't help?"

The silence stretched for so long I wondered if he'd left. I turned. He remained at the desk, fingers tapping, chin near his chest. He raised his head, a tortured look in his dark eyes. "I can't ask her again. I don't want her to think I'm stupid."

"You aren't stupid, Blaze. I've told you that before. You're smart about a lot of things that aren't measured in a classroom."

"Like ball," he mumbled.

"Yes. Like ball. Like how to get along with people. How to follow the rules and lead others to do the same."

He shrugged. "That's nothing."

"It's something many people never learn. And you're a hard worker, too. In the gym. In the classroom. At home." I winced, knowing how Archie Clifton pushed his boy, deliberately leaving him little time to keep up with his classes. "Don't focus on the grades themselves. You just need to pass to graduate. That's all. Just pass. You have a bright future, Blaze. A diploma is part of that."

I took the seat next to him. "I'll find you some assistance. I promise. But you can't be afraid to ask, either."

"Yes, sir." He looked me in the eye, but both of us knew he wasn't convinced anything or anyone could help him. If he didn't have a breakthrough soon, I feared he'd quit school now, even with the end in sight.

"See you at church on Sunday?" I'd encouraged him to attend, but he wasn't a regular.

He shrugged. "If he'll let me. Chores that must be done right away seem to pop up every Sunday morning."

"I understand. You do what you need to do, but know this: God sees. And so do I."

Blaze loped out of sight, off to meet Nannie, I suspected. If only I could make the boy see his strengths for what they were: valuable assets given to him by God. But just like his tussle with numbers, no matter how often I pointed out the truth of his life, he couldn't make sense of it. Not yet. He'd believed too long the poison Archie Clifton spewed from his bitter heart.

During my lunch break, I pulled a second chair behind my desk — sat in one and propped my feet on the other. I leaned my head back, closed my eyes, and folded my hands on my chest. A nap would fill the time, and perhaps afford me a bit of peace. Maybe even a better mood upon awakening.

But moments after my mind stilled, a knock disturbed the quiet. My head popped up, eyes blinking in the light. My classroom door squeaked open.

"Mr. Vaughn? Could I speak with you a moment?" Lula Bowman stood arrow-straight, her chin tipped upward just a bit, her mouth set in a grim line.

I swung my feet to the floor and smoothed back the hair above my ear. I hadn't thought I'd see much of her at school after overhearing the conversation with her sister. I certainly hadn't expected her to seek me out. Then I remembered JC. My breath hitched. We'd had a good talk on Saturday. I sensed him beginning to trust me as a friend. I prayed the boy hadn't landed in any trouble.

"Of course, Miss Bowman. Won't you take a seat?" I offered the chair my feet had been resting on. She raised her eyebrows, shook her head, and remained standing as close to the door as possible, as if eager to make an escape. At least she didn't flit as near as possible, like Miss Delancey had.

"I'm here to discuss one of your students. Nannie Byrd."

"Nannie Byrd?" Not at all what I'd expected. I crossed the floor just to prove that I could, trying to make some sense of what those kissable lips could possibly say next.

"She was in tears over her geometry

exercises yesterday."

"I see." I stood an arm's length from her now. Her face flushed, but she didn't look away. Or move closer. "She's had trouble grasping polygons, but she seemed to be managing better than most."

Lula's eyes flashed. "She's not managing. She's floundering. And she'll be failing if someone doesn't take the time to teach her properly."

I stared for a long moment, the sourness of her words erasing her attractive features. "I *am* teaching her."

"Not well enough, apparently."

My jaw ticked as I shifted my weight from one foot to the other. If she were a man, I might have plowed my fist into her nose. But she was a woman. So very definitely a woman. I rubbed a hand across my mouth, allowing time to temper my reply. "And have you come to offer a solution, Miss Bowman?"

"As a matter of fact, I have come with an offer of help."

"Ah, help." I returned to the chair behind my desk, expanding the distance between us. "And how would you propose to do that?"

"I have extensive knowledge of mathematics, Mr. Vaughn. I could go over your lesson

153

plans with you —"

I laughed. Pink sprang to her cheeks. I leaned forward, palms flat on the desk. "I don't need your help to teach mathematics, Miss Bowman."

Her skin glowed brighter. "But you do need me to help Nannie. And I . . . I need . . ."

Her bravado melted into the vulnerability of a baby bird knocked from its nest. She intrigued me, this woman, first hard, then soft.

"Go on, Miss Bowman."

She blushed from her hairline to the white lace collar around her neck. "Apparently I'm the only option for a girls' basketball coach this year. Principal Gray said you could help me learn the game." Her lips pinched as if she felt a physical pain upon saying the words.

Principal Gray? He hadn't warned me.

She cleared her throat. "I'm proposing an exchange of sorts. I will help Nannie and any of your other students who need it, if you will help me learn the game of basketball."

I studied Miss Bowman for a moment. Coming to me had cost her — and not a little. That much I could plainly see. Must everyone who needed help be so all-fired stubborn about asking for it?

But could a music teacher really help my students learn math? Lula seemed confident in her ability. What did I have to lose? Time spent in her company meant the opportunity to work out the intricacies of her character while enjoying the view. And if she helped Nannie, Nannie would help Blaze, and I'd do anything to see that boy graduate in May.

"If you can figure out how to help Nannie, I'd be mighty appreciative."

At last, her shoulders lost a bit of their rigidity. "And I would be grateful for your help with basketball."

"You can count on me, Miss Bowman."

She angled her head slightly in my direction, then slipped through the doorway and down the hall. For the first time in a very long while, I didn't object at all to the thought of being in company with a lovely female schoolteacher.

17

Lula

Don drove to Dunn on Friday to eat supper with Jewel, her family, and me. I wished I hadn't burnt the crust of the chicken pot pie, but at least the filling tasted good.

"How about we pile in my motorcar and I'll take you to visit Daddy?" he said as he pushed away his plate.

My heart bounced in excitement. *Yes! Yes! Yes!* In spite of Daddy's sad condition, I ached to see his face, to talk with him. To know that he wasn't disappointed with me for temporarily halting my schooling.

I looked at Jewel. She bit her lip, glanced at the children. I could see the battle behind her eyes, wanting to go but realizing the effort.

"If you're not up to the trip, Jewel, let me take JC and Russell with me," I offered. "Daddy would love seeing his grandsons. There'd be plenty of nieces and nephews to care for Russell. And JC would likely enjoy a day on the ranch."

Both Don and Jewel agreed. Bundled in coats and blankets, the boys and I crowded into Don's motorcar and made the two-hour drive north to Chickasha. As I suspected, nieces and nephews spilled from the house at our arrival. Don's wife, Audra, kissed my cheek and led me inside.

"He's not doing so well, Lula," she whispered as we stood outside Daddy's bedroom door, just off the kitchen. "But I'm hoping the sight of you will cheer him up."

My heart sank, but I forced my mouth to smile. Audra patted my shoulder. "Go on. Sit with him awhile. We'll see to the boys."

I took a deep breath, sent up a silent prayer, then stepped to Daddy's bedside. I touched his shoulder, more bone than flesh. He turned his head. One side of his mouth lifted.

"Hi, Daddy."

He grunted or groaned or something in between. I sat in a wooden chair, held his hand. "I know it's been awhile, but here I am. Your baby girl."

Did he nod? I thought so. Best to keep talking, not think about the fact that he couldn't reply.

"I guess Don told you about Davy."

His gaze shifted to the floor.

"Jewel's sad, of course. But she has her kids to think of. And the new baby coming."

His eyes cut back in my direction.

"Didn't Don tell you about that?"

A garbled sound, as if his mouth were full of marbles.

I sighed. "Then I guess he also didn't tell you I'd come to help take care of her, did he?"

Frustration pushed air out my nose. Don would leave it to me to tell Daddy. He didn't like the unpleasant jobs. And though all my siblings didn't mind pulling me away from my studies, they'd known Daddy would be unhappy.

"But don't worry. I'll return to the university next fall, never you fear."

A slight squeeze of my hand. All he could give me now, but it was something. Not like my growing-up years when I was the baby that interrupted his plans. He'd left me to Mama until she wasn't there anymore. Then he noticed me, gave me the opportunity to be the one child to satisfy his dream of seeing his offspring educated. How could I deny that to my only remaining parent?

His wrinkled fingers intertwined with mine. I wondered what he'd say if he knew the rest — about music and basketball. Would he rage like he had when Don had left school to work as a ranch hand in the neighboring county? Or when Janice had announced her intention to marry at sixteen?

I didn't remember those incidents, but I'd heard about them all my life.

Daddy's eyelids fluttered closed. His breathing evened. And I felt only relief that I didn't have to reveal the current state of my life.

Don drove us home on Saturday afternoon. We waved good-bye to him from the porch, and then I hurried to church to practice for the next morning's service. Tears pushed at my eyes, blurring the notes on the page, while all the pain of the visit with Daddy seeped out through my fingers. After I finished the final song, I dabbed my cheeks dry with my handkerchief while a now familiar shadow slipped out the church door.

Sitting behind my desk early Monday morning, I brushed some paste onto squares of cardboard. To each one I was affixing a photograph cut from *Spalding's Official Basket Ball Guide for Women.* Examples of side throw and high ball, bad playing and line foul. I blessed Miss Elizabeth Richards of Smith College for her suggestion in the pamphlet to use the pictures in this way. If not for the girls' sake, for mine. Otherwise, how would I know if they were executing the moves correctly?

During the noon hour, I stayed in my classroom and studied the rules once more. Even though Coach Vaughn and I had agreed to help each other, I had no desire to appear ignorant from the outset.

All through the day, I fought a wooden gait, a squeaky voice, stiff fingers. When the final bell rang, my heart leapt into my throat. My hands suddenly itched to press the piano keys that created the notes that meshed into a piece of music. Something that stirred my soul and made me forget my fear of looking like a fool in front of these girls, this town. From what I'd seen when I peeked into the gymnasium, at least our audience would be minimal. God had granted me that small grace.

I gathered my books and the mounted basketball photographs and headed to the gym. My step quickened, my heart pounding against the confines of my corset. *You're doing this for Jewel and the kids,* I reminded myself over and over.

Warm, heavy air met me inside the mostly

bare room with the high ceiling, musty with a smell that reminded me of JC after he'd run home from the livery. My eyes watered. I put a hand to my nose. My gaze trailed the afternoon sunshine as it streaked the wooden floor from the windows in the west end of the rectangular building. Electric lights hung dark from the ceiling. The painted lines on the floor extended almost to each wall, with the exception of the east end, where a stand of tiered benches filled the space. Two poles towered on opposite ends of the floor, each with a rim and netting attached.

A gaggle of feminine voices approached, and I set my things on one of two benches along the north wall as the girls rounded the corner from some room in the back. They were all wearing black stockings and shoes, bloomers, and sailor middy blouses, hair tied up in knots behind their heads.

Nannie broke from the group. Her freckled face had never seemed so relaxed in our mathematics tutoring sessions as it did now. Deep dimples sank into full cheeks, framing her wide smile. She reached for my hand, pulled me into the circle of girls.

"Miss Bowman, meet the team. Gracie. Elizabeth. Rowena." She pointed to each in turn. "This is Mary, but we all call her Bill."

"Bill?"

Mary grinned. "It's my brother's name, but Pa can't ever seem to remember I'm not him." She giggled.

I suddenly felt at ease. "I know how that is. Mama was forever running through the list of my older sisters' names before she'd get to mine."

Nannie continued her introductions. "This is Foxy, or rather, Hilda."

"Your older brother's name is Foxy?"

They all laughed now. Except for Hilda. Her cheeks turned crimson.

"She doesn't say much, but she's cunning," Nannie said. "In a good way, of course."

I spied Hilda's grin before she ducked her head. At least neither of the girls seemed to despise their nicknames. But then I'd thought Fruity Lu endearing until I understood what people really meant. Scatterbrained. Stupid. Irresponsible. Everything I'd been fighting to overcome.

Nannie draped her arms over the shoulders of the two remaining girls. "This is Dorothy, and the baby of our group, Bess."

Bess, Rowena, and Elizabeth were in my music classes, but the other girls were as unfamiliar to me as basketball itself. What would they think of a coach who'd never even seen the game played?

The little confidence I'd mustered shriveled like an old apple. My feet screamed to run, yet I stayed, conjuring up Professor Clayton's shaky voice in my head. *"Work the problem again, Miss Bowman. You almost have it."* My chin lifted, even as it quivered, and I addressed the team.

"Ladies, I've been given the task of stepping into Coach Giles' shoes. And while I do not have his expertise, I will do my utmost to see that you understand the rules and forms of the game and that we play to the best of our ability."

Nods. Then a suffocating silence. Now what? The girls glanced at one another. I could read the questions on their faces.

"Do you want our doctors' releases now, Miss Bowman?"

I could have kissed Nannie. Instead, I nodded. "Yes, please." Each girl handed me a piece of paper indicating a doctor had declared her fit to participate. Of course I knew from the Spalding's guide that since we would play according to the girls' rules — a line game — we'd lessen the risk of any "bicycle" hearts due to strenuous physical exertion.

"Calisthenics now?" Nannie asked.

That sounded right. I wet my lips. "Will

you lead those, Nannie, while I arrange our next activity?"

The girls lined up and engaged in a series of stretches and twists while I chewed my bottom lip and studied the pictures on the cardboard.

Guards. Forwards. Centers.

Guarding. Shooting. Throwing.

I'd grappled to understand the pieces of the game but had no concept of the whole. It was like knowing the numerals but not the formulas to make use of them.

"We're ready now, Miss Bowman." Nannie rested her hands on her curvy hips, face expectant.

My mouth was as dry as a creek bed in August, but I managed to remember the first suggested practice activity: throwing.

"Make two lines facing one another, with about fifteen feet between you." I retrieved a ball from under the tier of seats. It felt cool and smooth and heavy in my hand. I brought it to my chest, then pushed it toward Bill. Instead of making a straight line, like I'd imagined, it sank toward the floor and bounced to Bill's feet.

My cheeks burned. I didn't know much, but I knew that wasn't correct. Then I heard the snickering and whispering behind me.

I whipped around.

A cluster of boys stood near the door, hiding smiles behind hands or turning laughing faces to the wall. I wanted to disappear. To crouch behind my team and let them shield me from the humiliation.

Fruity Lu would have done that. Lula Bowman would not.

I pressed my lips into a straight line as I put my back to the boys. "Chest throws, girls. Up and down the line."

They seemed to know what to do once I'd given the instructions. The ball traveled from girl to girl, their throws much more authoritative than mine. And on target. Until the ball sailed over Rowena's head, toward the boys. Rowena retrieved it from near the feet of a tall boy. He smiled down at her. She scampered back to her place and tossed the ball to Gracie, who had to lunge forward to catch it.

The sniggering behind me intensified. Mumbled words followed by loud bursts of laughter. I might not hold with the seriousness of a game with a ball in a gymnasium, but I wouldn't allow my girls to be ridiculed. I whirled, fists finding my hips. "Don't you have somewhere else to be?"

The bounce of the ball on the wooden floor echoed in the stillness, as if adding punctuation to my statement. But it didn't halt the boys' amusement. Elbows poked at ribs, eyes rolled toward the sky, lips twitched. I stalked across the floor, but as I reached the boy in front, Coach Vaughn stepped into the gym. Eyebrows arched, his gaze locked on mine. "What's going on here?"

Before I could answer, he spoke again, his eyes never swaying from mine. "Blaze?"

The good-looking boy in the center stepped forward and swallowed hard. "We, uh . . . we, uh . . ." His head bowed. "Sorry, Coach." He nudged the boy next to him. "Let's go get changed."

Tingles scattered through my chest, down my arms. Mr. Vaughn was only doing his job, I told myself. Yet he'd rescued me none-theless.

"Miss Bowman," Nannie called, "what should we do now?"

I turned back to my girls. "Side throws."

We completed our drills, then I dismissed my team. The girls broke into groups, hook-ing arms, chatting, retreating from the gymnasium. Mr. Vaughn lounged against the wall, one foot crossed over the other. Our eyes met. He grinned at me as if I were a pie just pulled from the oven instead of a colleague who'd asked for his assistance.

Warmth crawled up my neck, into my

cheeks. Did he think me like other women? Like the ones who hovered around him at church, seeking the favor of his attention? Did he believe my request for assistance to be a ruse? A ploy to become more familiar with him? I bent over to gather my things from the bench, to hide both my discomfort and my anger. Then a pair of men's shoes appeared in my line of sight. I looked up, found Mr. Vaughn's maddening grin again.

"If you want, stay for my practice. I'd be happy to walk you home and answer your questions afterward."

I pulled up to my full height, even though the tip of my head only reached his shoulder. "No, thank you, Mr. Vaughn. I'm doing just fine."

Bitsy Greenwood poked her blond head through the door of my classroom at noon on Friday. "I'm sorry I've missed you lately. How are your classes going?"

"Fine." Suspicion laced the word. While the pixie-like domestic science teacher had been nothing but kind in my few weeks here, I'd tried to avoid her. But she was like a butterfly, everywhere at once. Bitsy looked like a magazine model in her stylish blue dress, golden hair curled around her face. My dark locks had a more scattered look,

and my most stylish outfit shouted 1910.
"And how are your classes?"

"Piece of cake." She trilled a laugh. "Of
course, that's the advantage of teaching in
one school for seven years."

I picked up my handbag, wondering if she
would follow me down the hall.

After I'd shut my classroom door, she fell
into step beside me. "Of course, one of my
girls scorched her milk today. Not the most
pleasant of smells — or the easiest pan to
clean."

Ah, yes. I knew that odor only too well.
Cooking had never been my greatest talent.

She chattered about her students as we
climbed the stairs to the first floor. She
seemed genuine, not seeking my company
to gather gossip or elevate herself, but I'd
had so few female friends in recent years
that I had no idea how to respond to her.

"Bitsy!" Another female teacher waved her
over. I hurried toward the outside door, but
Bitsy stopped me.

"Come on, Lula. Join us. We won't bite."
Her arm curled around mine. "You remember Aggie. She teaches English. And Stella
— she's in science."

"Of course." I didn't, but I should have. A
woman science teacher was as unusual as
one in the mathematics department. Maybe

Stella and I could understand each other. I nodded, finally remembering to smile.

The women chatted about students I didn't know. I didn't pay much attention until they all fell silent, eyes fixed on a sight behind me. I twisted around.

Coach Vaughn was sauntering toward us. His face froze when he spied the group. Stella stepped into his path and talked with him a moment until he deftly slipped past her with a tip of his hat. I was pleased to discover he wasn't a capricious flirt. Stella sighed as she returned to us, eyes dreamy and far away. "Isn't he handsome?"

My mouth fell open. Had she, a science teacher, fallen victim to Coach Vaughn's pretty face?

"Last year when my door jammed and I was stuck in my classroom, he sat in the hall and talked to me until they found someone to work it open again. Not many men would do that for a girl."

Or maybe he was a flirt after all?

"That sounds like Chet." Bitsy this time. "I know most women cotton to him for his looks, but there's more to him than that. He's a good teacher, a good friend, a good son. He's loyal and trustworthy and dependable."

"I wouldn't mind just a pretty face." Stella sighed.

I rolled my eyes toward the ceiling, wishing I could take my leave and enjoy the noon hour alone.

Bitsy laughed. "You say that, but think about long nights in a house with a man who couldn't make intelligent conversation. Would you really like to just sit and stare at a set of well-formed features for years upon years?"

Stella shrugged. Aggie smiled.

"So have you spent your heart on him too, Bitsy?" I wanted to clap my hand over my mouth. How had the words escaped without my permission?

"On who? Chet?" Bitsy looked as if I'd suggested she eat a worm. "He's not my type."

Was she the only woman in Oklahoma besides me to feel that way? Maybe Bitsy and I had more in common than I'd imagined.

Her elfin face turned serious. "I want a man who knows how to laugh, how to have fun. Not a stuffy mathematician. The one I want is —" She blinked fast, whisking away the moisture I thought I'd spied in her eyes. Then she cleared her throat, tossed her curls, and put on a wide smile. "Now, are you eating lunch with us today or not?"

18

Chet

I stood in a shadowy corner of the gym on Friday afternoon, waiting for Lula's practice to end and mine to begin. After she'd snubbed her nose at my offer of help — which she'd asked for in the first place — I'd deliberately stayed out of her path. I didn't stick my hand in the same dog's mouth twice.

And yet, as those wide eyes studied pictures on cardboard and then tried to demonstrate correct form for the girls, I wished she'd been a bit more receptive to my company. More like Miss Delancey. Not too much. Just a little.

"Throw the ball here, Foxy." Lula stretched her arms in front of her, but as the ball neared her fingers, she squeezed her eyes shut and turned her face away. A short squeal preceded the *bounce-bounce-bounce* echoing throughout the high-ceilinged room.

She jammed her hands to her hips. A strand of dark hair dangling across her forehead flew upward with her huff. "Well, that's not exactly how to do it."

The girls looked at one another, Bill finally speaking up. "I think we can figure it out." She motioned to the others to get into their places and the passing drill began in earnest. The girls didn't have one bit of the trouble Lula did. I inched back into the shadows, laughter locked behind my lips, arms folded across my chest.

As the girls continued to pass the ball up and down the line, Lula dropped onto the bench. She chewed her bottom lip and swiped a hand across her cheeks. I pushed away from the wall, wanting to go to her, to help her, in spite of her infernal pride.

I thought of Ma's insistence that she could care for herself if I joined the army with Clay. Yet we'd left her on her own once before, Clay bunking on the ranch where he worked, me in school fifty miles away. We'd both arrived home one Christmas to find the house filthy and her health declining. Clay had moved home immediately. The following year, we'd all moved to Dunn for my job. Last year, Clay and I had purchased the small house. If taking care of Ma had taught me anything about women, I'd learned that those who declared they needed help usually didn't and those who claimed they didn't usually did.

My boys trickled into the gymnasium, dressed for practice. The girls giggled and whispered as they readied to leave. Lula moved more slowly, as if her limbs were made of iron.

I could brush past her, ignore the tightening in my gut. But I'd experienced the sensation enough to know where it came from. I'd have no peace until I did what needed to be done.

One of her books toppled to the floor, landed with a bang. I picked it up, held it out to her. She hesitated a moment before the tension in her face released and her full lips titled upward. "Thank you." She set the book in her stack and stood.

"Nannie's doing much better in class now. Thank you for your help."

She nodded but wouldn't look at me. Stubborn girl.

"I believe you originally mentioned a reciprocal agreement. You help Nannie, I answer your questions about the game."

Her head jerked up, hope and wariness in a fierce battle behind her eyes.

I shrugged, hoping my nonchalance would

shift victory in my direction. "You've done your part. Now why don't you let me do mine?"

Her eyes pinched into a squint.

"Please stay. Watch our practice. Note any questions you have, and I'll answer them whenever you have some free time."

She glanced down at her books, at the bleachers, at the boys. She wanted to accept my offer, I could tell. Two white teeth gnawed her bottom lip. "If you don't mind . . ."

"Hey, Coach!"

I flashed a quick smile, then jogged to join my team before she could finish her answer. When I glanced over at the bench later, I saw she'd chosen to stay.

While Ma meandered the aisles and talked with the other ladies who shopped on Saturdays, I strolled down Main Street, no particular destination in mind. Just enjoying the cooler temperatures and a few minutes of freedom from home and work. I stopped at the storefront boasting the white pole with alternating red and blue stripes. A shave would have been nice. I rubbed the stubble on my cheek and remembered Davy Wyatt's fate.

Maybe not.

Cupping my hands, I peered through the dark window. Two chairs, wood-framed with leather cushioning, sat tilted backward, as if ready for a barber to apply his blade to a customer stretched from headrest to footrest. Davy Wyatt hadn't had any idea a shave would usher him into the presence of God.

I shuddered. Yet it wasn't contemplating my own mortality that made me pause. I'd settled that long ago in the little Baptist church in Wetumka, Oklahoma. My eight-year-old chest had felt as hollow as JC Wyatt's eyes had looked on Wednesday evening at prayer meeting. Losing a father could do that to a boy. But then Mr. Slicer, the principal of our school, had invited me to church. I'd grabbed the lifeline he offered.

Mr. Slicer and I remained friends until he passed away. A strong man with a strong faith. Without his influence, I'd never have been able to overcome my grief and look toward the future. Nor would I have aspired to teach school, to influence the lives of my students for eternity like Mr. Slicer did for me.

I shook my head and continued down the sidewalk. Likely we wouldn't see another barber in town until at least spring. Give people a little time to forget. Though I doubted it would leave my memory any time soon. Not with JC around. Or his attractive aunt crossing my path at school and church.

I stared out over the bustle of shoppers, mostly farm families plus a few men in uniform with girls on their arms. I forced Lula from my mind and thought of her nephew instead. I wanted to be his friend as Mr. Slicer had been mine. JC still sought out my company at church. And the afternoon we'd spent together at the soda shop had been good. But only time would build a deeper friendship.

A horse whinnied on the street in front of me, making haste to the livery stable at the end of the block. I'd heard Mrs. Wyatt had sold the business. I hoped Davy had left his family in a decent financial state. One less thing for JC to feel responsible for.

The man in the buggy wrestled to unhitch the horse. I shook my head, feeling no regret over giving up an animal to board and feed in favor of an automobile, even if it did eat more gasoline than I desired it to.

A boy dashed from the shadows into the weathered livery. JC? Was he in trouble? My concern formed quickly into a prayer. And yet he didn't appear to be running away from anything. He seemed to be running

177

toward something.

I stepped into the street behind a wagon, turning my head to avoid the trail of dust.

It took a minute for my eyes to adjust to the dim interior of the barn. Mr. Timmons, the livery's new owner, groused at the young man returning the horse and conveyance while JC brushed down the mare. I held myself to the shadows, watching, listening. Mr. Timmons and JC didn't speak to each other except for a grunt or two on Mr. Timmons' part. Had he given JC a proper job?

"Help you, sir?" Mr. Timmons' gravelly voice startled me.

"No, I —" I shoved my hands into my pockets and shut my mouth. Best to think before I let words flood out. I nodded toward JC. "Good little helper you have there."

"He'll do till he tires of it." Mr. Timmons sighed. "All the lads do."

JC didn't pay us any mind. He picked up a shovel almost as big as he was and began mucking out a stall.

"I'll just say hello to the boy, then be on my way."

Mr. Timmons shrugged. "Whatever suits." The man tottered away without a glance back.

At the stall where JC worked, head down, intent on his task, I leaned my arms on the half wall and wedged one foot in the gap between the horizontal boards. "That's a man-sized job you've got there."

JC's head jerked up. He blinked, then grinned, drew up straight, small hand gripping the shovel handle until his knuckles whitened. "Yes, sir, Mr. Vaughn."

I pushed away from the stall. "I thought perhaps if you finished up soon, we could run down to the drug store for another soda. I heard they've got some of that Dr. Pepper from down in Texas."

The boy's eyes widened and his mouth stretched across his face. "Yes, sir! I'd like that."

"Meet me at the drug store, then. Fifteen minutes?"

His head bobbed, and he attacked the soiled hay like a Tommy going at a Hun.

I chuckled, sauntering back into daylight. Ma wouldn't begrudge more time in town to catch up on the gossip and to brag on Clay. And at the soda fountain, JC and I could converse on our own terms, man to man. Maybe JC was another reason God wanted me in Dunn, Oklahoma, instead of in a trench in France.

Mozart's Symphony no. 41 kept Ma and me company in the long Sunday afternoon hours. I enjoyed the rest those hours afforded, but by evening, I found myself ready for Monday morning, ready to work again. After a cold supper, I dropped another recording into place on the gramophone. Ma rocked and knitted. I closed my eyes, leaned my head back, and thought through my week. Math classes. Basketball practices. Church.

And Lula.

Ma started another recording, just as tranquilizing as the last. Then a pounding at the door bolted me upright. Ma stood, the half-finished sock trembling in her hands, her mouth turned into a deep frown.

Clay.

My first thought. Hers, too, I imagined.

I yanked open the door, expecting to see a telegram delivery boy.

Instead, it was Blaze. Blowing on his hands. Almost blue with cold. I pulled him inside and stood him next to the heater, then shoveled another load of coal inside it to ignite more warmth.

Ma quietly climbed the stairs. Was she still

shaken with fear for Clay or had she thought to give me privacy with my student? I wanted to believe the latter, but I guessed it was the former.

Blaze toasted his large hands and shuddered before turning his backside to the warmth.

"Where is your coat?"

"Left too quick to get it."

"Left where?"

"Home." He turned to face the heat again.

"Had supper?"

He shook his head before his chin dropped to his chest.

"Sit at the table. I'll heat up the rest of the soup we ate earlier today."

A few minutes later, I ladled the steaming broth and vegetables into a bowl. Blaze almost inhaled it. When he finished, he wiped his mouth with his sleeve and blinked up at me as if he'd forgotten anyone occupied the table with him.

"So what happened?"

He shrugged. "Pop's growling about me spending time at school and at practice. When games start, it'll get even worse."

I had my own feelings about Archie Clifton. I couldn't endorse Blaze's complaints about the man, but I wouldn't defend his pa, either. "Are you doing your part? Getting your chores done? Being respectful?"

"Yes, sir. Every day. Even if I have to get up at dawn or stay out till midnight. Nannie 'bout tore my head off when I fell asleep in history class last week, but I couldn't help it. What with working at home and studying and basketball —" He shrugged again.

Guilt pummeled me. I should tell Blaze to quit basketball, to focus solely on finishing high school. But I knew if he quit the one thing he enjoyed about getting an education, he'd never survive until graduation.

His slender fingers raked through his hair. "Maybe I should join up now. A soldier's life is better than what I got. Even a rat-infested trench in France!"

I rubbed a hand across my mouth, more to keep it shut than anything. I didn't blame him, really. The idea of putting an ocean between himself and his father probably seemed much more appealing than finishing school. But I knew Blaze well after three years of basketball. If I gave my opinion on the subject now, he'd determine to do the opposite, just because he could.

"It's always an option. 'Course they won't take you until you're eighteen without a signature from your pa. And as much as it rankles him for you to spend time at school, he isn't going to want to lose you to the army yet, either."

Blaze's jaw clenched. He knew his pa wouldn't let him go just as surely as I did. Too much work on their farm, and Blaze did most of it. But beyond that, Archie Clifton seemed to take some perverse pleasure in snatching away every vestige of happiness from his boy. As if he begrudged him every good thing.

It almost made me wish Blaze wore JC's shoes. Losing a father — growing up without him — seemed an easier lot than the one Blaze had been given.

19

Lula

By the Monday after Thanksgiving, my team of girls seemed to be getting the hang of the drills. Nannie, her feet spread wide on the floor, stretched her arms high as Bill tried to throw the ball around her to Gracie. Nannie managed to knock the pass out of bounds.

"Good job." I approached the girls, motioning for the others to join us. "Did you see how she watched the ball the entire time?" Everyone nodded. "That's what we must do when playing defense, but of course when we are the ones with the ball, we have to find a way around a player like Nannie."

"How?" Bill asked.

I frowned. While I was starting to understand the fundamentals of the game, I had yet to grasp the game as a whole. I needed to ask Coach Vaughn how the girls should balance the differing skills of defense and offense. "We'll talk about that tomorrow."

"But our first game is in a little over a month and we'll miss a week of practice for Christmas!" Rowena whined. I glanced behind me, thankful, for once, for the distraction of the boys clamoring into the gymnasium in their shorts and sleeveless shirts.

"Go on, now. The boys need the court."

The girls scattered. It took me a few minutes longer to collect my things. When I pushed open the gym door to leave, it banged to a stop, reversed, and collided with my nose.

"Ow!" I turned away, hand over my face.

"I'm so sorry!" Coach Vaughn turned me around, tipped my chin up. "Are you hurt?"

No moisture wet my hand, so I pulled it away and shook my head. "I'm fine, thank you." When I glanced up, I almost lost myself in the endless depths of concern in his dark eyes — until I reminded myself that I was no longer a silly schoolgirl mooning over a good-looking boy. That was Fruity Lu, not me.

Besides, as the weeks had passed, Mr. Vaughn gave me every reason to believe I'd misjudged him. He no longer looked at me with that wolfish grin I'd seen at my first practice. He'd been kind. Respectful. Answered my questions seriously and without judgment.

In fact, I had two pages full of newly scribbled questions stuffed in an old geometry book, waiting to be discussed.

"Could we . . . That is, I have —"

"More questions?"

I nodded. I sincerely wanted to understand the game, to perform well in the role I'd been assigned. In fact, the more I learned about the game, the more I wanted my girls to win.

Just like I'd won the Donally Award.

Chet glanced at his wristwatch, then at the knot of girls just beyond us, their voices a frenzy of whispers. Heat rushed into my face as he leaned closer. "I'll only be an hour or so if you want to wait."

I gulped, nodded. He joined his team. Nannie raced to my side, her fingers curling around my arm in just the spot where Chet's had been. The other girls swarmed around us, their giggles driving my spine ramrod straight. "Miss Bowman! Are you seeing Coach Vaughn?"

"No. Absolutely not. You know a teacher isn't allowed such dalliances."

"That didn't stop Miss Delancey." Gracie's snicker set off the others again.

Burning heat bathed my neck and spilled into my face. "Coach Vaughn and I are . . ." I blinked. What were we? Colleagues? Yes, that was it. "We're colleagues."

Nannie's round face wrinkled at the word. "Is that all?"

Foxy linked her arm around mine. Bess did the same on the opposite side. Then they moved forward, carrying me along with them.

"Don't you think they'd make a striking couple, girls?" Nannie's question sparked yet another twitter of laughter. And a lovesick sigh.

I couldn't let them get such nonsense imbedded in their heads. I pulled free. "I appreciate your interest, girls, but I'm not looking for a relationship."

Gracie's eyes grew as big as two full moons. "But Coach Vaughn's so . . . so . . ."

Bill's mouth curled into a saucy grin. "Miss Delancey dubbed him a rake because he didn't cotton to her attention."

Miss Delancey had set her cap for Chet? Envy pricked, surprising me like the sudden jab of a pin. I didn't like the feeling. Not one bit.

Chet locked the gymnasium door while I pulled my coat closer around me. The days had grown shorter. Darkness would accompany my solitary walk to Jewel's house. But even as I warded off the December cold, I inhaled it, savoring the sharp, fresh scent with smoke lingering on its edges.

"It'll be warmer if we walk while we talk." Coach Vaughn's voice startled me, reminding me I wasn't alone.

I bit my lip and glanced at the few stars winking overhead. Was he asking to walk me home, or just walk? He hadn't requested to walk me home since that first disastrous day of practice. The request I'd refused. Could I consent now without violating the conduct expected of a female teacher?

Surely it would be all right. He wasn't taking me on a date or anything, just accompanying me while we discussed school business. I took a deep breath and let it out in a stream of white. "We can walk."

His hand touched my elbow as we started forward. I stopped. "Coach Vaughn —"

"Call me Chet." His eyes stared into mine, darker in the dusky evening, but softer somehow, too.

"All right. But Chet?" My heart beat double-time.

He sighed. "Yes, Miss Bowman?"

I took a deep breath. "Lula. Just . . . Lula."

He grinned. Tingles crawled down my

arms and legs. I sucked in a chestful of air and prayed I could keep my heart from turning traitor to all my plans. I stared at the ground, swept almost clean of fallen leaves by the brisk north wind. "You don't have to walk me home. We can find a time to discuss my questions at school."

"True. But we're here now. And you do have to walk home either way."

I opened my mouth and shut it again. To decline his offer would be impolite. My feet fell into pace beside him. A new awkwardness stole between us. I wondered if he felt it, too. If he suddenly wished he hadn't suggested walking with me.

A horse and buggy passed. Then an automobile chugged by, leaving its acrid smoke behind. I waved the smell away from my nose and coughed.

"Don't you like the smell of oil and gasoline?"

"Not particularly." I had no love for the smell of horse manure, either. I preferred things clean. I liked to walk to where I needed to go. Bicycle, if I decided to.

He slapped his hands on his chest and took a deep breath. "It's the smell of progress. I love it."

A street lamp pooled its light around us. Chet stared into the distance, as if seeing something beyond a dusty Oklahoma street. He caught me looking and grinned like JC with a shiny nickel in his possession.

I blessed the darkness that once again cloaked our faces from each another. Chet had dreams, too. I'd glimpsed shadows of them in that faraway look. But he had something else — something I didn't have. He had peace about his current place in life.

I'd felt peace when Mama was alive. Then that peace had disappeared into the ground with her. The peace I'd imagined I'd find while accomplishing Daddy's dreams for me had never quite come to pass. My college diploma was nothing more than a paper with my name on it. Perhaps the peace would finally come with my next degree. Or maybe at the end of my days, looking back.

Yet Chet had it now, shining naked from his face.

I cleared my throat, searching for some topic of conversation to erase my unsettling thoughts. Basketball. Yes. That's what we were meant to be discussing. I knew the girls had to be protected from strenuous overactivity as well as the roughness of the boys' game — or so the Spalding's guide said. But there were still fundamental skills that crossed both games. Chet had taught me some of them, and I wanted to know even more to give my girls the best shot at winning.

We turned the corner. The blaze of another street lamp illuminated a poster attached to the brick of a building across the street. A white-haired man dressed in red, white, and blue pointed his finger at us, the text underneath his image reading *I want YOU for U.S. Army.*

"I guess you miss the other coach." As soon as I'd said the words, I winced. Bitsy had told me Chet hadn't enlisted out of duty to his mother, and that it was a source of contention between them. I didn't want to dredge up an awkward situation. I searched his face, wondering if my words had shaken the tranquility I'd glimpsed earlier. But his expression remained the same. Or almost. Did I spy a bit of wistfulness — or had the wind blown shadows across his face?

"Giles. Brian Giles. He's a good friend."

We moved forward. "Was it a good thing that he enlisted?"

Chet's hands disappeared into the pockets of his coat. "I can't think of any reason for it not to be."

"Except that he could get killed."

He frowned. "Except that."

Fresh grief over Davy pushed tears to my

eyes. At least Jewel hadn't had to send him to war, not at his age and with a family dependent on him.

I wanted to understand Chet from his own lips, not the tales of others, so I asked, "And having your friend join up didn't propel you to follow?"

He shrugged. "I have other responsibilities that preclude my involvement in the current crisis."

The words sounded rehearsed, as if he'd said them a thousand times.

He ran a hand through the thick hair that curved away from his forehead, then threw me an almost apologetic smile. "I take care of my widowed mother. I'm all she has now that my brother Clay has shipped out to France. I feel quite strongly that it would be wrong to abandon her for the glory of going off to war."

I let his words linger, thinking of Bo and the other soldiers I'd seen wandering about Dunn on leave from Camp Doniphan at Fort Sill. Did they make Chet feel as conspicuous as I felt among a gathering of new brides?

My heart bumped in my chest, and gooseflesh trailed down my arms. I stared at my mittened hands curled around my books — music, basketball, geometry. Quietly, I said,

"I've often had to stand on the firm ground of my convictions when others thought I ought to be doing differently."

He didn't respond. Inwardly, I cringed. Had I misunderstood and shared too much?

I raised my head. In the shadow of the streets, his gaze met mine. His eyes shone. "Thank you for telling me that," he whispered.

My foot turned on the uneven terrain. He reached for my arm. Steadied me.

"I appreciate your help," I said, wondering if he knew I meant it for more than keeping me upright.

And then we were standing at Jewel's front walk, without a word of basketball having passed between us.

20

Chet

All through basketball practices the week
before Christmas, my eyes strayed to the
empty seat on the bleachers where Lula
often sat during our drills, sometimes scrib-
bling notes on paper, sometimes watching
with her pencil tapping against her lips.

The basketball questions she'd posed had
been thoughtful. Detailed. As if she truly
wanted to understand the game. And yet it
wasn't those conversations that came to
mind when I thought of her. It was that first
time she'd let me walk her home. We'd
talked of other things, things more personal
in nature. And I'd begun to wonder what it
would be like to have Lula as a friend —
someone who understood my need to stand
by what was right, even if it wasn't what I
wanted or what others wanted for me.

And yet after that conversation our time
together had been spent discussing basket-

ball strategy and rules. I took it as a challenge to try to steer the conversation back toward more personal things. But while she maintained an amiable manner, Lula was a formidable opponent against my efforts to get to know the woman behind the sweet face and quick mind.

I blew my whistle to stop the boys' sprints. Two players flopped to the floor. One walked the court with his hands on his head. Several bent with hands on their knees. Blaze stood upright, barely winded, a grin covering his face.

After a quick word of encouragement from me, the boys gathered their things and began the slow exit. I clapped Blaze on the back. "Need any help with your homework?"

He shook his head. "I'm going to Nannie's tonight. She says Miss Bowman explained things six different ways, until she finally understood. Now she'll try to smash the information into my thick skull."

"Don't sell yourself short, Blaze. There's plenty in your noggin. Don't make up your mind beforehand that you won't get it."

"I'll try. Thanks, Coach." He jogged away as I locked up the gym, whistling "All the World Will Be Jealous of Me."

Let's suppose that the lips I found kissing a
  rose
Were to tell me to look in your eyes,
If I'd find there a light that for me only
  glows,
More and more would my heart realize . . .

Could I kindle such a look in Lula's
velvety brown eyes? I was far more familiar
with warding off marriage-minded females,
not wooing ones who sparked my interest.

I climbed into my Tin Lizzie. Thoughts of
Lula led me to thoughts of JC. I turned on
Main Street instead of continuing toward
home, past the empty barber shop, the dry
goods store, the grocer's. Was JC at the
livery stable this late? I eased my motorcar
to the edge of the street and cut the engine.

When I peeked into the dim barn, JC's
mop of dark hair poked over the wall of a
far stall. "Hey there," I called.

JC grinned. "Hey, Mr. Vaughn."

We hadn't had much chance to talk since
basketball had taken up most of my free
time, but over our few sodas, we'd forged
enough of a friendship to allow me to dig
deeper now. "How have things been going
at home? Everything all right between you
and your ma?"

"Yes, sir." His shoulders drooped a bit as

196

he returned to brushing down a gentle mare. "I've been doing what you said — reminding myself that Mama's more sad than I am."

"That's good. Thinking about others before yourself is the way Jesus told us to live."

His arm dropped to his side. "But it sure would help if Mama and Aunt Lula wouldn't treat me like I'm Russell's age. I'm the man of the house." He slapped his chest. "I can take care of things when Mama doesn't feel well and Lula's at school. Don't they know that?"

Not feeling well? I knew what it felt like to be a boy in a house with a grieving mother, but had Mrs. Wyatt's grief made her ill? I wondered if Ma knew. She seemed to feel an affinity with the young widow. Maybe she'd want to help out. "Your ma's been sick?"

JC lifted one shoulder, let it fall again. "She's gonna have another baby. In the spring."

My gut clenched. Was that why Lula had come to stay with her sister? I suddenly felt selfish for wanting her company for myself. "Then it's even more important that you be the man of the family, isn't it?"

"Yes, sir." Serious brown eyes met mine.

I had an idea for a practical way I might help the boy. More than just buying him a soda once in a while, or giving him advice. "What if I talked to your ma?"

A scowl twisted his dirt-smudged face. He wiped a sleeve across his dripping nose.

I held up my hands, anxious to salve his pride. "Not outright, you understand. Just in general conversation. I could let her know that you're ready to take on more responsibility for the family. But you have to remember, you can't just run out on them when you get upset. The man of the house doesn't do that, even when his insides ache so bad he wants to hit something. Or cry."

JC stared at the straw-covered floor. "I know. I've been doing better now that Aunt Lula plays the piano at church. Honest I have." He looked up, eyes pleading for me to believe him.

I smiled, encouraging his efforts.

He shrugged again. "But I guess you could talk to Mama for me. Uncle Bo certainly won't."

"Uncle Bo?"

"Pa's friend. He's around whenever he has leave from Fort Sill."

The man in uniform I'd seen Mrs. Wyatt introduce to Lula at church. I thought of the way she'd noticed the recruitment poster, of our discussion of Giles and Clay and my own lack of service. She wouldn't be the first to fall to the "khaki craze," as the girls at school called it. Was Bo why she wouldn't let me any closer than basketball?

"Don't you like him?" I asked, fighting down jealousy.

JC rubbed the horse's nose before stepping out of the stall and securing the latch on the door. "He's not my dad."

"No, he's not. And neither am I. No one will ever be your pa, but maybe he just wants to be friends, like you and I are."

His eyes narrowed as if my defense of the man roused his suspicions against me, too. I needed to find a way to ask Lula about Bo.

"C'mon, JC. I'll drive you home in my Tin Lizzie."

The boy's face lit faster than an electric lamp. If all it took to stay in his good graces was a ride in my automobile, we would be friends forever.

I thought I'd get a chance to talk to Mrs. Wyatt about JC at the Christmas concert at the high school, but she wasn't there. Only Lula attended, dressed in something soft and filmy, very unlike her usual school clothes. I couldn't take my eyes off her as she led her students in Christmas carols.

Nor were the Wyatts at church the following Sunday. Instead, Mrs. Wayfair sat at the piano, pounding out the familiar hymns of the season, albeit with less skill than Lula had done a few nights earlier.

Not until the next Sunday did Ma and I sigh in relief to see Lula in her place at the piano. After the service, Ma and Mrs. Wyatt spoke near the front of the church. I headed in that direction, but on my way there I spied Lula seated in a pew, one child on her lap, another smashed against her side. I wanted to stop, to ask how she was, tell her I'd missed her at practices, but I didn't feel comfortable doing any of that until I'd made good on my promise to JC.

Mrs. Wyatt stuck out her gloved hand. "What a pleasure to see you again, Mr. Vaughn. My son tells me you and he are quite good friends these days."

I glanced around to find JC. He sat with Lula now. "I hope so, Mrs. Wyatt. I remember what it's like to be a little boy without a father."

My gaze cut to Ma. A storm cloud seemed to have settled over the face that had been so agreeable moments before. I sighed. She hated when I referred to Pa in any fashion. But I couldn't worry about that now. "I'd very much like to talk to you about JC sometime, ma'am."

She laid a hand on my arm. "Call me Jewel, please. And I'd like that very much. Perhaps —" She glanced toward Ma. "Perhaps you and your mother would like to join us tomorrow night for a New Year's Eve dinner? We thought we'd celebrate new things to come. Good things." Her voice had dropped to a whisper, and her eyes glistened with unshed tears. I cleared my throat and looked down at my hat in my hands.

"We'd be glad to join you." The huskiness in Ma's voice surprised me.

I glanced behind me at JC and Lula. I certainly wouldn't object to some time in Lula's company, but I told myself I'd keep JC at the forefront of my mind.

We arrived at the Wyatt house Monday night with a custard Ma had baked that morning. Jewel thanked her while Lula flew from kitchen to dining room with a look of sheer terror across her face.

I couldn't help but grin — and wish I could follow her about the house.

Instead, Ma helped the women get the food on the table while JC's sister — Trula, if memory served — pulled me toward the living room. I settled on the sofa while JC dug out a checkers set and arranged it on the floor, and the toddler crawled into my lap and sat, thumb in mouth, head resting against my chest, just under my chin, completely content. The two little girls chattered simultaneously, competing for my attention. I hoped they'd call us to the table soon. I was used to high schoolers — I didn't have a strategy for handling such young children.

A knock at the door. Before I could lumber to my feet with the little boy in my arms, the girls raced from the room.

"I'll do it!"

"No, let me!"

The door opened while the girls argued.

"Uncle Bo!" they squealed in unison. They arrived back in the living room with a man in uniform holding each of them by the hand. The same man I'd seen Jewel introduce to Lula.

My gaze slipped to JC as I lowered his little brother to the floor. Arms crossed and eyes narrowed, JC watched Bo as closely as a mountain lion watches its prey. If this was "Uncle Bo," I was about to get a chance to make my own judgment about him.

Before I could extend my hand in greeting, Jewel bustled into the room. "Bo!" She held his hands in hers a few seconds longer than a simple greeting could account for.

"We're so glad you could come!"

Ma slid into the room after Jewel. Lula was nowhere to be seen.

Bo grinned. "After all the holiday passes, I didn't think I'd be able to weasel another. But I did."

The man nodded toward Lula when she appeared in the doorway. I glanced at JC. His scowl deepened. I envied him. It was the same look I wanted to wear.

Jewel pulled Ma forward. "I want you to meet my dear friend, Captain Bo Nelson. He and my Davy" — she pulled a handkerchief from her sleeve and dabbed at her eyes — "were lifelong friends."

Ma's eyes shone. "My son, Clay, is in the service, too."

Bo glanced in my direction. I shook my head.

Ma sighed. "No, my other son. He recently shipped out to France."

For some reason, this information made Lula frown. Then she blinked and cleared her throat. "Dinner's ready."

Jewel pulled Bo toward Lula. "Bo, dear, will you please escort Lula to the table? JC can bring me, and Mr. Vaughn can accompany his mother — just like one of our old parties!"

Bo offered Lula his arm. She blushed and

lowered her eyes.

My mouth turned as dry and gritty as sawdust. I crooked my arm for Ma but couldn't take my eyes off Lula. I hoped Ma and I could eat and excuse ourselves as quickly as possible.

But once our meal commenced, everything changed. Jewel and Bo drew Ma into gentle conversation and Lula hardly glanced at the man seated to her left. Of course, she didn't look at me, either. A cup of milk spilled. Lula mopped it up and dried the child's tears. The littlest one grinned and giggled, poking his finger into a pile of mashed potatoes. Of all the children, only JC remained solemn, darting a glance at me every now and again. I needed to find a way to speak to Jewel about him — and perhaps to Bo, as well. Though I didn't relish additional conversation with the man if he was meant for Lula.

"So tell us, Mr. Vaughn, have you been able to teach Lula the finer points of the game of basketball?" Jewel's mouth twitched upward. Lula kept her head down, eyes intent on her food.

"I believe she has things figured out. The season starts a week from Friday. I do hope y'all will come to some of the games."

Jewel gave Lula a long look. "I imagine we

will since my sister is involved. And of course you'll come to some games, too, Bo. Won't you?"

He dabbed his mouth with a napkin. "If I can get away, certainly. Although if the rumors are true, we'll ship out soon. I don't know if I'll be able to wrangle much more leave."

Jewel's face turned pale. "You'll go to fight?"

He nodded, lifted another bite of beef, then set it back on his plate again, something unspoken passing between him and the widow of his longtime friend.

Lula wiped Trula's mouth and then rose, stacking three empty plates to take with her into the kitchen. She reached for my plate just as I lifted it. Her soft, warm hand brushed mine on the rim of the dish. I wanted to grab hold, to not let go. But of course I didn't. She blushed deeply and scurried to the kitchen.

Why was she so timid around me? What treasures lived locked behind those dark eyes?

I pushed back my chair. "I'll help clean up."

"Absolutely not!" Jewel sprang to her feet and steered both Bo and me toward the front of the house. "Lula, please join us.

The dishes can wait."

A few moments later, Lula walked stiffly into the room, crossed to the fireplace, and stabbed at the wood with an iron poker. The ashy log splintered, sending a nest of sparks flying up the chimney. Then she wobbled to the stool at the piano and sat facing the keyboard, hands clasped in her lap, gaze fixed on her hands.

JC leaned on the edge of the instrument while Bo complimented the meal and the company. I pulled out my handkerchief and wiped my forehead. I needed to move away from the heat, but was it the fire or Lula?

I ran my hand over the top of the walnut cabinet that housed a phonograph, then let my fingers graze the keys of the piano. A sheet of music propped on the ledge above the ivories caught my eye: "All the World Will Be Jealous of Me."

"That's one of my favorite songs." I nodded toward the music. "Will you play it?"

She popped to her feet. "I really don't think that's appropriate for today."

I tipped my head. "Something else, then?"

"I . . . I don't —" She couldn't seem to catch her breath. "I'd better finish the dishes." She spun to leave the room, but Jewel caught her by the arm. "Mr. Vaughn, perhaps I will take you up on your offer to help your mother and I tidy the kitchen. JC, please help the children get ready for bed."

"Mama!" he whined. I silenced him with raised eyebrows. If he wanted to be the man of the family, he needed to help his mother when she asked him to.

"Yes, ma'am." He trudged off, his little brother in tow, both sisters following along behind.

"Bo and Lula can entertain each other, can't you?" Jewel grinned at the two of them. Bo returned the gesture, but Lula looked as if Jewel had asked her to climb on the back of wild bronco.

I knew I ought to follow Jewel to the kitchen, but I couldn't leave Lula alone with Bo. I slipped off my jacket and laid it over the back of a chair. Then I unbuttoned my cuffs and rolled my shirtsleeves toward my elbows. "Why don't you entertain Mr. Nelson, Jewel? I have great expertise in the area of dishwashing, so if Miss Bowman will lead the way . . ."

Lula brightened, and I took hope that my company was apparently not as odious to her as Bo's.

"Come, dear. I'll help, too." Ma wrapped an arm around Lula's waist and led her to the kitchen.

I took a step to follow, then remembered

JC and knew what I had to do. I cleared my throat. Jewel and Bo looked at me in surprise, as if they'd forgotten anyone else was in the room. I sat on the piano stool. "While we've got a moment, I've been hoping to talk to the two of you about JC. . . ."

21

Lula

Thoughts of our first basketball game of the season had me flustered. Or at least I told myself it was the basketball game. The truth was I couldn't think of New Year's Eve, of Chet at our dining room table, without feeling . . . undone. And the memory of him rescuing me from Jewel's matchmaking? It still left me breathless.

Only he hadn't followed me into the kitchen. He'd stayed with Jewel and Bo while his mother had helped me clean up. Did that mean he hadn't meant to rescue me at all?

Nannie poked her head into my classroom at noon. "You know the game's at the town hall, right?"

My mouth dropped open. The town hall? Not the gymnasium here at school? "Are you certain?"

She nodded, eyes dancing with excitement. "Coach Vaughn arranged it. We're to use the admission money to buy war bonds. The town hall has room for more people." She disappeared again before I could form a reply.

After my final class of the day, I ducked my head and trudged through the cold January evening to the town hall, the air fragrant with the scent of coming snow and billowing smoke from those keeping warm indoors. My heart bounced against my ribs like a basketball under Blaze's hand. Steady but firm and quick.

Even in the unlit hall I could make out the two sets of spectator stands placed along one side of the court taped off on the floor. Two poles with baskets hugged the walls at opposite ends of the rectangle.

The door opened behind me, letting in a wave of cool air, but it shut just as quickly. I turned, expecting my girls but finding Chet. The building suddenly felt too warm. I removed my coat and draped it over the bench where I would sit with my players.

Chet's hand cupped my elbow, and electricity jolted through my body, intensifying the steady thump in my chest.

"You look like you're going to be sick."

I blew out a long breath, wishing my nerves wouldn't show so clearly on my face.

He leaned closer. The scent of winter and gasoline mingled on his overcoat. "It's just a game. You'll do fine."

Eight chattering girls pushed inside and retreated to the far end of the large room before peeling off coats and scarves to reveal bloomers and blouses. Though Chet had put a bit of distance between us now, the girls giggled and whispered as they glanced in our direction.

Chet clicked the buttons on the wall, and electricity burst into the bulbs overhead, flooding the court with light. I shielded my eyes for a brief moment, then blinked the room into focus. My team clamored around me, adjusting the bows on the wide white bands that held back any stray hairs that might want to drift from their pins during play.

"This is it, Miss Bowman. Aren't you excited?"

"Do you think we can win?"

"Do I look good enough?"

I laughed at the last one. Foxy primped and preened as if she were getting ready for a house dance instead of an athletic contest.

When the other team arrived, I shook hands with their coach, a man of enormous height and few words. Chet's team, clad in shorts and shirts, climbed into the stands, stretched long legs in front of them, and leaned their backs against the row above to watch our game. Townspeople filled in around them. In the crowd I picked out a woman I'd gone to high school with, a man that had been friends with my brother Ben, Pastor and Mrs. Reynolds, and Mama's friend Annie Chiles. As a wave of nerves washed over me, I turned to the wall and wrapped my arms around my middle. Too many familiar faces — people who remembered me as Fruity Lu — for my comfort.

"All set, Miss Bowman?" Principal Gray's jovial voice didn't help my queasy stomach. He was the one who'd landed me in this mess in the first place.

Determinedly, I stood as tall as I could manage. "I'm ready."

Chet caught my eye. He inclined his head toward the girls from the opposing team warming up and then at my group clustered near the bench.

"Nannie, get the girls ready." I smiled thanks in Chet's direction. "We've got a game to play."

"We don't mind, Miss Bowman. Really we don't." Nannie walked beside me to the tiered benches at the side of the court after our game. Our loss. I cringed. We'd only scored four points. The other team scored twenty.

Blaze led the boys in a series of shooting drills as they prepared to begin their contest. Nannie had filled me in on Chet's deal with the school board. It was good of him to be so civic-minded and patriotic, but I found my stomach roiling with nerves on his behalf. Even if I was still new to the world of basketball, I knew that winning every single game was a monumental challenge.

Nannie wiggled her fingers at Blaze, but he didn't notice. She huffed, then turned her attention back to me. "It's not like we were any good even when Coach Giles was here."

I tried to accept that as a compliment, but I couldn't ignore that the crowd had snickered at my girls' attempts to pass the ball. Defend the ball. Shoot the ball. Anything at all, really. The other team had noticeably overpowered us the entire game.

My gaze drifted to Chet. He stood with his hands in the pockets of his pants, the matching brown jacket bunched up about his wrists. His attention never left the boys warming up on the court. I had more questions for him now that I'd seen an actual game played. My elbow tingled where he'd touched me earlier. Why did he have to keep chipping away at my resolve to keep men out of my life?

Nannie climbed higher in the stands to sit with her teammates. I remained on the bottom tier, alone, elbows on my knees, chin in my hands. The boys moved from one end of the court to the other. Dribble, dribble. Pass, pass, pass. Shoot. The other team caught the ball before it bounced out of bounds and took it to the opposite end of the court.

I took note of what resulted in a team scoring points and what didn't, hoping to apply some of it to the girls' game. But it wasn't easy. The boys ran the length of the court. The girls stayed within their allotted lines, two girls in each of the three zones, each playing either offense or defense, not both.

By the halfway mark of the game, my back and neck ached. I stretched my spine and dug my fingers into the soft places near the bone. Conversations grew louder in the absence of play, drifting to my ears.

"They look better than last year, that's for certain."

"We'll see when they have to play Edgewise at the end of the season."

"Missed the girls' game. Heard it was good."

I winced. Good?

"Good as in good for a laugh. Wonder if they'll score more than ten points the entire season!" A deep chortle, vaguely familiar.

My fists tightened. I almost turned my head to find the speaker.

Then his companion answered. "Especially since Fruity Lu's the coach!" A slap resounded. Hand to thigh? Hand to bench?

Didn't matter. It felt like a hand to my face.

My jaw clenched as I found the edge of my seat and gripped it as if to save myself from drowning. I shouldn't have come back to this town. I shouldn't have stayed. I shouldn't have agreed to teach music or coach basketball or play the piano at church. Not when my past reputation lurked constantly in the shadows.

I stared across the town hall, willing the mortification to recede before it spawned tears. If only I hadn't found my attention planted on the last person I wanted to witness my distress.

Chet.

He stared right back at me, eyebrows bunching as if in consternation. I needed to leave. To be alone. But before I could reach my feet, a soft hand settled on my shoulder.

"Do you want to come sit with us?" Bitsy

smiled at me, and I couldn't help but smile back. I followed her to the other side of the bleachers, away, I hoped, from those who refused to let Fruity Lu be forgotten.

Our boys won by ten points. I waited until the crowd around Chet thinned before approaching him. His grin widened when he saw me. I ducked my head, warmth crawling up my neck. "Congratulations. Your boys played well. At least, I think they did."

He chuckled. "They did indeed. I'm glad you noticed."

My head shot up, but his expression seemed amiable enough. In spite of my determination to limit my time in this man's company, I needed his help. I let my gaze wander over his shoulder, away from his dark eyes and oval face, the strong nose and masculine mouth. Things I'd long ago schooled myself not to notice about a man.

"I need a favor."

"All right . . ."

"I need you to teach me more about the strategy of the game. I don't want the girls to spend an entire season in disgrace due to my ignorance."

No smugness appeared in the set of his mouth or around his eyes at my confession. Instead, he seemed pleased. "I have a few things to finish up here, but if you'll wait, I'll drive you home and we can talk."

I stepped backward, flustered at the idea of riding alone with him. I could have explained our one walk together to anyone who'd questioned my motives. But climbing into his car was more . . . deliberate. I didn't want to violate my contract with Principal Gray. But I didn't want to refuse Chet, either. I wanted to learn strategy. And no matter how hard I tried to convince myself otherwise, I wasn't averse to spending time with Chet.

After stuttering an acceptance of his kind invitation, I retreated to a corner until the crowd dwindled. Even Principal Gray left with his family. Relief drenched me like a spring thunderstorm.

"Ready?" Chet pushed open the door and stepped aside to let me pass.

I murmured thanks. As we walked to his automobile, I said, "You've done wonders with JC. Thank you for that."

He shrugged. "I haven't done much. Listened, mostly."

"Jewel very much appreciated your telling her how he feels." The conversation that had kept him from joining me in the kitchen on New Year's Eve. How could I fault him for helping JC?

He kicked at a pebble on the ground. "I know how much it helps to have a friend who understands what you are going through."

I glanced sideways at him, feeling the layers of the statement. He understood JC. But he seemed to understand me, too. And I, him. Both of us walked a path the people around us did not understand.

"Yes, that makes a world of difference."

We fell silent, our steps in opposition to one another. His long and solid, mine clipped and light.

"How's Blaze doing in math class? Nannie's always worried about him."

"He's managing better now, thanks to you both. I believe he'll graduate if he stays on course."

A blast of chill wind shook my hat and rustled my hair. I pulled the collar of my coat around my bare neck and shivered.

Chet pulled a long draw of air through his nose and let it out through his mouth as we reached his motorcar. "I love autumn and winter. The cold, dark evenings in contrast to the warm, lit gym. Or town hall, as the case may be."

I almost laughed. Perhaps we didn't understand each other as much as I'd imagined.

He laid a woolen blanket over my knees before settling behind the steering wheel and starting the engine. "So what great basketball wisdom may I impart to you this evening?"

My gaze swept over the street, looking for someone who would recognize me and alert Principal Gray. Best get the questions asked and be done with it, in spite of my wish to take a long drive with him in the Ford.

"You watched the girls play. What am I missing in coaching them? Obviously they had little understanding of how to take the ball from the other team or keep it in our possession."

He didn't answer right away. Instead, he started whistling, the tune barely audible above the chug of the motor but familiar in an odd kind of way.

When words finally left his mouth, they came slowly, like uncertain steps. "I've watched you practice, and while you've taught them the technical skills, they seem to lack a passion for the game. The drive to succeed."

My chest puffed up with defenses but deflated just as quickly. If I acknowledged the truth, I'd noticed the same thing with my music students' performance at Christmas. They had hit the right notes, but the songs had not had heart. I'd thought my lack of fervor for either music or basketball wouldn't make a difference for my students as long as I taught them the basics. But I suddenly feared it had.

Frustration shook me as surely as the cold wind whipping through the open sides of the automobile. I hadn't sought either position, but the Lord had put me in the path to receive them. How was I to succeed at them if I had no hope of inspiring my students?

The motorcar stopped, and the engine silenced. Two downstairs windows of Jewel's house glowed bright, alerting me that she was awaiting my arrival.

Chet looked straight into my eyes. "I didn't mean to criticize. Please don't take it that way. You are doing the best you can in a difficult situation."

My vision blurred. Never had anyone known me as fully as it seemed he did by that one statement. I wanted to throw my arms around his neck and weep into his chest. Pour out all my insecurities. My hopes. My longings. Even the womanly ones I'd buried beside Mama. Instead, I fumbled to open the car door. At least in the darkness he wouldn't be able to see the wetness in my eyes.

"Lula?" He jumped out and raced around to help me to the ground. His fingers brushed lightly against my elbow.

Pride clogged my throat, but one corner broke away, letting the words past. "So will you help me? With the team?"

He stared into my face so long I wondered if he'd heard my questions. Then he blinked, stepped back. I almost stumbled forward.

He combed a hand through his hair. "I'll do what I can. Maybe if Blaze talked to Nannie —"

"No!" The harshness of the word surprised me. I moderated my tone. "I don't want her to . . . to think any less of me." In spite of another gust of cool night air, my face burned.

Chet shook his head and moved closer, leaning his face toward mine. "I wouldn't let anyone think less of you." He took my hand and placed it in the crook of his elbow. In an instant, we were moving again, toward Jewel's house. I thought about inviting him in, chatting a while longer.

But I dismissed the thought. I had to protect my job and the welfare of Jewel's family, even if I did desire, at the very least, to call this man my friend.

22

Chet

At the front door, Lula's hand slipped from my arm. I dipped my hat and bid her farewell, wishing I didn't have to. I jogged down the few steps to the yard. Then I stopped. Turned. She hadn't yet gone inside. It almost seemed as if she were feeling the same way I was, and it gave me courage.

"Let me take you to Lawton tomorrow," I called to her. "We'll talk about basketball. Maybe see a picture show. Eat ice cream." When had a prospect for a day delighted me more?

She didn't blink or twitch. She stood there, eyes wide. I moved a step closer. "Please, Lula?"

She rocked forward on her toes, her small tongue darting out and circling her lips. Then she took a deep breath, closed her eyes, and whispered, "I'd love to."

I didn't remember returning to my automobile or driving home. But suddenly I was in the house, peeling off my coat, hanging it and my hat on a peg by the kitchen door, dropping my leather case beneath.

"Ma?"

No answer. Was she angry that I was late? The light bulb blared overhead, but I saw no evidence of supper. The range was cold and the house beyond was dark.

"Ma?" I turned on lights, put a record on the gramophone — "All the World Will Be Jealous of Me" — and stretched out on the sofa. Had I really just asked Lula out? And had she said yes?

I sang along to my favorite song. When it ended, Ma still hadn't turned up, so I put a pot of coffee on to boil. Where could she have gone? Should I be worried? She had a few friends, but she rarely spent time with them outside of Red Cross meetings or church, though she *had* taken to stopping by God's house at odd hours.

My stomach rumbled, but even hunger couldn't dampen my spirits. I'd downed two cups of coffee by the time Ma bustled through the door.

"Sorry I'm late," she mumbled, immediately gathering eggs and bacon from the ice box and then slicing bread to toast in the oven. As the iron skillet popped and sizzled,

223

I retrieved dishes from the cupboard. She finally filled one plate, then the other. I carried them to our small table.

I placed a napkin in my lap as I inhaled the sharp smell of pepper and meat. My stomach grumbled again, but I folded my hands and bowed my head, saying a blessing over our meal before forking some eggs into my mouth, trying to appear hungry for food instead of for the hours to tick away until I could see Lula again.

Ma watched me, silent. Not a new thing. Our conversations had dwindled when Clay left. Long ago, when my father still lived, I remembered him teasing Ma out of her silent sulks. I hadn't had much success with the technique. But then I'd had only seven years to watch and learn from him, and most of those years I wasn't paying much attention.

Clay, on the other hand, could charm Ma into giving him the last morsel of food standing between her and certain death. Clay seemed more like Pa that way. Maybe just the mention of my brother would loosen her up.

"You reckon Clay's over there yet or still crossing the pond?" I sopped up the runny egg yolk with my bread.

Her eyes lit. Her mouth opened. Then one

corner of her mouth dragged toward the floor. "I couldn't say where Clay is, but you sure look like a hound that's been in the henhouse."

I bit into a slice of bacon, savoring the flavor.

"How did your game turn out?"

"We won." Easy enough. But her scrutiny made me nervous. "So where were you when I got home?"

She shrugged. "I ran over to the church."

"Oh? A meeting going on?"

"Not exactly."

"So you were . . . ?"

She dabbed her napkin to her pursed lips. "Can't I take in the peace of the church building if I have a mind to?"

"Of course." The last of my egg slid down my throat as I wondered if my prayers for her were on the verge of being answered.

"I saw that motorcar of yours earlier. At the Wyatts' house."

Perspiration dampened my armpits. I pulled at my collar, wishing I could open a window. "Our game was at the town hall. You remember — we're raising money for liberty bonds."

Ma's eyebrows arched, the same look she'd given me when I was a boy and had tried to hide some misbehavior. Like tip-ping over outhouses.

"I, uh, I also drove Lula — uh, Miss Bowman, home afterward."

She stiffened.

Why had I called her Lula? Too familiar. Too telling.

"She had some questions about basketball. Coaching, you know."

Ma picked at the food on her plate. "Did she now? I'm surprised a girl that serious about music would give much thought to something like basketball."

"Serious about music?" From what I could tell, Miss Bowman was serious about mathematics. That was the subject that made her face light up like a shooting star in the night sky. Not when she talked about music. In fact, had she ever talked to me about music? I couldn't remember her mentioning it — odd, now that I thought of it, considering it consumed her school days and her Sundays.

I couldn't quite reconcile Ma's comment with the times I'd observed Lula at the piano, either. She hit all the notes. Quite well, actually. But I'd never felt she gave herself to the music in any emotional sense. I'd assumed music was a job to her, a skill she possessed that allowed her to make a living.

"You're sweet on her."

My fork clattered to the plate. Ma and I didn't discuss matters of the heart. She'd never spoken of her feelings for Pa. Nor had she encouraged Clay or me to take a wife. Of course, I'd never given her much concern on that score. School and church and athletics had consumed me both when I was in high school and now. But Lula was changing everything.

Ma pushed away her plate and crossed her arms. "So you won't leave me to go into the army, but you'll cast me aside to take a wife?"

My mouth dropped open. She didn't mind if I left for France but didn't want to share me with another woman?

"For heaven's sake, Ma. I've only known Lula a few months." I slapped my palm on the table. "And if I judged correctly from our dinner with the Wyatts last week, you seem to like her, too."

Ma grumbled something as she cleared the table. I didn't even try to decipher her words. Instead, I began to imagine what it would be like to be married to Lula. To come home to love and peace. To conversation and laughter and comfortable silences. To a woman with dark hair and warm brown eyes accentuating the creaminess of her skin. To a wide mouth that looked so kissable when it pulled into a rare grin.

Yes, God had called me to care for Ma. But He'd also brought Lula into my life — and my church, my workplace, even my basketball world. He must've had a reason for that. And I intended to discover what that reason was.

I surveyed my slicked-back hair, then straightened the knot of my necktie and grinned at myself in the mirror. I felt like a schoolboy again. Something had smoldered to life between Lula and me. I prayed she felt it, too.

"I'm leaving, Ma." I grabbed my hat, donned my coat. Ma rocked in her chair, elbows on the wide arm rails, hands clasped, mouth in a decided frown. I wanted to walk out the door and leave her to sulk, but at the last moment, I relented, crossed the floor, and planted a kiss on her sallow cheek.

Though it didn't change her expression, it made me feel better. I'd tried. And besides, even Ma couldn't ruin this day. Thoughts of Lula already had my spirit soaring as high as an airplane in a clear sky.

Almost too soon I stood at the front walk leading up to Jewel Wyatt's house. I gulped down an onslaught of anxiety. I hadn't courted a girl since Grace Widmore, in high school — and that had only been sitting in her parlor on two Saturday nights while her parents looked on. Even then, Ma's disapproval drew me home again, in spite of the fact that Clay ran after every pretty face that looked in his direction.

I straightened my shoulders. Should caring for Ma preclude having my own corner of joy in the world? Joy in the form of a young woman with a pretty face and oodles of brains in her head? I grinned as I sauntered to the front door. I'd never been one to back down from a challenge.

Shrieks and squeals leaked out of the Wyatts' house, along with a peppy tune that filled in the empty spaces. My knock silenced everything. Mrs. Wyatt appeared at the door, her expression a question mark.

"Why, Mr. Vaughn! To what do we owe this pleasure?"

A swirl in my gut. Had Lula not told her of our outing? But then, why would she? Mrs. Wyatt's push for Lula to take interest in a man needled Lula the same way Ma's push to enlist did me.

"Who is it, Jewel?" Bo stepped out of the front room.

Every muscle in my body went on high alert. Had he come to see Lula, too?

JC squeezed between his mother and Bo and the doorframe. "Hey, Mr. Vaughn. Can we go get a soda today?"

Bo clamped one of his meaty hands on JC's shoulder. "I'm sure Mr. Vaughn has more important things to do, son."

A storm roiled across JC's face. Jewel might have taken to heart my admonition to treat JC more like a man, but apparently Bo had not. If I hadn't already committed the day to Lula, I'd have whisked JC out of the house so he didn't have to spend the afternoon with "Uncle Bo." But today wasn't about JC.

"I've come for Lula."

Jewel's eyebrows dipped toward her nose. When she glanced at Bo, my confidence faltered. I clasped my hands behind my back, suddenly thankful for winter and the reprieve from arriving with flowers in hand.

"Imagine that. Two of you here and Lula nowhere to be found!"

"Where is she?"

JC glanced back at his ma. "Johnny Wilhelm came with a telegram. Then Aunt Lula left. Said she'd be back later."

Jewel's nervous laughter sank my stomach further. "Well now. I guess that answers our questions. Do you want to wait, like Bo, or shall I just tell her you dropped by?"

Dropped by? We had a date. She'd agreed to go. Had Bo come at her encouragement as well or was his presence just a coincidence? Had she forgotten our hastily made plans, or did she regret saying yes to my invitation in the first place? Either way, she wasn't here now, and when she returned, Bo would be.

I wouldn't.

Whatever the reason for her absence, she'd made it clear where I ranked in her world. I slapped my hat on my head, determined that Bo wouldn't see my discomfiture. "It wasn't important. I'll see her at church tomorrow — or Monday at school." I stalked back to my Tin Lizzie.

Perhaps God was punishing me for eroding the edges of my conviction, for not keeping my attention completely on Ma. I didn't know. I only knew I wanted to drive and drive. Not stop until I'd left Dunn — and Lula Bowman — far behind. Then I wouldn't have to face Ma's questions or Jewel's look of pity. I could live life on my own terms, without thought of another.

Another. JC.

I reversed direction and motored back to Jewel's house. I'd take JC to Lawton. We'd spend the afternoon in the Kingwood Theater, then drink sodas at the drug store. Not

my planned companion for the day, but one
I understood far better.

23

Lula

I fingered the telegram crumpled in the pocket of my coat as the edges of the world blurred around me. I'd fled the house, not sure where I was heading, hop-stepping every so often, almost like a hiccup in my feet. I stumbled over a tree root but caught myself before I hit the ground. My feet carried me onward, until I'd arrived at the church building, pushed open the iron gate, and threaded my way around the final resting places of friends and family and strangers alike.

The path to Mama's stone had seared itself into my brain on that awful day we'd laid her in the ground. My knees hit the hard dirt in front of it. I brushed away debris from the name carved into the granite.

Martha Lou Bowman. 1850–1909. Beloved wife and mother.

I shifted, sitting with my arm draped over her marker, my head resting on the curve as if it were her shoulder. The cold of the stone bit into my cheek, mimicking the pain in my chest.

With a sigh, I pulled the telegram from my pocket, smoothed out the wrinkles, and read it aloud. " 'Donally Award yours if you return for winter term. STOP. Week from Monday. STOP. Accept? Professor Clayton.' "

The first moment I read the words, I felt the kiss of God for my obedience in choosing to stay and care for Jewel and her family, for accepting the teaching positions that made me uncomfortable. He'd given me another chance to fulfill my dreams, my destiny.

But the exhilaration lasted only a moment before disintegrating like sugar in boiling water. The winter term. A week from Monday. Before the baby arrived. Before basketball season ended. Before I fulfilled any of my obligations.

I pressed my fingers into the sides of my head, wishing I hadn't left so fast that I forgot my mittens. I couldn't choose. Either way, I'd disappoint someone. I'd abandon something I'd determined to see through to the end. If I didn't accept the award now, it would be gone forever. The little — if any — money I might save from this year would never cover a year's tuition. Nor living expenses. Without the Donally Award, I'd need another year or two of work before I could afford another year of graduate study.

Help me, Lord. Help. A ridiculously simple prayer, but neither my heart nor my mind could form a more complex thought.

The cold air blustered around me, as if irritated I stood in its way. I shivered, closed my eyes, and tried to picture Mama's face, her voice. But they refused to come. All I could hear was Daddy's proud bellow. *"Did you know my girl Lula is getting her college degree? She's going to be a professor, the first woman PhD in Oklahoma!"*

With the end of my scarf, I wiped the dampness from my face. I'd done everything I'd thought was right and all I had to show for it was a handful of shattered dreams. I bit my lip and let the icy wind slap me, hoping to dislodge some of the self-pity. But it only woke me up enough to notice the numbness of my body. I rose, stumbled toward the church. I needed sanctuary from the weather and the world.

"Please let it be unlocked," I whispered as I pulled the iron handle. It gave way under my grasp. I stepped inside.

The piano drew me. Ignoring the hymn list on the wall, I blew on my hands, massaged some feeling into my fingers, then let them roam over the keys as my feet had the streets.

Scales came first, one key, then another, each more complicated than the last, engaging my mind as completely as manipulating a set of numbers and functions. Before I could assert control over the music, the notes organized into a melody. An old piece. Bach? Mozart? I couldn't recall the details, but my fingers remembered. They started slow, a bit unsure, then gained speed and confidence. I closed my eyes, gave myself to the music I'd denied for so long.

My heart filled to bursting with the beauty of the sound, with the joy of bringing it to life. Of filling the room, from wall to wall, rafter to floor, and every crevice in between.

I grew warm, wished to shrug off my coat. But I couldn't stop. Not yet. Not until the end.

What was it Mama used to say? *"Music washes away from the soul the dust of everyday life."* Mama had declared I had a gift, but after she'd breathed her last I'd abandoned music altogether. Devoted myself to Daddy's dream. Convinced myself Mama would approve. But would she condone my picking and choosing? Denying one gift to pursue another?

I slammed both hands onto the keyboard. Discordance assaulted my ears. I hung my head as sobs shook my body. If only Mama could tell me what to do now.

A rustle shocked me to attention. A familiar shadow in the last pew. My stomach squirmed as I squinted, trying to make out the form. My heart crawled into my throat. Had Jewel followed me?

"May I help you?" My reedy voice in place of the rich music. The shadow rose, then disappeared, the bang of the door echoing through the empty room. Until finally, silence. And in the silence, a breath of peace.

God had given me gifts — in my head and in my hands. But He'd also asked me to be caretaker and provider for Jewel and her children. I doubted He'd condone my leaving them to placate my own desires, even if those desires would honor my father's wishes. That wouldn't be following Jesus' example of leaving heaven on my behalf. No, staying would require an act of faith — something I'd practiced very little of late.

I withdrew the telegram and stared at the stark words once more.

I knew what I had to reply.

■ ■ ■ ■

When I eased open the front door of Jewel's house, I noticed the quiet first. Had Jewel taken the children out in the cold? It didn't seem like something she'd do. I hurried inside, suddenly anxious about my sister.

"Lula?" A sleepy voice came from the living room. I blinked into the emptiness. Jewel's head appeared over the top of the divan.

"Jewel! What on earth are you doing?" I helped her sit up. "And you've let the fire die down."

"Don't worry. I have my own little heater." She patted the bulge of her stomach. "Anyway, JC mentioned you got a telegram before you went out. I hope it wasn't bad news."

I shrugged, wishing I could lay my head on her shoulder and pour out all my thoughts. Instead, I poked at the smoldering embers of the fire, then added more wood.

"I didn't know how long you'd be gone. I guess I feel asleep."

"I'm sorry." I sat beside her, my fingers straying to the crumpled paper in my pocket. I couldn't tell her, couldn't add my burden to her own.

The silence startled me once more. "Where are the kids?"

Jewel stretched with a pleasurable sigh, almost like the purr of a contented cat. "Bo came by after you left."

"Bo was here?" He'd taken to showing up at the strangest moments. He seemed to finagle more leave from camp than other soldiers, but why? Was it loyalty to Davy, or did he have another reason? I tried to spy an answer in my sister's face but didn't see anything beyond a bit of tiredness.

"He took Inez and Trula to get some things I needed at the store."

My eyebrows shot toward the ceiling. "Did he?"

Jewel's cheeks pinked as she shrugged. "He helps how he can. He certainly doesn't come because of your encouragement."

"Jewel." I hoped my tone warned I wasn't willing to travel that road at this moment. "I'm just surprised, that's all."

She sighed. "He was Davy's best friend. He feels a responsibility to look after us."

I grunted, still wondering if Bo's attentiveness to the Wyatt family had much to do with Davy at all. But I kept my observations to myself.

"Where are the boys?"

"Russell's upstairs napping and JC went to the picture show in Lawton with Mr. Vaughn."

My heart jumped into my throat.

Chet.

Lawton.

How could I have forgotten?

I framed my face with my hands, unwilling to expose my disappointment to Jewel. I'd given Chet an impulsive yes last night. A Fruity Lu moment if ever there was one. Yet missing our date stung with the force of an army of fire ants, and I could only imagine how Chet felt.

Jewel looked directly at me now, the accusation in her face pushing my gaze to the floor.

"Did . . . did he explain why he'd come?"

My sister frowned. "No, he didn't. Seemed kind of odd, though. Were you expecting him?"

Relief surged through me, which ignited even more guilt. "I'll catch up with him tomorrow or Monday."

"That's what he said, too." She looked thoughtful for a moment. "You know, Chet Vaughn would make a mighty fine husband."

I clenched my teeth to hold in a groan. I liked Chet. More than I wanted to. But even though I'd decided to stay and help Jewel, it didn't mean I'd upended all of my plans. I could still return to my education. Eventually. But that meant keeping myself unencumbered.

Still, I hoped Chet and I could continue to be friends. My forgetfulness had likely strained that tenuous thread. If Jewel poked her hand in the situation, I feared it might snap altogether.

I saw Chet from afar at church, but Sarah Morrison held all his attention. Then I waited for him on Monday, after practice, but Jewel had asked me to hurry home and Chet hadn't arrived at the gym by the time I felt I had to leave.

Three days passed. The longer we went without speaking, the more I feared it would be that way forever. I wanted to send him a note, but where? At home, his mother might see. At school, the wrong eyes and incorrect interpretations could lead to serious repercussions.

At noon on Wednesday, Nannie and three other girls flung open my classroom door and bustled inside. Today these girls were looking to me for help with mathematics, not basketball. I might have forgone a prestigious prize paying for graduate school and a position teaching at a university, but it didn't mean I had to give up my ambition altogether. I'd redirect it, for now. Inspire at least one of these girls to look for more from life than pretty songs and ball games.

Yet even I had come to find value in music again. In friendship, too. Even in a nonsense game like basketball. I didn't desire these girls to fritter their lives away, but neither did I desire for them to live a life like the one I'd created for myself. One of loneliness. Of studying every night. Of self-reliance. There had to be middle ground.

Three quarters of an hour later, I pushed away a loose strand of hair with the back of my hand, hoping to avoid smudging my cheek with chalk. "Do you understand it now?"

Nannie's brow crunched. "I think so. But I still get confused finding the square root of a fraction." She shook her head and glanced around at the other basketball girls who had expanded our tutoring sessions. "Maybe we're not meant to understand any of it. What good will it do when we leave school anyway?"

"In college, you'll build on this information to understand higher mathematics."

"College?" Nannie's laugh trilled. "I'm not going to college, Miss Bowman."

"Normal school, then. You could become a teacher."

"No way." The other girls echoed her sentiment.

I sighed. "Okay then, you might not need to find the square root of a number to calculate the number of jars needed to put up jam or to know if a length of fabric will be enough to fashion the dress you desire, but those things are numerical puzzles, too. The more you understand how numbers work, the better equipped you'll be to do the math you need."

They didn't look convinced, but they didn't argue, either.

I set down the chalk and dusted off my hands. "That's enough for today. We'll go over this again before your next examination. When is that, by the way?"

"Friday, I think," Rowena replied.

"I'll double check with your teacher." My insides squirmed at the mention of Chet. I might have been avoiding him. He might have been avoiding me. I wasn't sure. But between tutoring his students and basketball games, our paths were bound to intersect very soon, and I'd need to apologize for missing our day together. "Go on now. Get to your next class."

Smiles erupted as the girls gathered their things.

"See you at practice, Miss Bowman." Nannie waved good-bye.

The silence they left behind threatened to smother me, and I still had fifteen minutes until my next class would arrive. I sat on the piano stool. My fingers grazed the keys. Then they pressed a bit harder, one note at a time. I swung my knees under the keyboard, both hands moving now, touching white keys and black, sending the hammers pinging against the strings.

I no longer saw the numbers on the chalkboard or the notes on the sheet of paper in front of me. My senses recognized only music as my fingers picked up speed. Emotion surged like a swollen stream over drought-weary land. It settled, pooled, and curled into the dry crevices of my spirit like it had found the place it belonged. My soul calmed. My hands stilled. The notes lingered. I opened my eyes — when had they drifted shut? — to find my students in their places, wonder on their faces.

I stumbled to my feet. They stared as if they'd never seen me at the piano before. I cleared my throat. "Pull out a sheet of paper. We're taking a quiz."

24

Chet

Over the two weeks after Lula stood me up, we had only one conversation — about the date of my next math test. She offered no apology. No explanation. Angry just thinking about it, I slapped my hat to my hand before jamming it on my head and turning up the collar of my coat to ward off the bitter January wind for the short jaunt to where I'd parked my automobile. If Lula hadn't wanted to go out with me, why had she said yes in the first place?

Women. They all played games. Just different ones. Miss Delancey's was a game of chase. Was Lula's hide-and-seek? Whatever it was, I had no desire to take part.

I walked faster, shoving my hands into my pockets, growling under my breath. I felt a bit guilty for taking out my frustration on the boys during practice, but in the end it wouldn't hurt them any. We'd been playing well, winning. But half a season remained that would decide the fate of the Dunn High School basketball program, for we would never move forward without the proper facilities.

I only hoped that the school board kept their word. Unlike Lula.

"Don't you have a game to go to?" Ma asked.

Of course she paid attention now. When I wanted to be left alone. When I wanted to find an excuse to arrive at the town hall near the end of the girls' game instead of at the beginning.

"Didn't you want me to clear the ashes out of the stove?"

"Not right this minute. Tomorrow would have been soon enough."

"Well, I have time now." I dumped another shovelful of gray dust in the bucket, a thin cloud of grime rising to my face.

"You'll have to wash —"

"I know." I stomped out the door and dumped the ashes on the compost heap. I had no call to snap at Ma. I had to get Lula out of my head, return to the firmness with which I'd staved off practically every other female of marriageable age who had crossed my path. If Lula had been the one trying to capture my attention instead of the other way around, I wouldn't have had any problem whisking her from my mind.

"Sorry, Ma," I said as I came back inside. She nodded. I gathered my things.

By the time I reached the town hall, I'd settled a bit. My boys were lounging among the spectators. I greeted them with curt nods. One by one, they straightened, faces sober. At least I knew they remembered the stakes. We needed every win to force the school board to keep their end of the bargain. We were a team, just like our brothers and uncles and cousins holding bayonets and going over the top together. We'd do the same. Fight the battle. Win the war.

Students, parents, and teachers filled in the empty spaces in the stands, each one clinking their coin into the tin cups at the door. The team from Shady Grove eyed my players as they clustered on the opposite bench. I paced the area between the seats and the wall, watching, thinking, praying — anything to keep my eyes from straying in Lula's direction. But one piece of conversation above me stopped me cold.

"She's still a good looker. And not married if she's teaching."

I looked up. A ruddy-faced man seemed to be holding court with a few others.

Farmer types. Mid-twenties. Thick and broad. All with eyes sweeping toward Lula sitting on the home team bench. "Guess she hasn't made a catch yet, so look out. She's pretty and all, but not a brain in her head that I could ever see."

Not a brain? If they thought that, they were the senseless ones.

"I'm surprised she's still around. You remember when she took up with the debate club? Two weeks and she was gone again. Never could commit to anything."

"But that was because she was sweet on Randy Wade. Remember?"

A deep chuckle. "She always was the life of the party. Maybe I should invite her out sometime."

A new voice interrupted. "Who are you talking about?"

"Lula Bowman. You know, Fruity Lu." Guffaws rained down.

Fruity Lu? My eyes sought Lula on the opposite side of the court. I couldn't reconcile their descriptions with the woman I knew.

I had half a mind to find a reason to throw these dolts from the hall. But of course that wasn't really my place. I shoved my hands into my pockets and prayed for calm as I strolled in front of the stands. Then I rested one shoulder against the cool wall and crossed my arms. I'd keep an eye on that group after the game. And an eye on Lula, as well.

The whistle blew to end the girls' game. I still hadn't located Blaze in the stands. It wasn't like him to miss Nannie's game. Wasn't like him to be late at all.

I pulled Virgil aside. "Have you heard from Blaze?"

He shook his head. "But we talked about the game at school today."

My jaw clenched. Something was wrong. If I had to guess, that wrong had to do with Archie Clifton. I raked my fingers through my hair, not caring if it stood on end. "If he doesn't show, I'll count on you to lead the way tonight, Virgil."

"Yes, sir." The senior's Adam's apple slid up and down his thin neck. He returned to the team and motioned for them to gather round.

Part of me wished I had an assistant coach to entrust them to, leaving me free to check on Blaze. For no matter how hard I tried to tell myself it was nothing, I knew it was *something*.

Principal Gray slapped me on the back and started talking, but I could only hear

249

noise, not words.

"Could you run out to the Clifton place and check on Blaze for me?"

"He isn't here?"

I shook my head.

Principal Gray donned his hat, shrugged into his coat. "I'll pay Archie Clifton a visit. You and the other boys just keep to your task, get the job done."

"Yes, sir." I motioned my team over, spoke confident words of encouragement and prayed they didn't recognize the hollow ring. It wasn't that I didn't believe they couldn't win without Blaze, it just didn't matter quite so much compared to his well-being.

"Felix." I pointed to a freshie who had shown promise in practice. "Take Blaze's position at right guard."

"Yes, sir," he squeaked. He joined the other starters on the court.

The official blew his whistle and tossed the ball in the air. Virgil leapt up and swatted it toward Clem, who threw it to Felix. A few seconds later, the ball dropped through the hoop. I breathed a sigh of relief along with another prayer, for if I knew anything about Blaze, I knew he'd not miss a basketball game unless it were a matter of life and death.

Every muscle in my body clenched during the final three minutes of the game. When the whistle shrieked, I sank against the wall, spent. Two points. We'd won by two. But at least we'd won. The boys knelt around me, faces solemn, eyes questioning. I wished I had something grand to tell them.

"I'm proud of your tenacity. You stuck in there and made it happen. Good job."

Heads lowered, one by one, until only Virgil looked me in the eye. "Any word on Blaze, Coach?"

I shook my head. Virgil's head bowed, too.

"Get on home, boys. Enjoy your victory." If only I hadn't turned and seen Nannie's face splotched red from crying.

I loitered long after the game ended, hoping for Principal Gray's return. He never came. I hurried up the block to my car, head bowed against the swirling wind. Until a shadow caught my eye. A figure pushed away from my Tin Lizzie.

Lula.

I stopped, breath trapped in my chest.

"Hi, Chet."

She glanced around, her tongue darting across her lips. My heart drummed in my ears. Had she brought news of Blaze?

She took a tentative step forward. "I'm so sorry. For the other day. You know." She looked at the ground, took a deep breath. "I should have said that earlier, but I, well, I —"

Her gaze lifted to mine. "I got some unexpected news that day and —" She shook her head. A curl fell over her eyebrow. I wanted to tuck it back in place beneath her hat. I pressed my hands into fists to squelch the urge.

"What's wrong, Lula? Do you know something about Blaze? Tell me. Please."

She looked confused. "Blaze?"

White breath streamed from my mouth. "He didn't show up at the game tonight. You didn't know?"

She shook her head, looked away, and moved beyond reach. "I went home. I just came back to say I'm truly sorry — and I hope we can still be friends."

Friends. The word hit like a punch in the gut. Lula Bowman had no more interest in me than . . . than Archie Clifton had in Euclid's postulates. The sooner I got that through my thick skull, the better.

In the gray of predawn, I stalked Principal Gray's house for some sign of life. I hadn't

252

slept much. Not with concern over Blaze and reliving the conversation with Lula. At least with Lula I knew where things stood. She wanted to be friends. But I couldn't see my way clear to that. Not when her presence stirred feelings I'd long denied myself.

By the time light shone out a downstairs window, I'd convinced myself Blaze was fine. I'd been worried for nothing. But the moment my friend answered my tentative knock at the door, I knew it wasn't true.

Principal Gray invited me inside. His wife brought us coffee and then retreated to the kitchen.

"Well?" My nerves coiled tight, ready to spring if he kept silent another moment.

"I went out there, like you asked. Archie Clifton met me with a shotgun."

"A shotgun?"

"Of course, I'm not scared off that easily." He chuckled. "Archie Clifton thinks he's a tough son of a gun, but I was a sooner before I was a school teacher, so I have some grit in my back pocket, too."

I grinned, picturing Principal Gray at the helm of a covered wagon, racing for his plot of land. Maybe this would turn out better than I'd feared.

"Still, it took some talking to get him to let me inside and see Reed."

"But you did see him." I took a sip of coffee, hoping to calm the pounding in my chest.

"I did. He wouldn't say much, but who could blame him? Archie kept that shotgun crooked in his elbow while we talked — while *I* talked."

My teeth ground into one another. I had no understanding of a man who didn't want his child to have a better life than he did.

"Archie says he needs his boy on the farm. All day. Every day."

I snorted. "Of course he does. I don't have to be a brilliant mathematician to know that free labor plus sky-high grain prices equal cash in the bank."

"I know." Principal Gray rubbed a hand across his forehead. "But he and I made a deal, eventually."

"A deal?" Coffee sloshed onto the table as I set my cup down with a thud.

"Reed finishes this year of school — and basketball — with no more interference from his father. After that, he'll work two years for Archie as payment for letting him continue his education after eighth grade."

"And Blaze agreed to that?"

Principal Gray hesitated. "He did after I talked with him."

I leapt from my chair. "Why would you

encourage that? He needs to get away after graduation. He needs —"

Principal Gray held up his hand. "He needs a reason to keep going and get his diploma. If he thinks Archie will release him from his obligation to the farm after two years, he can see an end of things. That's all I wanted for him at the moment. A tangible finish line."

My lungs emptied.

"Look, Chet. I've known Archie Clifton a long time. I doubt he'll stick to his end of the bargain, which will release Reed from his. I'm just buying us some time. We've got to keep watch on the boy, though. Don't want him to do anything stupid in desperation."

"No, we don't." I took my leave, almost limp with exhaustion. I'd hoped for so much more than this for Blaze, but I had no control over the situation. I could only pray.

By Sunday evening, I fell into bed exhausted, but dreams of Lula made my sleep fitful. She laughed, spun away, playing the coquette as if she had suddenly become her predecessor in the music room. A tug at my arm turned my head. It was Ma, pointing into a trench. Brian Giles' tortured face stared up at me, unblinking. Clay knelt beside him, covered in mud. Shots pounded overhead. Everyone dove for the lowest point, crashing into one another. Then Lula's face appeared above me, her hand caressing my cheek, her lips moving toward mine.

I sat up with a start, heart pounding, chest heaving. A shaky hand reached for my wristwatch on the small table beside my bed.

Four thirty. Earlier than I usually got up. But sleep wouldn't return now. I let out a soft growl. What was this girl doing to me? I needed to focus on Blaze, on basketball, on Ma.

I threw back the quilts, let the unheated air smack me fully awake. I washed and shaved and shivered into my clothing, then stared into the small square mirror above my washbasin. The season was far from over. I would forever be crossing paths with Lula in the gym and at the town hall. I had to find a way to keep my heart safe.

After combing my hair into place, I shrugged into my jacket and tugged my shirtsleeves over my wrists. I'd take advantage of the early hour to spend some time in the gym, praying. Then I'd devote my day to instructing my students and encouraging my players. If Lula was around, I just wouldn't let the conversation veer in any direction besides math tests and basketball. Nor would I let my gaze linger on her sweet face.

25

Lula

I hurried out of the gym after practice, as I'd taken to doing after I forgot the date with Chet. It was nice getting home earlier. I had a chance to tidy the house, spend time with the children, help Jewel cook, wash the dishes, and then enjoy a bit of conversation with my sister after the kids went to bed.

So why did my thoughts constantly stray toward Chet Vaughn? He was a distraction I ought to be thankful to be rid of. I could go my way at the end of the school year with no regrets. Begin again the arduous task I knew only too well — earning and saving money for tuition.

And yet odd moments found me wistful, missing the way Chet and I used to talk about basketball or the students at school. But my apology had come too late, apparently. He avoided me. I didn't blame him — I wouldn't want to pursue a friendship with me, either. What kind of friend forgets an appointment agreed to only hours before?

While he still responded to my occasional basketball or math class questions, our comfortable companionship had disintegrated like frost in daylight. I'd said I was sorry, but I didn't know how to repair things between us.

The door to the school was just closing when a deep voice shouted my name against the late afternoon bluster. I turned, searched the street. A man jogged in my direction, his face lost beneath hat and scarf and raised coat collar. I took a step forward. Chet? Had he finally forgiven me? Then I froze.

Too tall to be Chet. Too broad. The coat flapped open to reveal a leg clad in khaki.

Bo.

Disappointment shivered my insides. Then my inner chill turned to ice. Had something happened to Jewel? To the baby? Panic surged from my toes to my throat.

I met Bo in the middle of the street, clutched his arms, and stared into his squinted eyes, trying to read his secrets before hearing the words. "Is it Jewel?"

"How did you know?" A strangled whisper. His scarf fell aside, revealing a face contorted with pain.

Oh, dear God, no. No. This was my fault. I should have been home more. Helping more. I grabbed the lapels of Bo's coat and buried my head in his chest. His arms wrapped around me, stilled the shaking.

"Lula?" Chet's voice.

My heart froze as cold as my nose. I raised my head, Bo's arms still encircling me. Only I wished I hadn't. Chet's focus moved from my face to Bo's hands, clasped at the back of my waist. My stomach dropped so far I feared it would drag me into a deep hole in the ground.

I jumped from Bo's embrace, hands flying up to cover my cheeks. But the expression that had been stony the evening I apologized now turned to steel. Chet changed direction.

I wanted to follow, to explain. But Jewel — I had to hear about Jewel.

Bo tugged at my coat sleeve. "I need to know how to help her, Lula. I need to know how to tell her."

I wiped away hot tears before I faced him. "What's happened to my sister?"

He blinked. "What? Nothing's happened to her. That I know of."

"Then what did you —"

"I know she misses Davy. I miss him, too.

260

But she's . . ." He toed the light dusting of snow on the ground. "I can't leave her to fend for herself."

Balled hands flew to my hips. "And just what do you think *I'm* doing here? It isn't like I don't have a life of my own to live!" I pushed past him, against the stiff wind. First, he'd scared me to death over Jewel, then he'd sealed my fate with Chet. A sob bubbled in my chest.

"Please, Lula." Bo's hand stopped me. "I . . . I love her."

His revelation poked a hole in my chest, let out all the air I'd been holding inside. He loved her. The bare anguish in his eyes testified to the truth of it.

First Davy, now Bo. They loved Jewel, wanted to protect her.

Why did that make me so envious? How could I be jealous of something I had no desire to possess myself? I'd long declared I wouldn't marry. I intended to pursue my studies, make Daddy proud. Show my siblings they couldn't dictate my life.

My jaw tightened. "You can't help her, Bo. She misses her husband."

His chin dropped to his chest. "I know. But I'd hoped . . ."

For the first time, I took a good look at Bo the man, not the pawn in Jewel's matchmaking game. My heart hadn't grown so hard as to disregard his feelings. In spite of my vows to abstain from marriage, Jewel hadn't made any such vows of her own, not even in her deepest grief. My sister had flourished as a wife and a mother. She'd been happy. She deserved to be happy like that again.

"You won't tell her, will you?" He sounded like JC asking me not to let Jewel know he'd eaten the last sliver of pie. My heart turned as soft as fresh bread. At least I no longer feared Jewel pushing him in my direction. I only hoped she wouldn't object to me pushing him toward her. A grin tugged at the corner of my mouth. For all the times she'd badgered me about men, it was time I returned the favor.

Another game, another loss for my girls. I didn't stay to watch the boys' game. The sight of Chet's friendliness with everyone but me cut too deeply.

On Saturday afternoon, I filled the church with the melodious hymns Pastor Reynolds had selected for Sunday's service. They felt different under my hands now. More than a collection of notes on a page. In the agony of losing the Donally Award — and losing Chet's friendship — my soul opened to the music like rain-soaked ground under a trowel.

And yet my senses remained on alert, wondering if my mysterious visitor would slink into the shadows today. But for the better part of an hour, I played to an empty room and for my own satisfaction — and that of Pastor Reynolds, ensconced in his small office behind the sanctuary.

A creak stilled my hands as my head snapped toward the back of the room.

JC shielded his eyes from the sunlight streaming through the tall windows lining the walls. "Aunt Lula? You coming home for supper?"

"Yes. I'm just finishing up."

"I'll wait." He slipped into the last pew, much like my other solitary listener. I ran through the final hymn with half my attention on the music, half on my nephew. I couldn't deny that Chet's time with him had helped him work through some of his grief. Their relationship made me happy. Except when it made me sad. Regretful of my forgetfulness.

The notes swirled about the room. JC's face relaxed while my guilt heightened. I needed to help my nephew, too. Not leave it all to Chet. Maybe that was the lesson God wanted me to learn. To pour my heart into

263

my own family, not lose it to a stranger.

As JC and I walked home together, I asked about school and the horses in the livery stable. His eyes lit with pleasure as he described each one — not only their appearance but their personality.

"Aunt Lula, can I ask you a question?"

"Anything." I rested my hand on his head as we walked.

"Do you think Uncle Bo is sweet on Mama?"

I hoped my face didn't show surprise. Was this why he'd been so antagonistic toward his father's best friend? I hadn't realized a boy his age would be aware of such things.

My observant nephew needed to know the truth. But Bo had revealed his heart to me in confidence. I had to honor that, too. I prayed for wise words. "Your daddy and Bo knew each other a long time, even before your daddy met your mama."

"I know. Daddy told me they met just afore the turn of the century, after Oklahoma Territory opened up and both their families came for the free land."

"I imagine that's right. Anyway, Bo knows that with your daddy gone to heaven, your mama needs a friend to help take care of her."

"She has you. And me. Isn't that enough?"

"Bo's nearer her own age than you or I. That makes a difference sometimes." I had no intention of getting into the complexities of the relationship between a man and woman with a ten-year-old boy. "What makes you think he's sweet on her?"

His shoulder lifted, then fell again. "Sometimes he looks at her the same way Bobby Fellman looks at Maria Tanner." He rolled his eyes heavenward, and we both laughed. But I didn't want to lose the moment to plow a smoother path for Bo, should he need it.

"You know, someday your mama might decide to marry again. It's hard to be alone with five children."

JC stopped, looked up at me with solemn eyes. "I know. Maria Tanner's mama died three years ago and she got a new mama for Christmas that year. I figured I'd better look out."

"I'm glad you realize it's a possibility, but don't set yourself against it just yet. Remember, God knows what you need even if you don't think you need it."

JC shoved his hands into the pockets of his coat and scowled. "Mr. Vaughn told me the very same thing."

Don took us for a quick visit to his ranch

on Sunday afternoon. When Daddy heard my voice, he turned his face to the wall. Janice told me not to think too much of it. Don's wife, Audra, said he barely took food now. Which didn't make me feel any better.

I stayed up late after we got home, scrubbing floors, trying to tire out my body so it would close down my mind and let me sleep. But a late night meant a groggy Monday morning. Just before noon, I scrubbed musical notes from the chalkboard with undue vigilance and prepared to work on indirect proofs with Nannie and a couple of the other girls on the team. But the thought of mathematics no longer brought the same satisfaction as before. Now it fueled visions of Chet instead of Professor Clayton.

I hadn't had much experience with men, except in my high school years. Back then, I'd willingly been the scatterbrained, happy-go-lucky girl, following Jewel's example of surrounding myself with laughter and music, ignoring anything that required too much contemplation. At least until the day I'd overheard Wes Granger talking to his friends. The day I'd returned to school after Mama's funeral.

A dark cloud had shrouded my world as I'd trudged off to school that autumn morning, an ache as deep as an oil well in my chest. Jewel had Davy to hold her while she cried. I thought I'd have my boyfriend Wes, but except for a brief nod at the funeral, he hadn't comforted me.

Maybe he was afraid of my brothers and sisters. Or Daddy, who had turned so gruff as to frighten even me. Maybe Wes feared the tears themselves. We were, after all, only sixteen.

With my head hung low, I crossed the spongy grass toward the corner of the schoolhouse, all of us still in one building in this brand new state of Oklahoma. I pressed my books against my chest to hold in the pain of a world without Mama. When I heard the voices, I stopped, not wanting to be noticed. Then Wes's familiar cadence rose above the rest. My heart soared as I listened, my name on his lips.

"Fruity Lu? She's fun, but I'd never settle down with a girl like that. Likely she'd forget to add sugar to the jam or to darn my socks."

My heart slammed to the ground and I froze. Wes couldn't have meant those words.

"Life would never be dull," one of the other boys said. Several chuckled. Heat rushed into my face. I swayed, put a hand on the schoolhouse wall and held myself steady. Surely Wes would defend me.

He laughed instead. "My brother says there are girls you have fun with and girls you marry. And if you marry the fun ones, they'll plague you with wanting to go dancing and be romanced all the days of their lives."

I took one step backward. Then another. After the third, I turned and fled to Jewel's house, ran past the spinning record on the Victrola and up the stairs to the room they'd declared mine. I threw myself on the bed and sobbed.

An hour later, I sat up, dried my tears. With Mama gone, I had to take care of myself. And I knew how. Daddy had always scolded me to leave off parties and dancing and music and apply myself to my studies. It was the only thing he'd ever wanted for his children — an education. If I made Daddy proud, I wouldn't need any other man's approval.

Not long after that, the predictability of mathematics filled the gaping hole in my heart. I grasped hold of its regularity and refused to let go. And sure enough, Daddy noticed. He talked to me when I came home for visits. He bragged about his little girl to everyone who would listen.

My students entered the room with their

usual clatter, bringing me back to life as Miss Bowman instead of Fruity Lu. The first thing I noticed was Nannie. She slouched into a desk near the back, arms crossed over her chest. The other girls glanced her way, but none spoke to her. Nannie didn't look at them. Her stare was fixed on something far beyond the classroom walls.

Had there been a rift between the girls? Over what? My stomach churned as we walked through the mathematical concepts, Bess and Foxy breaking into smiles of comprehension, Gracie and Rowena wrinkling their noses when they didn't understand. When I dismissed them, Nannie bolted for the door like one of Don's unbroken colts.

I pulled Rowena back from the others. "What's wrong with Nannie?"

Rowena rolled her eyes. "Blaze. He says he's quitting school and enlisting."

I shot a glance to the doorway where she'd disappeared. No wonder the girl was upset. Chet would be, too, when he found out. I lowered my voice. "Who else knows about this?"

Rowena shrugged. "No one, I don't think. We only know because Bill overheard Nannie and Blaze arguing about it. Can I go now?"

"Yes. Thank you, Rowena."

She scurried away, then turned back, her bottom lip caught between her teeth. "You won't tell anyone, will you? Nannie doesn't even know we heard."

I couldn't promise her that. This was too important. I had to do what I deemed best for both Nannie and Blaze. "You can trust me."

I held my breath, hoping that would satisfy.

It did. Rowena grinned and flounced away.

Blaze, quitting school? I shoved my papers into my satchel. Chet might live and breathe basketball, but I knew Blaze's graduation held just as high a place in his heart.

26

Chet

Rubbing the back of my neck, I paced my empty classroom. I had things to do before basketball practice, but I couldn't seem to settle into any of them. Lula continued to distract me, to haunt my dreams, even after I'd caught her in another man's arms. I needed to put her out of my mind, but my heart refused to cooperate.

The door clicked open. I spun around.

Lula.

My palms turned slick. I stumbled over my own feet trying to get to her, welcome her in.

She clasped her hands at her waist, her eyes stretching wide. "It's Blaze."

I tensed, suddenly rooted to the ground. "What about him?"

She wet her lips, took a deep breath. "He's quitting school to enlist. I thought you should know."

Enlist? Surely she was wrong. Surely —

She turned as if to leave. In a rush of adrenaline, I charged ahead, barricaded my body between her and the door.

She pulled up, stepped backward. I stopped close enough to her to speak quietly, far enough away to keep her from diverting my attention from Blaze. "How do you know this?"

Her gaze slid to the floor. "Nannie was upset during our tutoring today. One of the other girls told me they overhead Nannie and Blaze arguing about his decision."

I dropped into the closest desk, holding my head in my hands. "I told him not to. I asked him to be patient."

"I'm sorry." The gentle touch of her hand on my shoulder drew my head up. She no longer stood stiff and aloof. More like uncertain and tremulous. Over being here with me or the news about Blaze?

I groaned. "I want him to graduate. To know that he isn't stupid or worthless like his father tells him. When he has that diploma, he'll have a foundation no one can ever take away from him. He'll have a shot at a better life."

Lula pressed a hand to her mouth, lines appearing on her forehead and around her eyes as if I'd said something that upset her.

But I had no idea what.

I stood, shoved my hands into the deep pockets of my trousers. "Thank you for letting me know. I'll . . . figure something out."

"You're welcome," she whispered. Then she gave me one of her rare smiles. I reached for the desk, dizzy at the sight. "I thought you should know." She stepped toward the door again.

"Wait," I said.

She bit her lip. I closed the gap between us.

"Will you help me? With Blaze?"

"Help you? How?"

"If you and I and Nannie all talk to Blaze together, maybe we can make him see reason."

A tiny frown tugged at the corner of her mouth, but she nodded.

"You get Nannie and meet Blaze and me after the boys' practice. In the gym. Will you do that?"

"All right." Her frown deepened. "But we'll need to give him another option to consider, not just 'Don't do it.' "

I grinned. A smart girl, and not just in the classroom. I glanced at my wristwatch. "I'll think of something."

By the time the boys' practice ended this evening, I needed a foolproof plan to keep

Blaze in school.

"Let's go! Let's go! Let's go!" My voice bounced off the gym walls as the boys sprinted up and down the court. Even if Lula hadn't warned me about Blaze, I would have suspected a problem. He missed four shots I knew he could make in his sleep. He didn't get after the other boys to hustle. He refused to look me in the eye.

I walked the length of the court, praying with every step, as the boys ran again, up and back. Up and back. I'd settled on an idea. One I believed came straight from God. But would Blaze go along with the plan?

I blew my whistle. The slap of shoes on hardwood stopped, but the heavy breathing didn't. I called them into a huddle as they gulped air.

"Four more games. We have to win every single one to beat the school board's challenge, so we need to focus. Here." I tapped a finger on my temple and stared right at Blaze. He studied the ground. "Y'all get on home now."

The boys headed for the locker room.

"Blaze, I'd like you to stay behind for a few minutes, after you get dressed."

His head shot up, eyes wary. "Why?"

"Just some things we need to discuss."

He shuffled away. The other boys trickled out the door a few at a time until only Blaze remained. I paced in front of the small spectator area. The gymnasium door squealed open. Lula nudged a sullen-faced Nannie in ahead of her.

Nannie wrenched herself from Lula's grasp, rolled her eyes toward the sky, and plopped down on the bottom bench. Had she quarreled with Lula? We needed Nannie on our side, not working against us.

Lula motioned for me to walk with her to the opposite side of the gym. She glanced back at Nannie, keeping her voice low. "It's worse than we thought. Seems that now they've concocted a plan to get married before he leaves — for *both* of them to quit school!"

I itched to throttle the boy. It was one thing to compromise his own future. Quite another to involve a girl.

"We have to do something!" Lula's whisper rose in pitch.

"Obviously."

She glared.

"Look, I have an idea. But only one. If we go into this together, maybe we can persuade them to put off their plans until June."

She crossed her arms. "What are you

275

thinking?"

Blaze sauntered out of the locker room, saw Nannie, and stopped. He turned toward Lula and me, his eyes accusing.

"Trust me," I whispered to Lula.

We met Blaze at center court. "I thought it would be good for us all to talk." With one hand on his shoulder, I steered him toward Nannie and pressed him to sit beside her. Lula stood next to me.

I cleared my throat and clasped my hands behind my back. "It has come to my attention —"

A tug on my sleeve. I tried to pull away. Lula stepped in front of me, facing Nannie and Blaze. "Why don't we all go to my house. I'll make us some cocoa and coffee." She turned and slid a pleading look in my direction.

My neck lit on fire. Who did she think she was, taking over? I had this under control.

But then Nannie and Blaze glanced at each other. Nannie gave a slight nod. Blaze stood, fixed his gaze on Lula, and cut me out of the conversation altogether. "All right, Miss Bowman. We'll hear you out."

27

Lula

While Nannie and Blaze figured out how to squeeze into Chet's two-seater car, I charged down the street, over two blocks, up another three. Breathless, I ran into the house, gasping Jewel's name. As quickly as I could, I explained the situation.

Jewel nodded, her mouth tight. "I'll bundle up the little ones and we'll pay a visit next door."

"Thank you."

"I'll be praying, too. For all of you." The matchmaking shine I expected to appear in her eyes didn't. I pressed a kiss to her cheek before she waddled away, the children following like ducks behind her. Then I welcomed Nannie, Blaze, and Chet into the warm kitchen.

Fixing the coffee and cocoa gave me something to do — something besides congratulating myself that Nannie and Blaze looked less defensive sitting at the kitchen table than they did in the cavernous gymnasium. If only Chet didn't look so inflexible and authoritative. So much like my brother Don that I shuddered. Couldn't he see that a lecture would only stiffen their resolve to do as they'd determined? If he wasn't careful, his manner would drive them straight to the justice of the peace and the army recruitment office.

I situated the drinks around the table, my heart pounding in my ears. I wished for a mathematical formula, some assurance of a correct resolution to this problem. But there wasn't one. So I prayed for calm, for wisdom.

Nannie's hands sought the warmth of her cup and lifted it to her mouth. Blaze didn't touch his. I waited in silence, knowing I'd tried Chet's patience when I'd suggested this change of venue.

Chet didn't speak first. Blaze did.

"I know you won't like it, Coach, but I'm eighteen now. I can go where I please, make my own decisions. And I've decided I can't stay with him anymore." Blaze's fist connected with the table, punctuating the words. But his eyes had a fearful look, as if he expected retribution for even that small act of defiance.

Ignoring Blaze's outburst, Chet sipped his coffee. The tightness at the corners of his mouth gentled. My breath released, the thudding in my chest calming a bit. But my silent prayers became more fervent. *Please, God, let Blaze listen to reason. Let him not rush out and get killed and leave Nannie a teenaged widow.*

Nannie covered Blaze's hand with her smaller one, her jaw set firm, her eyes challenging mine, almost as if she'd read my thoughts. "I love him, Miss Bowman. And he loves me."

I lifted the cup to my lips, blew away the steam, and sipped before I answered. "I won't argue that with you. You are the only ones who can judge how you feel about one another. But you don't need to quit school. Even if Blaze were to —" I glanced at Chet — "leave, it doesn't mean you have to marry right this minute."

Her round face looked so young and vulnerable, yet she didn't yield. Her fingers gripped Blaze's hand more tightly. "If he's going off to fight, I'd rather be left behind as his wife than his girlfriend."

Blaze's mouth lifted, and his eyes cleared. My heart sank. Of course he wanted to marry Nannie right away. The poor boy needed to know someone cared. But this

279

wasn't the answer.

Chet stared into his coffee. I wanted to poke him, force him to join the conversation. He'd said he had a plan. The time had come to put it forth. My foot jabbed in the direction of his leg but caught only air. I drummed my fingers on the table until I couldn't stand his silence. "Let's say you do as you intend. Blaze leaves. First for training camp, then to France. How would you survive if something happened to him over there, Nannie? What would you do with no education and maybe even a baby on the way?" My face burned, but it had to be said.

Nannie's chin tilted upward. "My family would help. And even if they didn't, I'd figure something out."

My teeth ground into one another as I fought the urge to shake some sense into the girl. I turned my fury on Blaze instead. "Blaze, can't you see —"

Chet's hand clamped around my forearm, manly fingers crushing the fabric of my sleeve. And for some reason, I turned almost giddy. At least until Chet's smooth voice sobered me again.

"Has your pa gone back on his agreement? The one you made in the presence of Principal Gray?"

Blaze's head tipped forward, but just

barely. I ached for his pain, for the broken relationship with his father, for his shame in his father's lack of integrity.

"Tell me what happened, Blaze."

The boy's eyes met Chet's. "He said we had to break up the back forty, even though it's near frozen solid now." He cleared his throat, looked away. "I told him I'd do it Saturday, when I didn't have school. Or basketball. Then he —"

Blaze pulled his hand from Nannie's. Her eyes and mouth rounded. She blinked back tears. Blaze sucked in a long breath. "He swung at me. I put up an arm to shield my face, but before I knew it, I'd —" His eyes begged Chet not to make him continue.

Chet cleared his throat. "I understand your need to get away. I really do. But I don't think enlisting right now is the answer. I think you'll regret giving up on high school when you are so close to the end. Wait four more months. Get your diploma. Then if you still want to, you can sign up to fight."

Blaze shoved his chair back and bolted to his feet. "I can't live one more day with that man. You don't know how he is. I'm afraid next time —" He looked down at his fist, clenching and releasing. We knew what he feared. He didn't have to speak it.

Chet rose. "Just hear me out, son."

Blaze looked at Nannie. She bit her lip and nodded, eyes wide and frightened. Blaze corralled his chair and sat again, his expression as hard as the ground outside. I wished he could understand how much Chet cared — how much we both cared. We wanted good things for them.

Chet continued, "You can be stubborn about this — do it your way — or you can think about what's really best for you and for Nannie. Act on your convictions. Act like a man instead of imitating the mule you walk behind for your pa."

My body went as rigid as a newly starched shirt. Had someone said those words to me, I'd have dug in like those boys in France, determined never to give ground. But Chet didn't stop. He plowed ahead with a determination that would have made Blaze's father take note.

"If you just react to your father, he wins. Think about it. If we went into each game only responding to the other team's plays or to their defensive scheme, we wouldn't often succeed. Instead, we have a strategy. An offense. And we see it through no matter how the other team tries to stop us. Right?"

My eyes darted among Blaze and Nannie and Chet. Blaze nodded.

"I'm offering you a plan, Blaze. An offense. Finish school. Then enlist. Don't get flustered by the defense." Chet glanced at Nannie. "I won't even pretend to know what to advise you about the other, except to wait until you are both graduated. I imagine that's what your family would advise, as well, right, Nannie?"

Pink splashed across the girl's cheeks. She stared at the table. Blaze still hadn't consented to Chet's plan, but I felt Nannie's resolve crumble. Maybe Chet did, too, for he rushed into the gap.

"What if you only had to deal with school and basketball, not your father? Then could you make it to graduation before enlisting?"

Blaze's eyes crinkled at the edges, and his jaw ticked. When he answered, his voice croaked with emotion. "How? How could I do that?"

Chet's hands clamped down on the back of his chair. "What about your uncle Sal? Could you stay with him? I'd be willing to talk to him — them, explain how things stand."

Some amusement passed between them. Something neither Nannie nor I understood. But it lightened the mood. And gave me hope.

"Come with me. We'll drive out to Sal's after supper. If for some reason that option won't work, you can stay at my house. We'll talk to your pa together."

Blaze looked at Nannie for a long moment. An entire conversation seemed to pass wordlessly between them. Then Blaze spoke, careful and slow. "I'm still not sayin' I'll stay until graduation, but I'll talk to Uncle Sal tonight. On one condition."

Every muscle in my body tensed, but Chet seemed to relax. "What's that?"

A slow grin curved Blaze's lips. "That I can walk Nannie home first."

Chet laughed. "Go on, then. But Ma'll have supper on the table at six thirty, so you best hurry."

"Yes, sir." Blaze pulled out Nannie's chair. She pressed her cheek to mine before clutching Blaze's outstretched hand and following along after him.

As the front door banged shut, Chet lowered slowly into the chair. He sat unmoving, elbows on the table, hands almost covering his face. I gathered the cups, rinsed them, then leaned back against the sink and studied this man who defied all my judgments of him. His heart understood people in a way mine never had. And the beauty of his compassion rendered his pleasing face even more handsome in my eyes.

"You handled that perfectly."

"I don't know how. I was terrified the whole time. I'm still afraid he'll run away from his troubles instead of face them."

I picked up a towel, wiped the water that dripped like tears down the side of a cup. Chet's chair scraped the floor. I felt him draw near, glimpsed the tips of his shoes through my downturned lashes. He took the mug and towel from my hand and began to dry it.

"Thank you," I whispered.

"Hello? Anyone home?" Bo stuck his head in the kitchen. Chet retreated to the opposite side of the room.

"Is she here?" Bo asked.

I pointed. "Next door."

"Thanks." He disappeared.

Chet looked from me to the empty doorway, his forehead scrunched in confusion.

"He came for Jewel." I turned and began to stack the clean dishes in the cupboard.

"For Jewel?" Chet's hands landed on my shoulders. He turned me to face him. I couldn't look up for fear of what I'd read in his eyes. For fear of what he'd read in mine.

"Could we try this again, Lula?" His voice felt like a caress.

"Try what?" Did I breathe the words or actually speak them? My gaze crept from the floor to his chest to his face.

"The Red Cross dinner is a week from Saturday night. Sit with me. Ma's in charge of the tables. I'll arrange it with her." A grin tipped his lips, and my stomach fluttered. "And you can be sure I won't let you forget this time."

A second chance. I'd be a fool to refuse.

Chet jogged to his automobile. I stood on the front porch, wringing my hands, the conduct rules for a teacher — most of which had to do, in one form or another, with not courting — ringing in my head. But the Red Cross dinner and dance was a community event. And patriotic. Surely there would be no cause for alarm in that. Especially if we sat at a table with his mother.

I wanted to ask Jewel's advice but feared that would only embolden all her matchmaking plans.

"Lula! Where is your coat?" Jewel scolded, coming across the yard, the clamor of the children behind her.

JC peered past me. "Was that Mr. Vaughn?"

I nodded, clenching my teeth to keep them from chattering.

"Get inside. You can talk to Lula there." Jewel gave JC's behind a playful swat. He bounded up the steps but stopped at the door and held it open for his mother and me. Inside, I poked at the waning fire, trying to stir it to life.

"He didn't even stay to say hello?" JC dumped a log on the grate, dousing the tiny flame I'd coaxed to burn. I squeezed my eyes shut.

I shoved the log aside, blew on the embers. Fire licked at the dry wood and caught. I brushed off my hands, faced my nephew. "I'm sorry, JC. He had a lot on his mind tonight. But I'm sure you'll see him soon. Why don't you help me fix some pancakes for supper?"

"I wanna help," Trula called out, bounding up beside me.

JC turned away.

"Not this time, Trula." I took JC's hand. "I think JC is all the help I'll need."

JC grinned as he raced into the kitchen. He just needed a bit of undivided attention. The kind a boy like JC was used to getting from a father like Davy.

Jewel smiled. "Everything turn out all right with those kids?"

"We'll see. I think things are good for now. Where's Bo?"

Jewel's cheeks turned rosy, and her eyes wouldn't meet mine. "He was in the area on army business and just dropped by for a quick hello."

"Oh?"

"Aunt Lula, how many eggs do we need?" JC shouted from the kitchen.

"You'd better go see to him," Jewel said, bending to retrieve the coat and mittens that Russell had discarded on the floor.

I waited to make sure the weight of her belly didn't topple her over — and to see if she had anything else to say. But her silence lingered. If she could keep the secrets of her heart about Bo, I decided to keep mine about Chet. For now.

28

Chet

The strains of "My Country, 'Tis of Thee" pulled my ballplayers' attention to the music students instead of our half-time huddle.

"Look at me, not at them," I reprimanded.

Of course, I peeked that way, too. But all I could see was Lula's back as she directed the ensemble celebrating the National Week of Song with a patriotic tune. Patriotic music in the background as we raised funds for war bonds. Fitting, to be sure. But distracting.

"We've got to settle down and play. Blaze, try to get the ball inside, to Virgil. Clem, I need you to block out their center. He's scored too many baskets already." All three boys nodded. I looked each player in the face before continuing. "These guys won't give us anything for free. Now let's get this game back under our control!"

The singing stopped just before I finished

speaking, my final words echoing through the sudden silence. Lula turned and frowned at me as if I'd interrupted her students' performance instead of putting an exclamation point on their anthem.

But I couldn't spend time thinking about her now. We had a game to win.

The Bulldogs were down by three points. After all the boys' hard work, we faced the end of our undefeated season and quest for a new gymnasium.

Minutes ticked by. My boys tried hard, but still we trailed. I slouched on the bench, my eyes on Blaze as he took the ball up the court. If only I could call out a play or an encouragement, remind them to keep their feet moving and their concentration on the ball. But I couldn't. There was no coaching allowed during play.

Blaze to Clem to Virgil. Virgil bounced it twice, waiting for Flip, one of my shortest players, to break free from his defender. The ball swung in Flip's direction. Flip passed it back to Blaze, who shot it in.

34 to 35. I wished we were the 35.

We followed the Millersville boys back down the court, each of my players focused on the ball, on the player assigned to them, anticipating the next move. The building could have caught on fire at that moment and they wouldn't have noticed. I gripped a towel between my hands, pulling and twisting to try to relieve the stress.

Less than a minute. It appeared our whole season would live or die on the final shot. The pounding in my chest thundered in my ears along with the buzzing of the crowd.

The ball left a Millersville player's hands, arced upward. I couldn't swallow. Couldn't breathe. Blaze jumped up with it and batted it away from the rim before it began its descent. I shot to my feet as the crowd cheered. The referee gave me a warning look that told me to get a handle on my spectators. But I couldn't fault them.

Time for one more run up the court, one more attempt at a goal.

Jump ball.

Clem snatched the ball out of the air after Virgil's hand slapped the leather. He tossed it to Blaze. Blaze dribbled toward our goal, passed to Flip. My eyes followed the ball from guard to forward to center. Left and right. In and out. Then Blaze stood alone at the top of the key — just beneath the free throw line. Clem received the ball, flung it to Blaze. Blaze caught it, shot —

Scored! My arms flew into the air as the final whistle sounded. The boys from our bench rushed the court, all of them gathered around Blaze. I held back. I'd have my turn at congratulating him. I glanced over the crowd. Lula smiled at me from her seat, and I couldn't help but smile back. Then Miss Morrison appeared in front of me, her hand curling around my elbow.

"That was so exciting! However do you manage to stay so calm?" She flapped a lace hankie in front of her face.

I eased my arm from her grasp and pointed toward my team as I moved away from her. "Thanks, Miss Morrison. I have to go."

Then there were slaps on the back, hands pumping mine up and down. School board members. Fellow teachers. Parents. Miss Morrison, I noted, was pushed out of the way and looked none too happy about it.

I pressed through the crowd, seeking Lula. Then the sea of people parted. Instead of Lula, the weather-hardened face of Archie Clifton rose before me, the hostility usually directed at Blaze now turned full force on me.

"Coach!" Blaze's arm waved over the heads of those still in attendance, his back to his father, not yet aware of his presence.

I made my way to my team and started the congratulatory process again. But when my boys gathered around, I turned sober.

"You didn't give up. I respect you for that. Enjoy this victory, but remember we still have two more games in which to prove ourselves."

A chorus of "Yes, Coach" followed my words. Then I sent them off to change.

Blaze lingered behind. "How's it working out at your Uncle Sal's?" I asked him.

"It'll do." His mouth twitched into a grin. "Although Miss Delancey — or rather, Aunt Rachel, is a bit . . ."

I laughed, imaging Miss Delancey prancing about her new domain.

Blaze cleared his throat. "I guess I can make it until graduation."

I schooled my expression to neutral. He wouldn't want me to make a fuss. "Good. Mind if I ask how you came to that conclusion?"

His head dipped. "Nannie and I talked again. She thought it would be best to wait." He looked up. "She's smart. I trust her."

I nodded, thanking God for a girl with common sense. Then my gaze strayed over Blaze's shoulder. Archie Clifton's eyes bored into mine. "Your pa's here."

Blaze looked as panicked as a boy atop a runaway horse. I gripped his arm, wishing I could impart strength and courage with a touch. But I could only advise — and pray.

"He came to see you play. You ought to at least speak to him. Be a man, Blaze. Prove you have it in you to live your convictions without resentment toward those who don't understand or agree."

He nodded, but the fear didn't leave his eyes.

"I'm praying for you. Right now."

"Yes, sir." He took a deep breath and approached his father. With his every step, I battered heaven with my requests. For strength. For humility. For kindness and patience and rock-hard resolve.

The conversation lasted less than a minute. Mr. Clifton didn't look pleased when he left. Blaze threw his arm around Nannie's shoulder, his face tight and pale. Nannie tugged at his jersey. He glanced down at her adoring grin and relaxed.

My eyes sought Lula again. I'd hoped to share the excitement of the victory with her, but as I searched among the small clusters of fans that remained, she was nowhere to be found.

In spite of Lula's disappearance after the game the night before, I felt like a schoolboy on Christmas morning. Ma had arranged the seating at the Red Cross dinner and dance as I'd asked — and without an untoward look or comment. Lula would sit beside me, Jewel and Bo beside her. If only Lula would have agreed to let me drive her there and back. But she'd been insistent. She'd come with Jewel and Bo.

When she arrived at the town hall as promised, I inhaled at the sight of her, from the feathered round hat to the beige dress of lace that billowed out around her slim ankles. A shiny band of blue circled her waist.

"You look lovely." I lifted her gloved hand to my lips while she surveyed the athletic venue turned banquet hall. In just a few short hours, the seating and basketball goals had disappeared. Tables swathed in red, white, and blue bunting had taken their place. If only the army recruitment posters weren't staring down accusingly and the sea of khaki uniforms, soldiers from Fort Sill, didn't leave me feeling naked in my plain suit.

"Talking basketball, I see?" Principal Gray reached out to shake my hand. Lula slid her fingers from mine, stepped closer to her sister. I returned the principal's smile, but the glint of steel in his eyes put me on alert. Had one of my boys gotten in trouble? Had I forgotten to turn off the lights or lock up after our game last evening?

Before I could determine the cause, he sauntered away, greeting others, appearing amiable. I wiped a hand over my forehead, drying the thin glaze of perspiration. My nerves were too high. That was all. Like the boys at the start of a game.

Lula sat herself at our table and began talking with Ma and Bo about JC's latest antics. I sat down beside her, but Lula barely noticed. During the meal, she picked at her food, hardly ever looking my way. My chest tightened with disappointment. Maybe such a public venue hadn't been a good idea. Not if I desired intimate conversation with her.

After dinner, the band tuned up. Jewel's arms crossed her chest, and her eyes glistened — dark eyes so much like Lula's that the grief in them twisted my heart. Bo slid an arm around Jewel's shoulder and whispered in her ear. She nodded and stood. I hopped to my feet, as well.

"I'll see Jewel home. I assume you can escort Lula later?" Bo's expectant look told me we'd joined forces in our pursuit of the sisters. I nodded, glad to have him as an ally instead of an enemy. But Lula's chair scraped the floor right behind me.

"No, I'd better —" She wrung her hands, her gaze racing between her sister and Bo.

Jewel pressed Lula back into her chair. "You stay. Have a good time with the rest of the young people."

Lula's lips pressed into a tight line as she stared across the room. I glanced that way but couldn't figure out what had drawn her attention. The first song began. Couples crowded the dance floor. Bitsy Greenwood waved at us from Carl Whitson's arms. My back went stiff, wondering what Giles would think. But Lula relaxed into her chair, her expression loosening. "Of course you're right, Jewel. You go on. We'll be fine."

What had just happened? What had she seen? I looked back at my two friends, my colleagues, on the dance floor and scratched at the back of my head.

Women. Would I ever understand them?

A nudge from behind pushed me forward. I looked back. Ma. Eyebrows high, nodding toward Lula.

Did she mean for me to ask Lula to dance? I swallowed hard. Of course I wanted to. But did this mean Ma wanted that, too?

I extended my hand in Lula's direction. "Shall we?"

Her cheeks pinked, and her white teeth peeked over her rosy bottom lip. I wanted to yank her into my arms and never let go. But I stood patient. Waiting.

She rested her fingers on mine. A shy half smile lifted her lips as my hand settled at her waist, hers at my shoulder.

I blessed the crush of people that forced her closer, so close I could smell lilac soap on her neck. I couldn't take my eyes off her rosy cheeks, her quiet eyes, her bright lips. Was her hair done up in a new style? It seemed . . . softer somehow.

No longer was she the stoic Miss Bowman who'd arrived at school in October. Nor the haughty one who'd declared herself a better math teacher than me. This Miss Bowman had a vulnerability I found endearing. A spark of life that warmed me whenever I was in her presence.

We moved to the music while a singer crooned words of endearment. I held more tightly to her hand, pressed the fingers of my other hand into the small of her back, drawing her closer still. I stared into the depth of her eyes, hoping she read all my heart wanted to say.

Her gaze slid away. "Your boys played a great game last night."

My hold on her loosened. Either she couldn't read my feelings or she couldn't return them. Either way, I had no desire to make a fool of myself over her. Best to keep our conversation on equal footing. "Thank you. And your girls have improved so much."

Her eyes jumped back to mine. I tried to smile, but my face wouldn't override my heart. I wanted more than basketball talk from her.

"I . . . um . . ." She cast a sweeping look over the dance floor. "I've never watched anything quite so exciting as that game."

I shrugged. "We work hard in practice for games such as those. The boys proved themselves well. I am very proud of them."

"As you ought to be. I just hope my girls can acquit themselves as well by the end of the season."

"You only have two more games, but I think the girls have a shot at a win. They played especially well last night. Looks like you've had a good teacher." I winked, hoping to get back to our natural camaraderie.

Her blush deepened to red. "I told the girls I'd ask you if you could come up with some plays. Things we can do to direct the action instead of just reacting to the other team."

Now I couldn't quash my grin. Slow and wide. She'd been listening. Quite attentively, apparently. Basketball had been an easy illustration to throw Blaze's way because I knew he would understand it. I hadn't imagined it would work in the opposite direction with Lula — life explaining basketball rather than basketball explaining life.

Our steps adjusted to the rhythm of a new song.

"You did an amazing thing with Nannie and Blaze," she said. "I know I told you that before, but it's really true. Nannie seemed back to her old self last night."

I nodded. "Blaze, too. I doubt he would have led us to victory the way he did without some stability in his life these past couple of weeks. His uncle agreed to let him stay there until graduation. His pa couldn't complain much. Archie's always doted on his baby brother. And Sal is the only family Archie has left, besides Blaze. Having him living in town means he's spent a fair amount of time at my house, too."

Her eyes widened. "And your mother's all right with that?"

"Ma's actually quite good with the situation. Once she learned of Blaze's plan to enlist after graduation, she's fussed over him like a hen with a new chick. In the next three months, he'll get all the attention he's been denied since his own ma left. Of course, she refuses to address him as Blaze. It's Reed or nothing."

Lula laughed, really laughed. Victory

surged through my chest, every bit as heady as winning a close game. I wanted that feeling to last forever. I wanted to spend my life listening to Lula laugh.

29

Lula

The band took a break, but Chet didn't let go of my hand. I liked the strength of his fingers curled around mine. The warmth of his grip. It made a girl feel special. But just as that thought flit through my head, a voice oozed between Chet and me, thicker and sweeter than sorghum.

"Why, Mr. Vaughn. You aren't going to let one lady take up all your dances, are you?"

Miss Morrison's sly gaze sidled in my direction as she inserted herself between us. Chet's hand fell from mine. I suddenly felt empty. Especially when Miss Morrison angled toward Chet and cut me out of the conversation altogether.

I wanted to yank the lace and feathers right off her close-fitting hat. But I could control my temper, just as I had with Mr. Graham in my mathematics classroom. I stepped around her, placed myself at Chet's other side. He grinned at me, then raised his hand to rest on my back, near my waist. As if he'd soon lead me away.

"Principal Gray! Do come chat with us." Miss Morrison pulled Mr. Gray into our small circle. His gaze traveled to Chet's arm, then to my face. His disapproving look turned my knees to jelly.

"I . . . I think I'll sit for a while." I managed a weak smile for Mr. Gray. I couldn't even look at Chet. I stumbled back to the empty table, glad it sat near a wall, in the shadows. Maybe no one would see the mortification burning in my face.

When the music started up again, Chet led Miss Morrison to the dance floor. After a glance in my direction, Mr. Gray sauntered to the other side of the room. I blew out my held breath, slumped in my chair. Did the principal believe I'd violated the teachers' code of conduct? But other teachers were dancing together . . .

As a new song began, Chet slid into the seat beside me, his arm stretching across the back of my chair. He leaned closer. The scent of something spicy — his shaving lotion, perhaps? — filled my nose, set my head spinning. Did he know how intoxicating he was?

I couldn't tear my eyes from his lips as

they widened into a grin. "So tell me how a talented musician such as yourself ends up at college studying mathematics."

A coffee cup sat near. I clutched at it, stared into the dregs. "Are you sure you want to know?"

"I do. I promise." His breath caressed my cheek. I wanted to lean into it. Into him. But the thought of Principal Gray's stern eyes lifted my back from the chair, every muscle taut.

I wet my lips, tucked a strand of hair behind my ear. "I'm not a musician. Not in the true sense. I never had enough discipline. Never could see it through long enough to discover if I had any real talent." My finger traced a triangle on the tablecloth. "I had a reputation for flightiness in my younger years."

His eyes narrowed. "Fruity Lu."

I sucked in stale air, held it tight in my chest. Increased my death grip on the cold coffee cup.

Chet noticed. He pried my fingers loose, held them in his hand. "I heard it said during a game but couldn't reconcile it with the woman I know."

His gentle tone pulled the air from my lungs. My head dipped. "I tried to be like my sister, surrounded by friends, the life of the party. Flitting from activity to activity was part of that. But after Mama —" I swallowed hard, then spoke fast. "After Mama died, things like music hurt too much. I needed . . ." The words stuck in my throat. I needed attention. I needed love. But I couldn't say those things to Chet. "I needed a change."

He looked as if he wanted to speak, but he didn't. I pulled my hands into my lap. "I made my own way in college, against the wishes of my family. Except for Daddy. He encouraged me. In June, I received my bachelor's degree and a prestigious prize in mathematics to allow me to continue on to graduate school."

His eyebrows lifted. "So that's what you were doing when Davy died, working on your master's degree?"

I looked away from his kind eyes. I couldn't bear the idea that he might stop seeing me as a woman and begin seeing me as a threat. "And teaching a college class. There was even the possibility of coauthoring an article with one of my professors."

"And when you found out Jewel needed you, you gave up your studies and your work. You agreed to teach music and coach basketball."

I gave a hesitant nod. "Although *agreed* is

a strong word. I needed a job to support us. This was the only one I could find."

Something pulled my gaze across the room. Mr. Gray and Miss Morrison in close consultation, both looking in our direction. *A job I might now lose if I continue this tête-à-tête.*

I pushed to my feet. "And of course I'll return to those things after this school year ends."

The music grew louder. Chet grabbed my hand and grinned. "But this year isn't over yet." He started for the dance floor. I stumbled along behind him, tears pressing at my eyes. I didn't want to draw attention, to cause a commotion, but I also didn't want to expose myself to Principal Gray's scrutiny. I needed this job more than I needed the pleasure I felt in Chet's embrace.

Then Chet stopped. I pushed up on my toes and peered over his shoulder. Towering and thick, a man blocked our path. Face like flint. Eyes smoldering like coals.

"You high-handed backside of a mule! Who gave you the right to take my son from me?" The bass voice bellowed across the room. The music faltered. The buzz of conversation ceased. Principal Gray inched through the frozen crowd. Mrs. Vaughn stood nearby, eyes wide, hand covering her mouth. Was this Archie Clifton? I prayed Blaze and Nannie were nowhere in sight.

Chet let go of my hand. Stood taller. "I didn't take your son. You agreed to let him stay with your brother. After you reneged on the agreement you made with Blaze and Principal Gray. Remember that?"

Chet's anger seemed to push back those who'd crept close. I wanted to yank his coat to pull him back, too. Remind him that men like Archie Clifton weren't worth arguing with. But I couldn't move any more than the others could.

Archie's leathered features twisted. "There's nothin' in the pages of a book he needs to know to walk behind a plow."

Chet stepped forward, hands fisted at his sides. "Unless he doesn't want to walk behind a plow. At least, not your plow."

"Why, you —" Mr. Clifton raised his meaty fists. Women screamed. Mr. Clifton swung. The pop of flesh meeting flesh, bone meeting bone. Chet fell backward, his foot crushing mine. I stumbled, hit the ground, feared my dinner might land there beside me. Instead, I found Chet in my lap, shaking his head, holding his jaw.

How dare Mr. Clifton strike Chet! Chet had only ever helped Blaze. He didn't deserve Mr. Clifton's scorn any more than

Blaze deserved his father's tongue-lashings. I scrambled from underneath Chet. He sat on the ground, dazed. I found my feet just as Archie reached for Chet's shirt front. I stepped between them, heart exploding against my chest in thundering beats. "If you want to hurt Chet, you're going to have to go through me," I said, my voice far stronger than I'd expected it to be.

The man's arm fell limp. Then he roared. "This is none of your business!"

Several men stepped forward to restrain him. He turned on them like an angry bear.

"I think it *is* my business, Mr. Clifton." My voice remained steady in spite of the tangle of anger and fear inside me. "You see, I've been helping Reed with his mathematics, so if you have an issue with Mr. Vaughn, you have one with me, too." It wasn't a complete lie. I helped Nannie, who helped Blaze. But he didn't need to know that.

Chet groaned behind me. Mr. Clifton looked confused.

"Mathematics. You know numbers? Figurin'?" I tipped my head. A snicker nearby drew a look of pure hatred from Mr. Clifton. Distraction. Leverage. "I trust you agree that your son ought to know how many acres you plant, how much seed is needed for each acre, what price is to be paid for the crop, and how much profit is needed in order to sow again next season?"

"Of course I do, but he knew that much learnin' four years ago. He should have quit school then. And no schoolmarm can tell me different."

"That's a shame, Mr. Clifton." I laced my fingers in front of me, slowly, calmly. "Because Oklahoma is an up-and-coming state that needs educated men to help her grow strong and successful. Blaze — Reed — needs all the education he can get, in the classroom and out of it. Mr. Vaughn has taught him the value of having a plan and sticking to it, both in getting a diploma and in the sport of basketball. And if Bla— Reed — chooses to enlist after graduation, he'll learn even more about life and people and sacrifice."

Chet stood next to me now. Mr. Clifton cut a glance in his direction.

"Did he tell you he's enlisting?" Something like fear lidded Archie Clifton's angry eyes. At the bottom of it all, did he actually care for his son?

Chet stepped forward, shielding me from Archie. "He's mentioned it. But he wants to finish school first. I won't apologize for helping him do that."

With a growl of rage, Mr. Clifton charged forward. Hands grabbed from all sides, holding him back, then dragged him from the town hall. Chet never flinched. At least not until he turned to lead me from the building, too.

"I'm sorry it ended like that" was all Chet said when he dropped me off at Jewel's house. My hands had trembled in my lap the entire drive, his mother squished between us, chattering about how the confrontation had almost given her the vapors. He didn't even look at me as he tipped his hat and left me standing on Jewel's porch.

Was he unhappy that I'd stepped in? Uncertainty roiled like a spring storm in the western sky as I slipped into the house, locked up, and clicked off the one lamp still glowing.

On Sunday morning, I left the oatmeal cooking on the stove and fled the house when my sister shuffled into the kitchen, telling her that I needed to practice the hymns again before the morning service. When I sat at the piano in the gray predawn light, the tension I'd been holding released through my fingers. Classical music. Popular music. Hymns. Each one seemed to express what I couldn't say in words, to explain myself to myself. Only when I looked up at the numbers on the wooden board did I realize that I wasn't alone.

The shadow woman slipped away again before I could see her face or ask her name.

I'd wanted my first meeting with Chet after the dance to take place in public, but also away from the prying eyes of my girls, their imaginations as rampant as Jewel's. But I didn't see him at church. Neither him nor his mother. It wasn't as if I didn't look. I did. Far too often.

Bo's presence at our Sunday dinner kept Jewel's mind off my evening with Chet. And yet a part of me wished to spill the details to her, to ask her opinion as to what it all meant. I didn't trust myself to read situations between men and women in the same way I trusted myself to read numerical equations or musical notes.

By Monday afternoon, my fingers ached from endless cantata practices. Basketball ought to have been a welcome relief, but my anxiety spiked as I wondered when Chet would arrive, how I should act, what I should say. My mouth went dry. My hands turned damp. And I remembered all the reasons I didn't involve myself with men.

I strode onto the court, where my starters were attempting to block a pass from under the basket into the center area. "You can't just stand stiff, girls. You have to watch the ball. Try to anticipate where the girl who has it will throw it next."

I set myself near Rowena. Arms straight over my head, legs wide apart, just like in the picture from the Spalding's guide. "Now, pass the ball to Bill."

Rowena grinned, held the ball at her chest, and pushed it toward Bill. I jerked my arms down, fingers reaching to grab the slippery leather sphere. But it passed too fast. And I twisted too far. I couldn't stop my momentum. My feet tangled. My knees buckled. I landed in a heap on my side.

"Oh my goodness! Miss Bowman, are you hurt?" Nannie yanked on my arm, trying to help me up. I pushed to my knees, trying to roll the kink from my neck. Then a larger hand reached down to assist me. I looked up. Into Chet's grinning face.

Bill and Rowena snickered behind their hands. I'd look foolish to refuse, so I set my hand in his and hopped up as quickly — and as modestly — as possible. I brushed off my skirt, then turned my attention immediately to the girls. "Obviously, that isn't quite how it's done, but you get the idea. Don't just stand there. Reach for the ball. You have to want possession of it more than the other girls."

A picture of Blaze as the ball jumped into my head, the tenacity with which Nannie would defend it or pursue it if another girl wanted possession. The way I felt when Miss Morrison wiggled her fingers and batted her eyes at Chet.

My heart fluttered, thoughts straying to places I didn't want them to go. After the basketball season ended, Chet and I wouldn't have a legitimate excuse to spend time together. I'd be forced to stand aloof, watching other women, women like Miss Morrison, jostle for position beside him at church.

I ordered the girls back onto the court to try again.

Of course, after basketball, I'd need to be home more. In just a few weeks, the babe would lie in Jewel's arms instead of extend her stomach.

"Better," I called out. "Now do it again." I chewed my bottom lip, trying not to look to see where Chet had gone. I didn't hear him breathing behind me. Had he left? I turned my head, caught his grin from the corner of my eye. I whipped back around, then blew the whistle and dismissed my team. But they didn't head for the changing rooms.

"Miss Bowman?" Nannie glanced at the other girls. My body pulled tight. If they teased me about Chet, I'd —

"Our last game — the one against Edgewise?"

"Yes? What about it?"

"My cousin plays on that team and, well, the girls and I were wondering if we — the girls on both teams — could host a supper for the boys — both teams — in the domestic science room after the game. A kind of celebration for all of us reaching the end of the season."

"And hopefully to celebrate our boys' perfect record, too," Bill said.

The others nodded.

My tension eased. "I think that sounds fine. Do you need me to secure permission?"

"No, we asked Miss Greenwood and she was fine with us using her room. We just wanted you to be there, too. To celebrate with us."

"Of course." I said it matter-of-factly, but my insides melted in the glow of being included. They knew the Lula who got excited over a difficult equation. The Lula who knew — and cared — little about basketball yet had come to value it for their sake. The Lula who taught them music not

314

as a frivolous add-on but a serious pursuit. And they liked her anyway.

The girls scattered. Chet sauntered toward the boys' locker room, scanning the gymnasium from one end to the other. I wanted him to pass right on by. I also wanted him to stop, take my hand, stare into my eyes.

I had no idea what I wanted. I only knew that in spite of the code of conduct my job required, the sight of him set my heart spinning like Russell's whirligig. But Chet plus me equaled — what?

Not knowing the solution to an equation tied knots in my stomach. Or did I fear the sum total more?

"I . . . I had a good time Saturday night." My voice echoed through the empty gym. I wished I could tug the words back into my mouth, but they lingered there between us.

He shifted his weight.

"Your . . . your jaw doesn't look too bad."

He raised his hand, rubbed the place where Archie Clifton's fist had connected with his face.

I held my breath. Then his eyes met mine. Sure and steady. My knees weakened. Would this be the end? Or a new beginning?

Of course we couldn't be together. Or could we? Couldn't a girl change her plans, her dreams? Could God be showing me a different way than the one I'd been focused on for so long?

Words I knew I shouldn't say scalded my tongue. I had no power to keep them inside. "Would you come to supper at Jewel's house after the game this Friday?"

A slow grin lifted his lips. "I thought you'd never ask."

30

Chet

As I walked into the school building on Thursday, Blaze cavorted around me like an overexcited puppy. "We can win these last two. I know we can, Coach. Me and the guys, we want to win them. For you. And for the Dunn Bulldogs to finally make a name in the state in basketball."

His mouth kept moving, but I quit listening the moment I spied Lula, her coat collar pulled up around her slender neck, cheeks bright with cold. I fell into step beside her, Blaze still talking, his head bobbing between mine and Lula's.

She glanced at me, smiled bewitchingly. The game on Friday couldn't be over soon enough for me.

Principal Gray blocked my way while Lula continued on to her classroom. I watched her descend into the basement before turning my attention to my mentor and friend.

"Do you have time to talk later today?" he asked.

"Yes, sir. I have a free class period at two."

"Fine. Fine." He slapped me on the shoulder. "I'll see you in my office then."

I jogged up the stairs to my classroom, trying to ignore the foreboding poking my gut. Likely he wanted to talk about the last two games. Or maybe Archie Clifton had stirred up trouble over Saturday night's tussle. Though, of course, *he'd* punched *me,* not the other way around.

Shifting the papers on my desk, I found my schedule, noted my meeting with Principal Gray. Then I turned my attention to mathematics. If only the subject didn't bring to mind a pretty little music teacher two floors below.

Standing over me, Principal Gray rubbed two fingers across his crinkled forehead. In all our interactions over the past four years, such an expression had never crossed his face in reference to me. To Miss Delancey, yes. To foolhardy students, yes. My stomach churned.

"I've tried to overlook this, Chet, but several people have spoken to me about your behavior over these past few days, and I fear I can't ignore it any longer."

318

I stiffened. "My behavior, sir?" The encounter with Archie Clifton rose up in my mind. I would not let that man bully me the way he did his son. "I stand behind everything I said to Mr. Clifton."

Principal Gray shook his head. "Not Mr. Clifton, Chet. Actually, I applaud you and Miss Bowman for standing up to the man. And therein lies the problem."

My heart sank. I should have protected Lula from the undignified fray. I'd spent all my energy berating myself for my carelessness. I'd stayed on the ground too long. Put her in harm's way.

Yes, she'd held her own. I'd thanked God for her strength of character more than once. And thanked Him that she didn't seem to hold my actions against me as I'd feared she might. "I know I should have stepped in earlier. I'm sorry."

Principal Gray sighed and sat. "You still don't understand, do you?'

I blinked at him, bewildered.

"You and Miss Bowman spent the evening dancing with only one another, then you sat together without any other company."

What in heaven's name was he accusing us of? My mind blanked, his words bouncing off the surface like a basketball off a wooden floor.

Then I swallowed. He was suggesting exactly the thing I'd intended when I invited her to sit with me that evening. She'd been cautious. Now I remembered. And yet she'd let go of her reservations. Why? I thought back, trying to picture the circumstances. Jewel and Bo leaving. Lula looking out over the dance floor.

Bitsy and Carl.

"Yes, we danced together, just like other female teachers danced with male ones."

Please, God, don't let me have ruined everything.

"Yes, but your . . . exclusivity indicated more than a working relationship. You were observed huddled together, alone, in a dim corner. And seen leaving together in your automobile, too."

"With my mother sitting between us!"

Principal Gray's expression softened. "I know, Chet. I'm not saying I agree with the insinuations. I like Miss Bowman. And I think of you as a son. But the rules of conduct are more strict for a female teacher. And they exist for this very reason. We must have no hint of moral impropriety among our teaching staff. The school board is insistent about that."

Everything in me wanted to fight back, to prove our integrity. But I knew it would do no good. Unlike Miss Delancey, Lula wasn't deliberately flirting with me. No, it was the other way around this time. If I didn't amend my behavior, Lula would find herself without a job. Without a reference. With a stain on her record I feared would be impossible to remove. I couldn't do that to her, no matter the cost to my own heart.

I pushed up from my seat. "There is nothing untoward happening between Miss Bowman and me. We work together. Nothing more. And I assure you, we will not be seen in each other's company, except on the basketball court, ever again."

He nodded. "That's all I needed to hear."

I couldn't focus on my final class of the day. Nor could I bring myself to visit the gymnasium during the girls' practice, no matter how much I wanted to see Lula. Just see her. For when we spoke, I'd have to do what was best for us both. I'd have to tell her we couldn't spend time together.

By the time I reached the gym, the girls were scattering, the boys arriving. I chatted with Virgil. Then Flip. Then I sent them off to change.

The boulder sitting on my chest reminded me of the day Clay's draft notice came. The disappointment of knowing I wouldn't be the one off on an adventure, redeeming the family name. I would be the one to do the hard thing. The right thing.

Like now.

I darted behind the bleachers, bowed my head, and begged God for the strength to let go. After all, Lula had made it clear she had every intention of returning to her other life once the school year ended. When I finished talking to God, I peered through the slats. Lula was on her way toward the door, her neck craning this way and that.

Hope tried to rise. I mashed it down, refusing to let myself be weakened. Best get this done. Quickly.

Long strides carried me around the seats. I met her at the door. "I'm glad I caught you."

She smiled up at me, open, eager. I looked at my feet. "I hope you'll forgive me, but I must regretfully decline your dinner invitation."

I heard her intake of breath and raised my eyes.

She stared, parted lips trembling just a bit. "Maybe — maybe another time, then? Next week perhaps?"

I stared at a spot on the wall behind her. "I'm sorry. I can't. You understand."

Confusion flickered across her face. "No,

I don't understand. Perhaps you ought to explain."

How could I make it clear I didn't desire to end our relationship? To admit aloud that others believed us to be "keeping company" seemed improper.

When the light in her eyes dimmed to something I recognized as resentment, my mouth turned as dry as chalk. I wanted to tell her I'd made a mistake — of course, I would come to dinner at her house. But I couldn't. To cause the death of her future, her dreams, would be to prove myself a greater coward than my father.

31

Lula

"Back already?" Jewel pressed the heel of her hand into the lump of bread dough on the kitchen table. "I figured you'd be at least another hour."

I couldn't look at my sister. Not after her excitement when I'd told her of my dinner invitation to Chet — and his acceptance. She'd squealed and hugged me and squealed again. Then she'd started planning the menu for Friday night. JC had grinned wide, his eyes taking on a spark of life that had been missing for months.

Two days ago, sheer happiness. Now I ached with remorse that I'd said anything at all. To Chet or to Jewel and her family. My arms and legs felt heavy and swollen. I wanted to creep up the stairs, crawl under the covers, and cry myself to sleep. But I couldn't. So I kissed Inez on the mouth, rubbed noses with Russell, and pulled Trula's braid before looking around for JC. A lump sat in my throat. JC would take it the hardest, I feared. I didn't want his friendship with Chet to tarnish in light of the man's sudden change of heart toward me.

"Where's your brother?" I asked Trula.

Jewel brushed the flour from her hands, the fine white powder falling like snow to the floor. "He was digging around in the garden. I told him to quit. He yelled that he was tryin' to help. Then he ran off."

I slipped a calico apron over my clothes and lowered my voice. "Remember what I was like after Mama died, Jewel? I seemed to be in everyone's way. And I was older than JC."

Jewel frowned, then rubbed a streak of flour across her nose. "That's true. I guess I need to pray for more patience." She divided the bread dough, plopped each piece into a loaf pan, and slid them in the oven. Soon the yeasty smell would permeate the house. Light bread was a rare treat. I wondered what had put Jewel in such a generous mood.

"You feeling all right?" I quartered the white flesh of potatoes, then dropped them in the pot of water.

"I'm good." But she sounded tired.

"Are you sure?"

She leaned against the sink. "Trula, go set a record on the phonograph. We need some music around here."

My heart lurched. A sappy love song. That would be Jewel's choice. Something that reminded her of Davy. But I couldn't bear it. Not today.

Please, Trula, please. Put on something quiet and soothing. But of course the first notes that crackled thorough the brass speaker confirmed my fears.

> I was jealous and hurt when your lips
>   kissed a rose,
> Or your eyes from my own chanced to
>   stray;
> I have tried all in vain many times to
>   propose,
> Now at last I've found courage to say . . .

Just before Jewel could trill "All the world will be jealous of me," I threw off my apron and bolted for the door.

"Lula! Where are you going?" Jewel called after me.

"I'm going to find JC."

I found JC in the livery stable, as I figured I would. But he wasn't working. He was sitting on a low stool in a dark corner, chin in his hands, dirt streaking his face.

He didn't even look up when my boots crunched over the dry straw littering the ground. I knelt next to him, breathing in the peculiar smell of little boy sweat. Like a puppy still wet from a romp in the creek.

"Anything I can do to help?"

His eyes slashed in my direction, then returned to the ground. "No," he grumbled through his fingers. But a moment later, his arms dropped to his sides and he turned to face me. "Why can't she understand I'm the man of the house? I have to help her!"

Tears clung to his lashes as he blinked. He swiped his face with the sleeve of his coat.

I reached for his hand. He resisted, then relaxed. "She's trying, JC. I know she is. You just have to be patient with her." *Like she's trying to be with you.*

His lips curled into a snarl. "I've been trying to help her for months! How long do I have to be patient, Aunt Lula?"

My mouth twitched, fighting a smile. Likely it already seemed forever since his world had changed. He couldn't yet comprehend the thought of the years that stretched out in front of him.

I sat with my back to the weathered boards, draping my skirt over the mountain of my knees. "I know it feels like it's been a long time, but remember, you're not even eleven yet. It hasn't even been a whole year."

He slumped against the rough wall of the barn. A horse whinnied two stalls away. I remembered Davy here, working with the horses, the people. He never met a stranger. Rarely wore any expression but a smile. Jewel and JC had Davy the longest and missed him the most.

I pushed to my feet. "Your mama made bread to go with our potatoes and green beans and bacon for supper. I imagine the house smells mighty fine about now." I ruffled his unruly hair, tipped his head back. "Let's go tell her how good it is. I'll help you practice being patient some more."

Before I knew it, he'd pressed himself into me, his spindly arms tight around my waist, his shoulders shaking, tears wetting the front of my dress. "I — just — want — my — daddy — to — come — home."

I held him, my throat doughy with emotion. "I know, sweetheart. I wish I could make that happen for you and your mama."

His body stilled. "Mr. Vaughn says God can help me, but it's hard when I can't see Him."

"I understand." How many times had I felt that way myself? And yet lately, God felt

328

near. Especially when I gave myself over to music. Could JC have something inside him like that? Something that would help him feel the presence of God?

I hesitated, my own faith so weak through the years, yet growing stronger with every day I'd been back in Dunn. How had I not realized that until now? Even with Chet's skewer of my heart, this had been a good year. A growing year. One drawing to a close in a few months.

Time was short. JC needed my help.

"When do you feel closest to God, JC?"

He looked up, his face scrunched in thought. "When you play the piano."

I sucked in a breath. I couldn't be here for him forever. But what if Jewel could find her way back to the instrument eventually? That might help them both. Until then, I could oblige. I could use my musical talent for yet another good thing. "Think we have time for a private concert before supper?"

"So what happened between you?" Nannie asked, standing before me in her dark bloomers and white middy blouse, feet planted wide apart, hands on her hips. It felt as if I were holding the basketball and she were trying to take it from me.

I looked at the empty bleachers to my

right. "I don't know what you mean." From the corner of my eye I saw her eyebrows shoot toward the ceiling. I walked toward the team benches. She bounced along beside me.

"Look, Nannie, it wasn't appropriate for Miss Delancey to discuss her personal affairs with her students and it isn't appropriate for me, either. Besides, there was never anything 'between' us. Everyone knows that female teachers aren't allowed to keep company with men. Your imagination has run amok."

Nannie huffed and crossed her arms. I envisioned her foot stomping the ground, too. Like Inez when Trula wouldn't let her play dolls. "I thought you and I were friends."

"We are, Nannie, but I am your teacher and your coach. There are boundaries we can't cross right now." I set my things down, avoiding her eyes.

"Blaze says Coach Vaughn's barking at the team like a dog who's lost its bone. He never did that before."

I dropped my backside to the bench. I didn't want to know about Chet. It had been hard enough to keep my mind off him.

Her eyes narrowed. "What did he do?"

Heat splashed my face, turning all my

fight to ash. "It doesn't matter."

Nannie sat next to me. "But you still like him."

I nodded, fingered the belt at my waist.

"Then show him."

"Show him?"

Nannie rolled her eyes. "Get his attention. Do something he can't help but notice."

What would Chet notice? Right now he saw only basketball, especially since he refused to look at me. Basketball plus . . . what . . . equaled reestablishing our friendship? I dared not hope for any more than friendship.

". . . and Blaze says when they win, they'll —"

Win. Chet would notice that. Until this moment, the idea of winning a game had been a hazy thing, nice if it happened but not vital to my existence. Suddenly winning mattered. It mattered as much as it had to hear my name announced as the winner of the Donally Award.

No, victory now mattered more because it involved my team. All of the girls had worked so hard.

"Nannie, we have to win a game. Tonight or next week. It's all we have left. We. Have. To. Win. Do you understand?"

Nannie grinned, then hugged me with a

small squeal. "That'll do it. Let me talk to the girls. It's not that we haven't been trying before, but we'll work even harder." Her eyes brightened with a mischievous twinkle that frightened me a bit. "Who knows? We might come up with a secret weapon."

She scurried away, left me limp on the bench. I had just put my heart, my future, in the hands of a group of girls.

Maybe I hadn't killed crazy Fruity Lu after all.

We suffered another loss, but the score was close. For the first time, I found myself hopeful.

All week I studied everything I could find about the strategy behind basketball.

One win. That's all I wanted. A gift to Nannie. To Blaze.

To Chet.

A gift that said I understood them a little better now and was thankful for their help.

I remembered Chet's words about offense and defense and having a game plan. I hadn't stuck to that as well as I ought, changing course in the middle of games based on what the other team did. But no more. Now we would stand our ground.

I gathered the girls before they changed for our last practice on Thursday. "What did we talk about this week?"

Rowena's arm shot into the air, her hand fluttering. "I know! I know! We have to stick to our plays, no matter what."

"Even when it seems they aren't working," Bill chimed in.

I nodded. "And?"

A smile burst out on Nannie's face. "And don't let up. Give your all the whole game."

"Exactly." I looked over my team. Blondes, brunettes. Even a redhead. Eyes of every hue. Unique personalities and intelligences, each with her own strengths and weaknesses, hopes and dreams. I'd learned that every one of my girls could be unrelenting in at least one area of her life. Now I needed them to transfer that tenacity to the basketball court.

"I'm proud of each one of you for your effort this season. I believe we can log a victory tomorrow night right alongside the boys."

The girls cheered, but my stomach tightened. Could a win on the scoreboard really help me gain victory over Chet's heart?

32

Chet

I brooded over Lula. The hurt in her eyes as she'd avoided me these past two weeks. The pride that kept me from telling her I'd pulled away to save her job. Her reputation. Because I cared too much instead of not enough.

By Thursday, my brain needed a different occupation. "Any news from Clay?" I asked Ma at supper.

She shook her head sadly. I regretted asking. Now she'd mope around the rest of the evening. I wasn't sure my nerves could stand the strain.

If only I could be as good as Clay at making Ma happy. But that had never been a talent of mine.

As I scooped food into my mouth, I wondered what kind of meal Clay had today. Bitsy Greenwood was always putting together packages full of goodies to send to

Giles. The thought made me sit up straight. "Ma, would you like to make up a package of treats for Clay? I could get it in the mail on Saturday."

Ma looked thoughtful as she picked up my empty plate and hers. "Do you think a cake would last the whole trip over?"

I leaned back in my chair. "I'm not certain. Why don't I ask Jarvis Grand, the postal clerk? He usually comes to our games, and he ought to have some idea."

"I'll need to stop at the store to pick up a few other things."

She took our dishes to the kitchen. I thought of a few items I'd slip in the box to Clay, too. Then my mind drifted back to Lula. I sighed. The idea of the package for Clay had kept Lula off my mind for, oh — I glanced at my wristwatch — a whole two minutes.

I wandered over to the gramophone, turning the crank and then setting the needle on my newest recording. The Original Dixieland Jazz Band played "Livery Stable Blues."

As my toe tapped to the rhythm, I thought of JC. After the season ended tomorrow night, I wanted to spend more time with him. At the livery stable. Or over in Lawton. Not at Jewel's house. Or even church. Those places were too close to Lula.

Ma frowned as she picked up her knitting and settled in the chair farthest from the music. "Can't we have some real music tonight?"

I knew some said jazz was of the devil, but I found the rollicking beat helped relieve the pressures of the day, even if Ma didn't care for it much. "This *is* real music, Ma. Played by real musicians. Down in New Orleans, I believe." That's what the man in the music store had told me when I'd bought the record that day in Lawton with JC.

"Doesn't sound decent."

I closed my eyes, ignored her dramatic sigh. But when the phonograph needle stalled at the end of the recording, I took a different record from its slip. One Ma would prefer.

Mozart's Symphony no. 41 filled the silence between us until we bid one another good-night.

My mind refused to quiet. Just before midnight, I threw on my Levi's and a flannel shirt and walked the quiet streets of Dunn, enjoying the moderate temperature. Not spring yet, but not the bitterness of winter, either. The chill slapped me further

336

awake, though I warmed with every step.

Yet even after three brisk blocks, the unease that had pulled me from my bed didn't abate.

Lord? Is this You? Are You trying to tell me something?

My heart pounded with every flick of a tree branch in the breeze. I tried to name the feeling that crawled over my limbs, through my chest, and rattled my brain. Not fear, exactly. More akin to the dread that arose when the sky grew green, when the nearest storm cellar looked like heaven. That moment when you closed the shuttered doors over your underground hideout, slid the brace in place, and prayed it would hold.

But why? As much as I wanted to win our last game, I knew it wasn't life or death. And as much as I'd wanted to spend more time with Lula, she wasn't the only woman in the world, even if she was the only woman in years I wanted to pursue instead of hide from. Yet she'd be gone in a few short months anyway.

I kicked a small stone. It tumbled over the path, bounced off the trunk of a tree, and rolled to the bottom of a short stack of stairs. The ones leading into the church.

I glanced at the parsonage next door. Completely dark. As it ought to be. I shuffled up the steps, knowing the door wouldn't be open. But it gave way under my grip. I stepped into the building, then felt my way to a middle pew and sat hidden in the darkness. The howling cyclone inside me fell quiet in an instant.

My elbows found my knees.

"I feel You here, Lord. Closer than in my bedroom at home." I rubbed my forehead as if I could iron out the wrinkled thoughts beneath the skin. No matter. God knew what troubled me. Or rather, who.

Faces flashed through my mind like scenes in a moving picture show. I prayed for Ma. Clay. Giles. Blaze. JC. Even Lula. All while holding tight to my conviction that each one had been brought into my life for a reason.

Lord, You've entrusted my heart with the care of so many. Please guide me toward how I can best help them.

Despite my lack of sleep, excitement flooded through me with the light through my window Friday morning. The promise of a brilliant taste of spring, the prize at the end of basketball season.

And yet a sheen of sadness colored the day, too. For Blaze, Virgil, Clem, and Glen, this would be their final game. I'd miss coaching them, watching them play. I knew others would rise to take their places, but these four had come to my team as freshies my first year of coaching and would always hold a special place in my heart.

Sopping up my gravy with a biscuit, I ruminated on endings and beginnings, trying to shove aside the fact that I'd ended something that had never quite begun with Lula. My stomach soured. I escaped to the kitchen to wash my face. No sense giving Ma the chance to question.

But she followed me anyway, dumping the dirty plates in the sink full of water. "I'd like to attend the game tonight."

I paused. She'd come to a few games before, when Clay had been here to bring her and to sit with her. But she hadn't come since he'd left. I wondered what spurred her interest now. Blaze?

"All right. I'll be home after school. We won't need to leave again until a half hour before the game begins."

"Oh." She plunged her hands into the water and scrubbed a plate. "I thought we'd go to the girls' game, too."

The girls' game? My jaw sagged. She'd never wanted to attend a girls' game before. Never had quite approved of girls and athletics. "Are you sure?"

She shrugged as she lifted a plate and let

the excess water drip into the sink. "I'd like to see what all the fuss is about."

I wanted to throw my hands in the air. The one thing I'd determined not to do today — see Lula — was the one thing Ma wanted to do.

Yet I couldn't deny Ma's request. In spite of her ongoing prickly behavior, she'd softened some in recent months. And she seemed to genuinely like Lula.

"If that's what you want, we'll go to both games. I'll be by after my last class. You'll be ready to go?"

She nodded, giving me one of her rare smiles. Maybe in spite of my pain over Lula, God was doing something good in my life, after all.

33

Lula

"Is everything in order, Bitsy? What do you need me to do?" I held on to the doorframe of the domestic science room, trying to catch my breath after running up from my classroom.

Bitsy laughed. "The girls have everything ready to go. I've just supervised."

My gaze roamed over tables set with dinnerware, pots and pans scattered about the counters.

Bitsy gave me a playful shove out the door. "Go on. I told them I'd clean up. The girls need you over at the town hall, not here."

I wanted to throw my arms around Bitsy as if she were my sister instead of a casual friend. It was like I was sixteen again: Fruity Lu, giddy over the prospect of a pleasant evening in the company of friends. And one particularly handsome face I hoped and prayed would notice my efforts in the sport he loved so much.

If he sought me out after our game — our win — no one could criticize his behavior. One coach commending another. I could imbibe his nearness even if I couldn't indulge it. If he showed up to the team dinner afterward, I'd bask in his presence all the more.

As I arrived at the town hall, the girls marched out of the makeshift dressing room, their arms linked, whispers and squeals in abundance.

I clapped my hands. "Let's get warmed up, girls. We have a game to win."

Nannie flashed me a smile. "Don't worry, Miss Bowman. We've got this."

Her flippancy didn't inspire confidence. I pressed my fists to my hips and watched my team run through their drills. Rowena seemed to be limping a bit. Had she hurt her foot? Her ankle? Then I noticed a gleam at the toe of her shoe. "Rowena, come here a minute."

The bow in the center of her head flopped as she ran to me. "Yes, ma'am?"

"Let me see your foot."

"My foot?" Too innocent.

"Your foot. The left one. Lift it up here."

She glanced back at the others who stood watching, then lifted her foot. I grasped the bottom of her shoe, peered at the toe. A small spike of silver protruded from the end. I pressed my fingertip against it.

"Ouch!" I stuck my finger in my mouth, partly to cool the pain, partly to keep from exploding at Rowena. I counted to ten — or at least to six. "Why on earth do you have a pin sticking out of your shoe?"

Rowena's chin dropped to her chest. "We heard about other girls doing it."

"Doing what?"

"Putting pins in the ends of their shoes. You know, so if the other team gets too close, you can prick them. After that, they stay farther away."

I groaned. "Call the girls together."

They gathered around me, glancing at one another. Fearing, probably, that I'd ask them to tattle.

"I don't care whose idea this was, but I want you to go to the dressing room right now and remove every pin from every shoe. Do you understand me?"

Mumbles of "Yes, ma'am" accompanied shuffling feet. I wanted to shake some sense into each one of them. And yet the moment they disappeared from sight, I had to slap a hand over my mouth to keep down the laughter.

Pins in their shoes. I shook my head. What

would these girls come up with next?

Foxy and Bill took their places to defend against the Edgewise team's shots. Rowena and Nannie stood at the opposite end, ready to shoot for the hoop, while Dorothy and Elizabeth covered the center third of the court to pass the ball from defense to offense without having it stolen and returned to the other team.

I almost forgot to breathe as Dorothy and one of Edgewise's centers jumped for the ball to start the game.

Edgewise scored first. Then we made a basket. Then they scored and we missed. They missed and we scored. Back and forth. I didn't take my eyes off the ball. Neither did my girls. With fierce concentration, they were down by only two points at the half.

I gathered the team into a huddle. "Y'all are doing great. But Dorothy, we need to move the ball out of the center more quickly. And Bill, you've got to block that short girl's look at the basket."

Solemn nods. Then a cheer rose from the stands. We all turned. The boys' team hooted and clapped in our direction. My girls flushed, giggled, and poked one another in the ribs. I bit my lip, loving the boys' enthusiastic display but hoping it

344

wouldn't distract my girls from the goal. Chet would understand. He'd calm his boys in a minute.

But the noise continued on, Chet nowhere in sight.

Odd. He usually wasn't far from his team before a game. I craned my neck, searching the crowd, but couldn't locate him.

I called the girls' attention back to me. "Focus on the game. You can do this. And no matter what the scoreboard says at the final whistle, I'm proud of all you have accomplished."

After a moment of wavering, I put Gracie in to play for Rowena. The six girls trotted back out on the court, each to her respective zone. The others sat near me on the bench.

The whistle blew to start the second half, but I couldn't get Chet out of my mind. Where was he? His game would start soon after ours ended. Besides, what was the point of my team winning if he wasn't there to see it?

I mentally slapped Fruity Lu and her need to be noticed. My girls needed to win for themselves. For the satisfaction of setting a goal and reaching it. I needed their win for exactly the same reason.

■ ■ ■ ■

The basketball rolled around the rim, then slid down through the net. Air whooshed from my body. A tie game. Minutes left to play.

Every girl focused. Every girl intense.

"You can do this!" I whispered, wishing that willing it in my head would cause it to happen on the court. But I'd learned that coaching wasn't like working a math problem — or even teaching one. I couldn't do anything to help them get the result I desired. Only watch. And pray.

I almost laughed. Pray about a basketball game? Had I come that far in these few months? And yet I knew I had. Praying about things that involved my heart, not my head. I'd given up things I'd enjoyed, like music, to gain approval from my father — approval that would last only for his lifetime. If I continued on my path to please him, what would I really have on the day they lowered him into the ground beside Mama? A day that seemed to be quickly approaching.

A whistle. A foul. A free trial for a goal by Edgewise. Dorothy jumped at center court after the ball went through the hoop and

Elizabeth caught it and threw it to Foxy, who pivoted, raised her arms overhead, and lobbed it to Gracie.

Patient offense by Nannie and Gracie. Then good defense from Foxy and Bill. All while Dorothy and Elizabeth used the center section to thread the ball from offense to defense and back again. That's all we needed. Each pair of girls responsible for their third of the court, hemmed in by the uncrossable lines.

Another basket on our end. The Dunn Lady Bulldogs were up by one. The ball went from one of Edgewise's guards to one of their players in the center section of the court. Dorothy ran right at the girl, arms stretched over her head, only a slim space between their bodies.

The other girl frowned, trying to pass the ball to her teammate, but Dorothy wouldn't give way, eyes on the ball, arms moving. Elizabeth stayed as close to the other center as a flea on a dog. The girl jumped, sent the ball arching over Dorothy's upraised arms. Elizabeth turned and batted the ball out of bounds. Edgewise won the jump ball. Their forward received the ball and tossed it toward the basket. It banged off the rim and landed in Foxy's hands.

She bounced the ball once, passed it to

Dorothy in the center. Dorothy passed to Elizabeth. Elizabeth to Nannie. My hands balled into fists, every muscle in my body tense. Rowena scooted toward me on the bench and threaded her arm through mine.

Nannie tossed the ball to Gracie, just out of reach of the defending guard, then Nannie ran to stand beneath the basket. Gracie turned, threw it to Nannie. With both hands, Nannie raised the ball overhead, jumped. The ball sailed from her hands, bounced against the backboard, and slid through the net.

Rowena squealed, squeezing my arm, bouncing her feet against the floor. The referee turned. I shushed Rowena's enthusiasm. Nannie stood with her toes at the line while Elizabeth jumped for the ball at center court. An Edgewise guard retrieved the batted ball, flung it to her teammate. Gracie snatched the ball out of the air and launched it toward the basket.

Score!

The crowd cheered. The timekeeper put his whistle in his mouth but didn't blow. I held my breath. Another jump, then the ball traveled to the other end of the court. Foxy stood between the girl and the basket. They both left the ground. Their arms hit. The referee blew the whistle, called Foxy for a foul.

The forward from Edgewise stood at the free throw line, directly across from the basket. She bent her knees, swinging the ball toward the floor then hurling it up with both hands. It banged against the backboard, the rim, and then rattled through. Bill jammed her hands on her hips, frustration twisting her face. One more shot for Edgewise. Right on target.

Still up by three, we only needed to keep possession of the ball until the game ended.

Dorothy made the jump again. Flesh slapped leather. The ball shot to the left. Elizabeth stretched long and secured her fingers around it. A pass to Nannie. One dribble. The whistle shrieked, the timekeeper waving his arms overhead.

I fell back against the wall. The other girls launched from the bench to embrace their teammates.

Twenty-four to twenty-one.

We'd won. We'd really won!

The girls jumped and cheered. They pulled me from the bench, all talking at once. Joy on every face. Their utter bliss a far greater reward than I deserved.

In that moment, I understood what I hadn't before. That the subject of my work wasn't as important as the act of doing it well. Giving my all. Seeing it through to the end. Music. Basketball. Mathematics. I didn't have to apologize for any of them. I didn't have to leave off one to do well at another. Each had its own time and place.

As the revelation settled in, my eyes strayed to the stands. A band of disappointment squeezed my chest. Chet hadn't witnessed any of it.

34

Chet

I ran.

Fast.

Hard.

Over the darkening roads, out of town.

Ran until every breath knifed my chest and my heart felt as if it would explode.

Then I stopped. In a random field. Hands on my knees, seeking air for burning lungs before dropping knees to the ground, hands cradling my head.

"No. No. No. No." Each word a moan. Each moan a prayer. All while the scene replayed, over and over and over again.

I'd motored home after school. "Hurry up, Ma! The girls' game will start in a little while."

"You don't have to shout," she said from the stairs, her hand on the rail, her feet searching carefully for each step. A hat I hadn't seen in years sat at a jaunty angle on her head, and she wore her best Sunday dress. In the old style, hem brushing the floor. For the second time today, she'd surprised me.

"Don't you look nice."

"Oh, pshaw." But her cheeks grew bright all the same.

I grinned. Maybe I'd spent the night worrying over nothing. Maybe today's games would usher in Ma's transformation and I'd simply been given notice in advance.

"Let me get my handbag. Then we can go." She lifted her skirt just a bit and headed to the kitchen.

A knock at the door turned me in the opposite direction.

"Yes?"

A wide-eyed boy extended a yellow envelope. A hollow feeling plunged into my middle. I fished in my pocket for a coin, dropped a nickel into the boy's empty palm, then took the telegram. He tipped his cap and dashed away.

"Who was —" Ma's voice died as her eyes locked on the envelope. Her hand crept to her throat. Her face turned gray. "What does it say?"

"I don't know."

Ma wobbled to the sofa. I eased down beside her, lifting the yellow flap. *Please, dear God. Please not Clay.* I couldn't form any other words, any other thoughts.

Sliding the sheet from its envelope, the typewritten words stared up at us, stark and black.

Deeply regret to inform you that Lieu Clay P. Vaughn died of a respiratory illness Feb. 28th. McCain, Adjutant General.

Ma grabbed the sheet of paper and crumpled it in clenched hands as her high-pitched wail filled the room over and over and over again, like the cry of an agitated hawk. My teeth ground together, the ripping agony of my heart as great as Ma's but without the freedom to let loose.

She fell into my arms, her body quaking with every labored breath. I stared over her head. My steady focus on the horn of the Victrola anchored me to earth. Clay was gone. Gone. He'd never return to Dunn. My chest cinched, Ma's small fists beating against it. But I couldn't feel her anger. My entire body had gone numb. I couldn't even find tears to cry. Only a hard stone of aloneness in the center of my belly. And a smoldering fire to *do something* — anything — to avenge Clay's death.

Ma pushed me away, red-rimmed eyes as

lethal as a bayonet on the end of a rifle. *It should have been you.* The words in her eyes were as clear as the ones on the telegram from the adjutant general.

And perhaps she was right. If I'd gone instead of Clay, Ma would still have the one son who mattered to her. But neither Clay nor I had been given a choice. The draft notice had come. Addressed to my brother.

"Can I get someone for you, Ma? Pastor Reynolds? One of the Red Cross ladies?"

She grabbed the lapels of my jacket. "I. Need. My. Son."

She didn't mean me. She meant Clay.

"I'm so sorry, Ma."

"You aren't," she spat back. "Clay's dead and you're smug that you're here, out of harm's way. Just like your father. No courage."

My body stiffened. She had no idea the courage it took to stay behind. To accept a different path than the one of adventure and glory, even if it did mean the possibility of death. It had been right for Clay to go. And right for me to stay.

She slumped back on the sofa, covering her face with her hands. I sat stiff beside her, waiting for whatever would come next, wishing I could escape to grieve my brother on my own.

Suddenly, she calmed. An eerie calm. Like the eye of a storm. "He committed suicide. Did I ever tell you that?"

Air disappeared from the room. Pa? Did she mean Pa? He'd deserted his army base and was shot for his cowardice. At least that's what Ma had always told us, the shame she'd tried to cover over every day since then.

"They were due to leave, to go fight. He got scared, lit out for home. Or so they told me. They caught him, brought him back to stand trial." Her head traveled back and forth like a broken gate in a strong wind. "He wouldn't even face his own cowardice, wouldn't take his punishment like a man."

"Oh, Ma." From the time I knew of my father's fate, I'd pitied him. I'd believed him flawed, but not truly a coward. Until now. Hearing the truth was like losing Pa all over again. Only worse. Now I knew the full shame Ma had carried. Added to the grief over Clay, it was too much.

And so I ran.

I knelt in the dirt until the stars shone bright overhead and my limbs ached from strain, then disuse. I stumbled back into town like a cowboy on a Saturday night after payday, willing my mind to clear, my vision to focus. When it did, I stood almost nose-to-nose with Uncle Sam, his finger pointed at my face.

I want YOU for U.S. Army screamed the words beneath him.

I stared into the earnest eyes of the white-haired man, his top hat sporting a band of white stars on blue. My jaw tightened. My fingers curled into my palms.

I'd held to my convictions with a stubbornness that made the Rock of Gibraltar look like a dislodged pebble. But if Ma needed someone to make up for Pa's cowardice, I would be the person to do it. For her. For Clay. Maybe even to prove to myself, once and for all, that I wasn't anything like him. I'd defend my country without fear. And if I died doing it, what would it matter? Ma would be vindicated. And there were very few people who would grieve me.

35

Lula

Bitsy bustled around her domestic science classroom, supervising the last-minute preparations for supper. A few minutes later, the Edgewise girls arrived, shy and awkward, to add what they'd brought for the party before all the girls would return to the town hall to watch the boys' game. Nannie chatted with her cousin, then with the others, until girls from both teams mingled like old friends instead of remaining separate.

I envied them that — their easy way with one another. I'd opened my heart to Chet, but he'd slammed the door in my face after making me think he'd flung it wide open. An ache pulsed in my chest. I wrapped my arms around my middle to hold the pain in place.

Chet would have joined his team by now, ready to finish out their season with a win.

Proof that basketball was a viable sport, one the community should support with their presence and with their coins — and eventually with a brand new gymnasium.

"Miss Bowman?"

I spun to find Blaze motioning to me from the shadows beyond the door. He should have been at the town hall, warming up. He had an important game to play. I stepped out of the room, fear snaking toward my throat. "What is it?"

He shifted his weight. "Coach hasn't shown up."

"Hasn't shown up?" Alarm magnified my voice. I clapped a hand over my mouth, then pulled Blaze out of sight of the doorway. "What do you mean he hasn't shown up?"

Blaze frowned. "I don't know. I only know we need a coach. And we — the boys and I — decided it ought to be you."

"Me?"

Blaze grabbed my hand, pulled me after him.

I glanced back. Nannie stepped through the door, wide-eyed. Both teams of girls clustered behind her.

"But, Blaze, I don't know anything about —" My feet stumbled to keep up with his lengthy stride. Out of the building, down the street. The speed of our pace tore at the pins holding my hair. The knot behind my neck drooped. Soon it would unwind altogether.

"Blaze! Stop!" At last I planted my feet and refused to move.

He jerked backward. His gangly hands settled on my shoulders. "We know what to do, Miss Bowman, but we're required to have a coach on the bench. Please, won't you be our coach? We have to hurry."

The fear in his eyes killed any hesitancy I had left. After all Blaze had been through, I would not let him down now.

I hardly knew how I got in the door, to the bench, through the jump ball. Had Chet's motorcar overturned? Was he lying unconscious in a ditch somewhere? Had something happened to his mother? To their house?

With every image, the weight in my chest intensified, doubled by the continual back and forth of the scoreboard. Chet was in trouble. I knew it as surely as I knew one plus one equaled two. And all I could do was watch his team win or lose. I couldn't even make a difference in the outcome.

Midway through the first half, I pushed aside my worry over Chet and focused on the game. We'd slipped behind by three points. Virgil crouched with one hand behind his back in the center circle, waiting for the referee to toss the ball and blow his whistle. He leapt at the sound and swatted the ball to Clem. Clem dribbled and then tossed it to Blaze. Blaze dodged one opponent, then another. He jumped, the ball rolling off his fingertips and swooshing through the net.

Edgewise's lead was cut to one.

Back to center court. Another jump ball, this time with Edgewise taking control. When the timekeeper announced the halfway mark, I let out my breath as the boys slouched on the bench, sweat trickling down the sides of faces red with exertion.

Blaze spoke softly to the boys while they rested, each one nodding gravely at his instructions. Blaze's intensity mesmerized me. Not just fervor for the game, but concern for each player. The corner of my mouth lifted. Whether Chet knew it or not, he had nurtured a heart like his own.

The thought bore down with searing pain as I noticed the crush of spectators, seated, standing, each of them having plopped their nickels into the coffers of the war bond fund. Chet had done it. He'd given the town a rallying point that supported both our boys in uniform and our future generations.

What would keep him from witnessing his triumph?

The Chet I knew would not abandon his team, even in the most dire of circumstances. He'd have sent word, if nothing else. Which meant something terrible had happened to *him*. A wave of nausea washed over me. I bit my lip, prayed the burning liquid would remain in my stomach rather than rising up my throat. The last thing these boys needed was for me to be sick on the court. But I couldn't think of Chet without becoming ill, even if he had spurned my attempt at friendship.

The game resumed. The score remained close. Clem dribbled off to the left, near our basket. Then he went down on the court, holding his ankle. The referee called time out. Blaze and Virgil hoisted Clem between them, helped him limp to the bench.

The boys circled around me, the scent of their sweat almost sending me into a swoon worthy of Fruity Lu. The referee approached. "You'll need to send your substitute to check in with me before play resumes."

I nodded, looked to Blaze. "Felix," he said.

The freshie jumped up from the bench, hopped in place, and tugged at his shirt, then his shorts.

"You'll do fine," I told him, having no idea if he would or not. The boy followed Blaze and the others out onto the court, speaking to the referee before lining up to take the jump ball at the place where the time out was called.

I held my breath. Felix swatted, but missed. The tall boy from Edgewise batted it to a teammate. Up and down the court they ran, trading baskets. The timekeeper announced the three-minute mark.

Three minutes. Still down by one. With a win, our boys would secure a new gymnasium as soon as the war ended. With a loss, they would become just another Dunn Bulldogs basketball team, though one with substantially more wins than losses.

A basket for Dunn. A basket for Edgewise. A miss. A score. A score. A miss.

How many seconds remained? I felt sure I'd fly apart with the strain. Blaze held the ball. He turned. Jumped. The leather sphere left his hand and sailed toward the basket.

Thunk.

Off the rim. The whistle sounded. I hung my head. It was over. We'd lost.

When the boys came to the bench, I'd have to shoulder their disappointment somehow. Over the game. Over Chet. But

362

the boys didn't arrive. I looked up. Blaze was standing at the free throw line. My heart jumped. The whistle had signaled a foul, not the end of the game! We still had a chance.

A movement caught the corner of my eye — someone stepping apart from the crowd. My head jerked left. Archie Clifton stared at his son, jaw bulging, every line in his weather-worn face etched as if in stone. A picture of agony — the anguish of a parent for a child he couldn't help.

My gaze swung back to Blaze. He lobbed the ball in an arc toward the net. It slid through the hole, hit the floor. Blaze shot again.

I let out a long breath. We were ahead by one point. I looked at the timekeeper. He held up a finger. One minute remaining.

Edgewise won the jump ball. Passed to their left wing. Passed it again. And again. An off-kilter shot. Virgil grabbed the ball. From one boy to another it flew. A bounce here. A bounce there. Then suddenly the ball reached Blaze's hands. He raced up the court. Two boys from Edgewise blocked his view of the basket.

In a flash, Felix was on Blaze's left, the ball on the freshie's fingertips, and then in the air. The timekeeper's whistle blared as the ball sank toward the basket, cleared the rim, hugged the net.

The crowd erupted from their seats, rushed the court. Archie Clifton followed the surge. Reached his son. Greeted him with a clap on the shoulder and a shake of the hand. The man's lips moved in speech, and a smile lit Blaze's face.

Only then did I slip away to find Chet.

I ran toward the Vaughns' house first, my hairpins pinging to the ground at an alarming rate. By the time I saw his Model T, my hair had streamed out around my shoulders, whipped and tangled by the wind.

No light shone from the windows. My hand brushed the cold metal of his car, clinging to the hope that its presence assured his safety. Then I charged up the steps and pounded on the door. "Chet? Where are you, Chet?"

I stopped. Listened. Was that a groan from inside? I rushed into the dark house. A shadowy figure rose from the sofa at my entrance, but the rustle of fabric told me it wasn't Chet. In fact, as the specter sat down again, head bowed, its size and posture struck me as familiar.

Was this the mysterious person who listened while I practiced at church?

Groping in the dark, my hand finally landed on a light switch. *Click.* The room brightened in an instant. Mrs. Vaughn's desperate eyes met mine, haggard lines creating furrows around her eyes and mouth, as if she'd aged six years in the six short days since I'd seen her last.

"What's happened? Where's Chet?"

Her gaze drifted toward the open front door. Everything inside me froze. Chet was dead. It was the only explanation for his absence, for his mother's despair.

And in that moment, I knew I loved him. No matter that it was impossible or that I'd told my heart no. I loved him, and I didn't want to live without him. My legs gave way. I dropped to the sofa.

Like a child with a forgotten plaything, Mrs. Vaughn held out her hand, a ball of paper resting on her palm. I smoothed it flat and forced the typed words to pierce through my anguish.

Clay.

Clay was dead.

Not Chet.

My heart soared, then plummeted. *Oh, Chet. I'm so sorry.* To lose his brother in a place so far away. No comfort in a body, a funeral. At least Jewel had that with Davy. A time to say good-bye, to digest the reality.

Instinctively, I pulled Mrs. Vaughn into my arms. I had only my presence to offer as comfort, but it was apparently more than Chet had given her.

Anger flared. How could he leave her alone? He didn't even have the excuse of feeling obligated to be with his team, for he hadn't been there for them, either.

"Where is he?" My words were quiet and calm, the opposite of those in my head.

She eased from my embrace, her focus refusing to leave the hands fumbling with a limp handkerchief in her lap. "I . . . I said terrible things, told him what I swore I would never reveal." With a shuddering breath, she finally met my eyes. "I'd determined my boys would make up for what their father did, no matter what. I thought it would make me happy. But I've found that bitterness is a deadly disease, Miss Bowman. It spews its venom in the worst possible moments."

What was she talking about? Make up for what? A wad of tears hung in my throat. My heart pumped faster. Maybe Chet had a reason to run.

Mrs. Vaughn clutched at me, clung to me. "Find him for me. Please. If I hadn't been such a stubborn old woman, I'd have only lost one son today instead of two." She slumped into me as if she'd used up every ounce of strength.

I wanted to run, to do as she bid. But I couldn't leave her like I'd found her. I removed the hat askew on her head and helped her stretch out on the sofa. I stroked her hair and kissed her forehead as if she were Inez or Trula, not a woman near to my mother's age.

She held my hand to her damp cheek, gratitude shining in her eyes.

"I'll find him and bring him home, Mrs. Vaughn. I promise."

I burst into Jewel's living room. "Mrs. Vaughn needs you. Her son died. In France."

Jewel's face blanched. "Where's —" She tried to rise, but couldn't gain the momentum. Then I noticed Bo. He helped her to her feet.

"I don't have time to explain. Please, just go to her."

Bo picked up his hat. "I'll motor her over. JC can watch the little ones."

"Thank you." I dashed back into the night. Main Street was dark and silent. At the livery stable, I heard only the nicker of horses, no human presence.

Could Chet have taken refuge outside of

town? Walked to Fort Sill? Gone to the town hall in search of his team?

I went to the town hall first and yanked open the door. Only a scattered few remained. Principal Gray spied me and frowned. His forceful stride brought him near. "Miss Bowman, I —"

"Chet — have you seen him?" I almost yelled.

"No, he still hasn't —"

"I'm sorry. I have to go." I turned and ran toward the school. The gym.

Even if he'd gone elsewhere to work through his personal pain, he'd eventually find his way back there. His place of peace. And pride.

Tripping over unseen impediments, stumbling down dark streets, I tried to pray. But no words emerged except *Jesus, oh, Jesus. I love him. Oh, Jesus, help me find him.*

I reached the gym, pulled at the doors. Locked, every one. My legs trembled. A sob burst from my chest. I eased down onto the stone steps, the evening chill seeping through layers of clothing and numbing my body. I covered my mouth, despising my weakness.

Crying over a man. One who loved a silly game. But also a man who loved his students and his mother. His brother. Even JC. A man whose friendship I'd come to cherish against all odds.

I lowered my head to my knees. How could a few short months uproot all I'd built my life on?

My hope is built on nothing less than Jesus' blood and righteousness.

I sat up straight, the words as clear as a pane of glass. The storm inside me died. Had I done that? Had I built my life on a rock that wasn't solid? That wasn't Jesus? Had I been stubborn, like Nannie and Blaze, instead of steady in conviction, like Chet?

Whatever else I had or hadn't accomplished, Mama wouldn't be proud of that. She'd taught me the story of the wise man and the foolish man from the time I'd been tiny — and made sure I knew what it meant.

But after she'd gone I'd decided that music and laughter and someone to love and cherish meant a sandy spot on the beach, while academic success and Daddy's attention assured me an unmovable foundation. Now I stood in a whirlwind, fearing my entire life would go *splat* at any moment. I covered my face with my hands, wishing tears would come and cleanse the heart that had veered so far from the truth.

My eyes remained dry. "I want You as my

foundation, Lord. Nothing less."

Peace ebbed through my tired soul, and for the first time in years, I had hope my prayer had been heard. I glanced heavenward. "Help me find Chet. Please."

Clouds hid the light of stars behind their bulk. My hope vanished — the same sinking feeling as confronting a mathematical equation whose answer remained beyond reach.

"When all else fails, start again at the beginning."

Thanks, Professor. I surged to my feet. Start over. I could do that. Grabbing hold of my granite tenacity, I retraced my steps to Jewel's house to begin the search for Chet once more.

36

Chet

I paced the dark aisle of the church. Clay and I had talked about this possibility — that something might happen to him. It was a huge part of the reason I had agreed to stay with Ma. But now something *had* happened. And I'd abandoned Ma when she needed me most. I'd run away. I was still running away.

I glanced at the enlistment papers in my hand, then dropped into a pew halfway toward the front and hung my head. "Forgive me, Lord. I didn't even ask You. I didn't even ask." I tasted the salt of tears, understood at once Peter's anguish at his betrayal of Jesus. Hadn't I just done the same thing — abandoned the trust bestowed on me by my Savior?

If only He would appear, fix me breakfast on the shore, and tell me to feed His sheep. Then perhaps I'd know that I, too, was forgiven. That I, too, still had a purpose to fulfill. Until then, I had to accept the consequences of my rash actions, whatever those might be, knowing full well I deserved every bit of trouble I received.

If only Pa . . . If only Clay . . . If only Ma . . .

No. It was my doing. All of it. After years of quiet discipline, one rash decision would change the course of my life. I'd signed my name, given my word, said I would go fight.

What would happen to Ma? My students? My team?

I slammed my fist down on top of the pew in front of me. The game. I'd missed the game. I'd let down my team. Had they still played without me? Had they won?

Principal Gray would find another coach. My students would get another teacher. But Ma had no other sons. If I could be certain of Ma's welfare, then I could face my death with less remorse. For I felt certain death would be the end result of my enlistment, as it had been for Clay.

Time passed. Fast or slow, I had no gauge. My body grew stiff from the chill. Breath hissed in my lungs. I would brave the consequences of my actions. And yet even that resolve didn't fill the hollowness inside me. The emptiness reminded me of the days after we'd learned of Pa's death. Ma co-cooned in her bedroom. Clay and I huddled together in a dark corner of the barn. Only now I didn't even have Clay.

There'd been no funeral for Pa. That made sense now. And once Ma had again found the light of day, we'd moved to another town, one that didn't connect us with my father's sad history — at least the version she'd told my brother and me.

To earn money, Ma washed other women's clothes, her hands turning red and raw. There was always an iron heating on our small stove, except when it was needed to cook supper. Years of scraping by. Financially. Emotionally. Yet she had carried the burden alone. For so long.

She'd watched her son go off to war, hoping his honorable service would erase the shame of his father's actions, only to have him die untried.

For years I'd prayed for Ma to see that only God could heal the wounds that festered inside her, but I'd never imagined her pain to be so deep, so wide. Why would God allow Clay's death now? Hadn't it demolished any good He'd yet accomplished?

Creak.

Rusty hinges groaned behind me, same as they had when I'd sought refuge in the church. I didn't want to talk to Pastor Reynolds, or anyone. Quick steps clicked up the aisle before I could slip into the alcove leading to the side door. A whiff of lavender accompanied the shadow.

Lula bent to her knees in the aisle. Her soft hand cupped my cheek.

"Oh, Chet." My name caught in her throat. I tried to turn away, but her touch held firm. Had she come to berate me? I'd done enough of that to myself. I didn't need her help.

"I thought . . . I thought . . ."

Was she crying? I grasped both of her hands in mine. Surely no other tragedy had befallen her family. "Tell me." More of a breath than a whisper.

"You . . . you didn't come. You didn't — I went to find you. I found your mother. She —"

I tightened my grip on her hands. "What about Ma?" Could I bear any more guilt?

She shook her head. "Jewel's with her. But you weren't there and the boys —"

I shut my eyes, clenched my teeth. They'd lost. My hands fell from Lula's. I stared at my feet. "I'm sorry. I'm so sorry. It's all my fault. I wasn't there. It's all my fault."

"Chet." She forced my face toward hers again, but she couldn't make my eyes meet

374

hers. "Listen to me. You don't understand."

"No," I mumbled. "No one understands."

Her hands pressed into my cheeks. "Blaze was worried. We were all worried. He . . . he came for me. I sat on the bench, acted as the coach in your place."

My eyes jumped to hers as a soft stream of moonlight shot through the tall windows. "You?"

"Yes, me." Her touch fell away. "My girls won tonight, I'll have you know. I can do whatever I have a mind to do. And I chose to put my mind to basketball."

I almost laughed at her vehemence. I could have if my heart hadn't shattered.

"You would have been so proud of Blaze." Her voice softened, spread over me like a buffalo robe on a frigid night. I wanted to curl into it, receive its warmth. "Blaze coached the team, really. I didn't do a thing. He was . . . amazing. And when they won —"

My head jerked up. "Won?" A current sparked in my brain, lifted me to my feet. I yanked Lula up with me. "They *won*?"

Her head bobbed up and down. I threw my arms around her, laughter ringing through the empty space. A giggle near my ear awakened my senses, the warmth of her breath on my neck, the smell of summer on

375

her flesh. I ought to step back, pull away. Instead I inhaled, drinking her in as long as she'd allow, still marveling that she'd come to find me.

As I peered down into her face, the reflection of the moonlight caught the edge of tears shimmering in her eyes like lake water in midsummer. Her lips parted. I lowered my mouth toward hers even while telling myself I shouldn't.

Would I feel the crack of her hand to my cheek? I hesitated only a heartbeat, waiting. She flinched forward. Our lips met, hers as soft and sweet as ripe berries, just as they'd been in my dreams. Her hands pressed against my chest before creeping to my shoulders, circling my neck. I pulled her closer, held her tighter. Never wanted to let her go.

Light saturated the room. We jumped apart, blinking at the brightness. I flung Lula behind me, felt her head press into the space between my shoulder blades, as if she could disappear from view.

"Chet? What are you —" Pastor Reynolds' head tilted, his brow wrinkled.

I let out a long breath, felt for Lula's hand, and pulled her to my side. No sense trying to hide.

"Miss Bowman?" Pastor Reynolds' eyes

slashed back and forth between us. "I don't understand."

"I . . . I came in to . . . to . . ." She glanced at me, eyes wide in a plea for help. Not blame. Not disdain. I wanted to sweep her into my arms again, cover her precious face with kisses.

Instead I squeezed her hand. "She found me here, sir. I'd —" I hung my head, lowered my voice. "We learned today that my brother, Clay, died in France."

The pastor's hand landed on my shoulder. "I'm so sorry for your loss."

"Thank you." I glanced at Lula, her face almost bloodless with fear. I thought of Principal Gray's warning. Of Pastor Reynolds' place on the school board.

Pastor Reynolds scratched his head. "Lots of people out there looking for you, son. Did you know that?" His gaze slid to Lula, and I could read his thoughts as clearly as if he'd spoken. Lula and I. Close together. In the pitch-black church.

I kept my eyes steady on his, eager to convey our innocence. Pastor Reynolds frowned. "This is a bit . . . disconcerting, to say the least."

I'd hurt Lula by discarding her dinner invitation in order to stave off this type of situation. Yet I'd brought it down on her just the same. I needed to drop her hand, deny everything. But I couldn't. Not again. Never again.

"We've done nothing wrong, sir. Nothing. I'll explain that to whoever needs to know."

Pastor Reynolds' eyes pinched into a squint. "I haven't said anyone's at fault here. Yet."

Lula's fingers tightened around mine. I might have failed Ma and my team, but I would not fail her. I would find the courage to be the man I'd thought myself to be.

37

Lula

Pastor Reynolds told us to go, to find Mrs. Vaughn. Chet and I navigated the dim streets, my hand still captured in his. He told me everything. His mother's excitement over the game. The telegram. Even the revelation of his father's suicide. That he trusted me with such knowledge stole my breath. Perhaps he'd had a change of heart about me — about us — since abruptly declining the dinner at Jewel's house. I could only pray so.

We rounded the corner leading to his house. He stopped. I plowed into the back of him, nearly knocking him flat. Light blazed from every window of his home. Three motorcars sat in the yard. A welcoming party I suspected neither of us wanted.

Chet's focus remained tethered to the house. "I don't know what else to do but go inside. We haven't done anything wrong, you know."

Flames of heat rushed into my face. Had he already forgotten about our kiss? That certainly didn't uphold the standard of conduct expected of a female teacher. And I doubted any school board member would think highly of Chet's involvement, either. Thankfully, Pastor Reynolds wouldn't take the situation to the school board tonight. But he hadn't said that he wouldn't do that come tomorrow. If he did, the reputation I'd worked so hard to establish would be in tatters. Fruity Lu would arise and live forevermore.

Chet lifted my chin with his fingers. I tried to avoid his eyes, but they held me as surely as his arms had in the darkness of the church. "I realize this is all my fault, Lula. I won't let anything happen to your job. I promise."

I knew he meant it, but I also knew he couldn't keep his word. Not about this. It was beyond his control.

"If the school board insists on your removal, I'll . . . I'll . . ." Suddenly, he stooped down on one knee. "Marry me, Lula."

My heart reeled. He didn't mean it. As much as I found I wanted him to, I knew he didn't. And I couldn't decide which felt worse — to be passed over or to be proposed to as an honorable duty. Neither made me feel loved. Wanted. Valuable.

On Christ the solid rock I stand, all other ground is sinking sand.

I tilted my chin upward as the words from the hymn played through my head. The Lord was my hope. I'd made that commitment earlier this evening. Not Chet. Not my own mulish adherence to a plan. If I stood obstinately on anything, it had to be on the rock of His Word. All else would falter, would fail. And yet, I'd trusted my own way so long, could I learn to trust another so quickly — even if the other was God?

I had but a moment to choose. Chet's dark eyes, alive with emotion and concern, drew me. I wanted to let them hold me.

I dare not trust the sweetest frame, but wholly lean on Jesus' name.

Peace settled the flutter inside me. I didn't have to run after something to fill me, as I had after Mama died. I didn't have to make any rash decisions. I could trust God to carry me — and

my sister. "I can't, Chet. I'm sorry."

Disbelief, hurt, and anger flickered over his face. He dropped my hand and stalked toward the house. Standing alone on the newly sprouting grass, I knew Chet would never propose to me again.

I half expected Pastor Reynolds to relieve me of my accompanist duties when I arrived at church early Sunday morning. But he didn't mention school or contracts or clandestine meetings in dark places. His silence gave me the boldness to ask if we could sing the hymn that had been replaying in my head since Friday night, the one that had found its way out of my fingers most of Saturday. The more I heard the words about Christ being my rock, the more I hoped they'd stick in my heart.

Pastor Reynolds gave me the nod to begin. I stumbled through the first two songs, my attention on the back door, watching for Chet and Mrs. Vaughn to arrive. In all the hullabaloo of the Vaughns' house Friday night, Chet and I never had a chance to say good-bye. Or thank you. Or even, I'm sorry.

By the time we reached our third hymn, I'd accepted Chet's absence, though it stung. In the light of day, didn't he recognize his impulsive proposal — and my refusal — for what they were?

The opening notes to "My Hope Is Built" birthed new shoots of faith in my heart, tender, like green sprouts from the dark soil seeking the warm sun. The second verse

rang through the building on a choir of
voices:

When darkness veils His lovely face, I rest
    on His unchanging grace;
In every high and stormy gale, my anchor
    holds within the vale.

The third verse passed, then the fourth.
Each bolstered my spirit, until the final
notes of the chorus churned through every
pore of my body. *All other ground is sinking
sand.*

The sermon in the song stayed with me
all through the service, overpowering even
Pastor Reynolds' carefully crafted words.
After the closing song, I joined Jewel in the
pew, waiting for the crowd to thin before
she navigated her large belly through the
narrow aisle.

"They aren't here."

Jewel patted my hand. "Louise was nearly
sick with worry that night. And they are
grieving. Give them time."

I rested my head on Jewel's shoulder, then
lifted it again. "She told you? Everything?"

Jewel nodded, her eyes sad. "JC, take the
children outside." She pushed to her feet as
they left. "It will take time for them to heal,

but now that the truth's out, maybe they can."

I wet my dry lips. "Even with Clay gone?"

"Louise loves Chet, but I think she's been jealous of him."

"Jealous?"

"He moved forward, didn't stay stuck in his father's past. She couldn't get over it. Clay seemed more willing to live in that place of shame with her."

Shame. I thought of Daddy. All my family. Of the shame they'd endure if the school board ousted me, effectively ending my career as a teacher at any level. Would I be able to move forward after that, leave the past behind? Fear jittered down my spine. "How heartbreaking. For all of them."

Jewel took my arm, waddled toward the door. "Yes, but the Lord is in the business of mending broken hearts. It's His specialty." We stopped at the door. She looked out over the lawn. Then her face brightened. I followed her gaze to Bo — Russell in his arms, Trula and Inez tugging at his hand, JC nearby, frowning but not scowling.

"And has He mended your broken heart, sister?"

A flush broke out over Jewel's rounded face. "Yes, I think He has. Or at least I can say that the process is fully underway."

■ ■ ■ ■

I expected Principal Gray to arrive at my classroom door and order me from the building. First one hour ticked by. Then another. By my third class of the day, I attacked cantata rehearsals full force, assuming I'd be there to see our performance through.

The teachers' lunch table didn't include many male teachers any longer — most of them had gone off to war. Bitsy plopped down beside me. "The games Friday night were so exciting, Lula! But we missed you at the team dinner afterward. The kids had so much fun!"

She continued gushing, the others joining in. What little appetite I had fled. I excused myself, wondering if the conversation would turn to Chet and me in our absence. An uncharitable thought, to be sure, for Bitsy had never been one to gossip, though I didn't know the others as well.

I piddled around my classroom, guessing Chet wouldn't stop by. But when my door clicked open, I whirled in expectation.

My hope plummeted back to earth. Only Nannie, with Blaze following sheepishly behind.

Nannie motioned him forward, hands on her hips in her sassy way. "I told Blaze if he could have you on the bench during the basketball game, he could come himself and let you tutor him in math." She nodded at me, all business.

Blaze's mouth tipped into a wry smile. My lips twitched. No wonder Nannie was besotted with the boy. Sturdy build, flawless features, and natural charm — and he did what she told him to do.

Her expression melted into adoration as she clung to his arm and stared into his face. "Besides, I'd rather be his girlfriend than his teacher."

Blaze blushed to the roots of his hair, returning her love-struck gaze with one of his own. I covered my smile, but needn't have, for they'd ceased to notice me at all. I cleared my throat. They both startled.

"I'd be happy to help you, Blaze." I wanted to ask what had happened with his father after the game, but it felt . . . intrusive.

"And you'd better do what she says," Nannie scolded.

"Yes, ma'am." Blaze grinned down at Nannie, looking for all the world as if he would kiss her then and there.

My mouth warmed with the remembrance of Chet's lips on mine. A pang of regret stabbed. Perhaps I should have accepted his proposal, taken the piece of himself he'd offered.

Stop it! Like the proposal, the kiss was the result of the overwhelming emotion of the moment — of Clay and his mother and the basketball game. I was simply . . . there, looking needy. Maybe his absence now didn't so much reflect the hurt of my refusal but the relief that he hadn't inadvertently tied himself to me for life.

38

Chet

As I paced my classroom, warm air dampened the flesh where my collar circled my neck. Should I seek out Lula? Apologize to her? I'd kissed her. Gotten caught. Put her job in peril. Then spouted off a rash proposal to win her favor.

Yes, most other women — women like Miss Delancey or Miss Morrison — would have jumped at the chance to score a husband. But not Lula. Likely she despised me now for such a heedless, arrogant action. As if marrying me would solve everything. I snorted. No one deserved to be involved in the mess I'd made of things.

And yet I couldn't forget our kiss. The way she'd leaned into it. Didn't resist. The warmth on my neck intensified. I sucked in a breath. I didn't want that to be the last time my lips met hers. Not when for the first time since Pa's death I'd felt . . . at home.

I shook my head, eager to dissipate the images. Even if I risked more time alone with her to apologize, I'd then have to tell her of my enlistment. And the terror of that held my feet fast.

Ma's reaction hadn't been anything like I'd expected. First she'd wailed and locked herself in her room, didn't come out until the sun started its descent on Saturday. Sunday had been even worse. She cajoled, badgered, nagged — this time trying to get me to undo what she'd wanted so badly before.

Then she quit. Went silent. No reproach in her eyes, only sadness. Disappointment.

I couldn't bear the thought of disappointing Lula, too.

Air. I needed fresh air.

Shoving my hands into my pockets, I descended the stairs. I glanced at the stairwell leading to the basement classrooms — to Lula — and hurried past the temptation.

Outdoors, a gentle spring breeze cooled some of my anxiety. I breathed in the clean smell of the new grass, circled the stout trunk of an ancient oak tree, then kicked at a piece of loose bark near the base. Enlisting had seemed the right course in the moment. If only I'd consulted the Lord for confirmation instead of my grieving heart.

What had been done was done. I couldn't fix things with Lula or Ma. But Blaze —

I took a deep breath. Sal had come by on Saturday afternoon and told me Blaze had moved back home that morning. I'd stared, drop-jawed.

"But he —"

Sal chuckled. "Arch couldn't resist coming to watch his boy play ball after all. And when he saw the whole town behind them, Blaze leading the team to the win?" Sal shrugged. "Guess it reminded him to be proud of his son instead of critical. I think he loves the boy, just doesn't know how to show it."

I wanted to hear the whole story from Blaze — about his father and the game. And I needed to congratulate my team on a job well done. Apologize for not being there to witness it. Explain my enlistment, too. Perhaps I owed them that most of all.

Even though the season had ended, I asked the boys' team to join me for a post-game talk that afternoon. I cranked open the windows in the gymnasium, hoping to circulate the freshness of early March after the musty closeness of winter.

But the air felt heavier than before. And scented with rain. I glanced into the sky. Clouds roiled over the gray surface. To the west, the verdant sky edged toward black.

The first spring storm. I cranked the windows closed again and waited for my team to arrive. I'd make my speech quick, send them home before the deluge.

The boys trickled in, most eyeing me with the distrust I knew I deserved. I'd let them down. As a coach. As a man. My chest tightened.

Was this how Pa had felt, sitting alone in a cell? Did he recognize what he'd done — and hate himself for it?

I cleared my throat and ran a hand through my hair as I stood before them. "As many of you have no doubt heard, on Friday afternoon I received word that my older brother, Clay, died in France."

Two boys squirmed, and the rest sat frozen.

"I understand Blaze did a fine job leading you on my behalf."

Blaze's head dropped lower, and his finger scattered the dust on the empty floor beside him. A rumble overhead shook the room. Best get on with what I had to say.

"I'm so proud of y'all. You didn't just go from a losing season to a winning one. You won every single contest. Your tenacity inspired an entire community and even secured a large war bond purchase from the town of Dunn and the promise of a new gymnasium for those who will come behind you — or for some, yourselves, should the war end as quickly as we hope."

Felix looked me in the eye and nodded. The others kept their gazes averted. Blaze stared at the ground.

The outside light dimmed. I couldn't see the boys' faces clearly anymore. Maybe that was best for finishing out my speech.

"Finally, I need to tell you that I won't be around next season."

Several exclamations sounded at once. Blaze's head rose slowly. I held up my hand as thunder grumbled overhead and a flicker of lightning flashed through the windows.

"I've enlisted."

Silence.

"But, Coach —" Felix shot a shocked look toward the rest of the group. Blaze lowered his head.

I clapped Felix on the shoulder. "I'm sure Principal Gray will do everything within his power to find you a good coach for next year."

"Like Miss Bowman?" Glen's question was followed by a few snickers.

My jaw tightened. "Whoever it is, I expect you to give them your best, as you have for me."

Their chorus of "Yes, sir" echoed in the gymnasium.

Another boom of thunder overhead. Another crack of lightning.

I jerked my head toward the door. "Y'all get on home now. Looks like we're in for some rough weather."

The boys gathered their books with solemn faces. I followed them outside, eager to be in our storm cellar should things turn bad, anxious for Ma not to endure the storm alone.

The wind shrieked in through the door when Blaze opened it. Each of us pushed against its force, one step at a time. I clapped a hand over my hat to keep it from flying away. Then Virgil tapped my shoulder, pointed to the sky. We looked up, every one of us. A cloud column rose in the west. How far away, I couldn't rightly say. But too close for comfort. Especially since it seemed to be rotating!

"Get back inside!" I yelled.

No one protested. We slammed the door shut. Barred it closed. Then I led the boys to the basement. We crammed into the custodian's closet, prayer sprinting through my head. For us. For our families. For the entire town of Dunn and those residing in the tents at Camp Doniphan, in case this weather extended there, as well.

Then I cracked the closet door and listened. Rain slapped the windowpanes. The boys sat on the floor, silent. Then the ping of hail on glass.

Blaze stood next to me. "You think it'll be a twister?"

I shook my head. "I wish I knew. If it doesn't get worse in the next few minutes, I'll go up and scout around, but it looked like it was coming right toward us."

As we stared into the darkness, I wondered if Blaze was worried about his pa in the dugout on their land. Did they even have a storm cellar? Of course he'd be worried about Nannie and her family, too, as I was about Ma — and Lula and Jewel and her kids.

"I'll just go up real quick —"

A loud whoosh like a speeding train filled the building, shook the walls. I pushed Blaze back into the closet, slammed the door, and held it closed, the knob biting into my hand, my arms aching with the strain.

Would I ever see Ma again? Or Lula? Would we emerge to a world unscathed or one in which tragedy met us around every corner? I squeezed my eyes shut, started to pray. I thought I was saying the words in my head, but soon discovered I was speaking aloud. Asking God's help. His protection. Several boys mumbled along, sending their own petitions to the Almighty.

And then everything stilled. Including our voices. Leaving only the panting of breath and the beating of hearts in our ears.

My arms relaxed and the door eased open. I glanced down at my wristwatch. What had seemed an hour had been mere minutes. I swallowed hard, praying others in town had seen the signs early enough, found shelter. I poked my head into the hallway. Ceilings and walls remained in place. I motioned the boys out of the closet. We inched up the stairs, bunched like a herd of cattle. Some broken glass crunched underfoot, but I sighed with relief that the building appeared intact.

I pushed open the front door of the school. A few high clouds skated across the blue sky. Branches and leaves littered the ground. The boys broke away, each in the direction of their own homes. Blaze remained at my side.

"You heading out to your place?" I asked.

Blaze shrugged. "After I check on things around here."

Which meant he wanted to be sure Nannie was okay.

"I'll be glad for your company, then." We walked forward in silence.

Half a block later we saw two houses, flat as pancakes.

Our steps slowed.

A motorcar on its side. A bicycle mangled at the base of a tree, one wheel spinning.

I broke into a jog.

Shards of glass. Splintered fences. Downed trees.

I started to run. One block, then another, Blaze keeping pace.

Surely Ma had made it to safety.

Then I saw my Tin Lizzie, half buried in the side of the house.

"Ma!" I ran to the storm cellar, yanked on the door. It flew open, unbolted. I called down into the darkness.

No answer. Only the faraway cry of a baby, the bark of a dog.

"Ma? Are you here?" I climbed over broken boards and mangled metal, and through the hole smashed in the side of the house. I reached the stairs. The structure had been compromised. I screamed for Ma again. I couldn't go up. If Ma were upstairs, she couldn't come down.

I stumbled beyond the dangling front

door, out to the stoop. *Dear God, what do I do now?* A bird chirped as if nothing out of the ordinary had occurred.

The church.

If there was trouble, Ma would go to the church. I sprinted in that direction, noting vaguely that Blaze had vanished. To go to Nannie's house, no doubt. I ran down the block, past pristine houses alongside others that seemed to have endured a stampede of wild horses.

I found the church untouched, the late afternoon sun streaming through the high clouds and surrounding it like a halo.

The door creaked open as usual. I stepped inside. The rush of air flickered the flames of dozens of candles illuminating the room. "Ma?"

Then Lula stood before me, eyes wide, face white. Alive. Unhurt.

I grabbed her shoulders, ready to pull her into my embrace. Her hands clamped over my wrists, held me away. "She's here, Chet. Your mother's here."

She continued on, but the words made little sense in my ears. I only knew she'd told me Ma was alive.

"Hush now. It's all right." Lula's gentle hand stroked my head as her arms circled my body. I clung to her, noticing, finally,

the heaving sobs that pierced the quiet.
Then realizing that terrible noise was me.

39

Lula

Mrs. Vaughn held her son, but her gaze locked on mine.

Thank you, she mouthed. Gratitude from soundless lips that could apply to so many things. Bringing her to the church. Comforting her son. Music shared in the dark sanctuary over the past few months.

"Lula!" Jewel. She sounded calm, but with an edge that pulled me through the commotion of the church to reach her. She grabbed my hands and squeezed, JC hovering near, his face gray with fear. "We were worried sick. I had the children in the storm cellar, but we didn't want to bar the door for fear you'd need to get in. JC held it shut until the wind stopped." She beamed at her son, who seemed to grow two inches with the praise.

"I'm so sorry." I hugged her, then helped her to a pew. "I knew Chet was still at school. I was — I got worried about his mother."

Questions gleamed in Jewel's eye. I refused to acknowledge them, to admit I cared what happened to Chet's mother because I cared about Chet.

Because I loved him.

The thought scraped over my raw heart, igniting a new wave of pain. He was here. In this room. Safe. But I had no claim on him.

I forced my thoughts to the loved ones in front of me. Jewel and JC. I brushed a strand of hair from my face, tucked it beneath a hairpin. "Where are the other children, JC?"

He swallowed, glanced at Jewel. "I couldn't let Mama come here alone. I sent them next door."

I tousled his hair and smiled down at him. "Good job, JC. You took care of everyone."

He huffed out a huge sigh and then grinned, some color returning to his cheeks.

Then Jewel grimaced, her hand skittering over her round stomach. A deep inhale. A slow exhale. I swallowed hard. Oh no. Not here! Not now!

"You ought to be at home." I tried to hoist Jewel to her feet, but she wouldn't budge.

Her face hardened. "I can't." She spoke

through clenched teeth. "Get. Doc. Adams."

JC's eyes grew round and frightened. Mirroring mine, I imagined.

Jewel hissed as she sucked in air. "Now, Lula."

I couldn't move. How would I find the doctor in this chaos? He could be anywhere. A hand seized my arm. I spun around, peered into the face I needed most.

"Ma told me what you did for her, Lula. Thank you." Gratefulness softened Chet's eyes, turning my knees to jelly. I wanted to wilt into his arms, but Jewel's groan snapped my mind back to the moment.

I pointed out the door. He let go, clearly confused. "It's Jewel. I have to find the doctor." Reason fled. I clutched his arm. "Help me. Please."

A guttural cry rose above the squall of voices. Mrs. Vaughn rushed across the sanctuary and knelt beside my sister.

With a hand at the small of my back, Chet propelled me through the curious onlookers. We reached the door, anxious to be free from the crowd. The door opened before I could touch the latch, bringing me nose-to-nose with Miss Morrison. She blinked, her eyes and mouth both round. But as her gaze roamed over my shoulder, she smiled.

"Why, Chet! Fancy finding you here." She

401

stepped forward, forcing me back. But I had nowhere to go. Chet remained rooted to the ground behind me.

"Did you come to help?" Chet's voice sounded friendly, but I could hear the edge, the same tightness it had when his team didn't do as he'd instructed.

"Of course! Isn't this just awful?" She skirted around me, tried to take Chet's arm.

"Good. They need help. Now if you'll excuse us." Chet urged me into the gold-washed world. I looked for his automobile, couldn't find it in the cluster of cars near the church.

"It's buried in my house," he said, as if reading my mind. His pace increased. I tried to keep up, taking two steps to his every one, worrying about Jewel with every heart-beat. I glanced back at the church. Miss Morrison stood in the yard, arms crossed, watching us go.

When we arrived at Doc Adams' house, my lungs struggled to draw air. Chet was barely winded. No visible damage here, but no occupants, either. A window opened next door and a gray-haired woman poked out her head.

"He's over on Tenth Street. A boy hit with flying debris."

Chet sprinted away. I flew after him, a

hand at my side trying to stop the pain that skewered with every breath. We reached Tenth Street. Doc Adams had departed. Needed over near Mifflin Avenue, someone said.

Exhaustion, frustration, and fear swirled into a wail. I leaned against the porch railing of the house where we'd stopped.

Chet's hands cupped my face. "We'll find him, Lula. We *will*."

I nodded in spite of my tears, my fears.

On Christ the solid rock I stand.

I grabbed his hand. "Pray," I breathed.

And he did. "We need direction, God. Help us to know where to go, what to do." Chet spoke as if God stood at his side. I almost expected to hear an audible answer. Though no voice replied, the solidness of Chet's faith anchored my own.

Twenty minutes later, Chet rushed back into the church, Russell in one arm, Inez in the other. I followed, Trula grasping my hand so as not to get left behind.

I pried her fingers from mine and attached them to Chet's suit coat. "Wait here," I whispered before sweeping past Miss Morrison, nearly knocking her flat. Why was that woman always in my way?

Outside Pastor Reynolds' office, low

voices murmured through the closed door. A long grunt. Quiet. Then the piercing wail of a disgruntled babe.

I leaned my head against the door, tears of relief and joy and sorrow mingling on my cheeks. *Thank you, Lord. Thank you for my —*

My head popped up. *Niece or nephew?*

Without a sound, I slipped into the room. Jewel lay limp on a pallet on the floor, Doc Adams attending her. Mrs. Vaughn scooped water from a basin over the squirming, screaming ball of flesh. "It's another girl. And she's beautiful."

She wrapped the child in an old shirt before placing her in Jewel's arms.

"Davina." Jewel stroked the pink cheek with the back of her fingers. A tear slid down her face and baptized the fuzz on her daughter's head. She smiled, wiped the place dry.

"Is she — ?"

Doc Adams patted my shoulder, eyes still on baby and mother. "A little on the small side, but she looks fine."

I knelt beside Jewel and my new niece, pushed back the sweat-soaked hair around my sister's face. I couldn't utter a word. My heart was too full. Missing Mama and Daddy. Missing Davy. How much more did Jewel ache with their absence?

404

Jewel laced her fingers through mine. "JC told me to stay put while he went to find you, but I didn't listen. Imagine that." She smiled wryly in my direction before she gazed at her baby again. I wanted to laugh. Jewel had never been the obstinate one. That had been my role, and I'd played it better than any starlet of stage and screen.

She took a jagged breath. "I'd never have forgiven myself if stubbornness would have cost me this child." Jewel's attention returned to me, eyes brimming with tears.

A loud, familiar voice came from the front the sanctuary. "Where? Where is she?"

One look in Jewel's eyes and I knew what she wanted me to do. I sprang to my feet, quickly reaching the sanctuary, where Bo was turning circles in the aisle, eyes wild. I grabbed his arms, shook him still.

"Bo. Listen to me. She's here. She's all right."

He calmed, finally seemed to see me. "She's all right?"

I nodded. "The baby, too."

Doc Adams answered our timid knock at the door. I led my nieces and nephews to their mother's side, their eyes wide with wonder and a bit of fear. Bo held back, as if unsure of his reception. I nudged him forward. Jewel propped the baby up a little.

Russell reached. Bo grasped his little hand, guided it gently to Davina's head. Inez popped her thumb in her mouth and pressed into Bo's side. Trula cooed to her sleeping sister while JC's grin encompassed them all.

Then Bo's focus moved from the baby to Jewel.

I leaned against the wall. The love shining from Bo's eyes left me breathless. Mrs. Vaughn and the doctor had vanished altogether. I ought to leave, too, but the scene held me captive. What would it feel like to have a man look at me that way? To have Chet look at me that way? With such obvious devotion.

And like a flash of light in a dark sky, I realized Jewel didn't need me anymore. Nor did JC, Trula, Inez, or Russell. At least not in the same way as before. I wrapped my arms across my chest. It was what I'd wanted — to be released to go back to my old life. To resume my course to make something of myself. To make Daddy proud. But like the tornado through the streets of Dunn, these past few months had broken apart the life I'd so carefully constructed. Splattered it to the ground.

For the first time, I asked myself what Lula Bowman really wanted.

Bo and I corralled the children while Mrs. Vaughn — Louise, as she'd insisted I call her — cooed over Davina and fussed over Jewel. "I'll take good care of them until the doctor says they can be moved home again."

And I knew she would.

I spied Chet near the pulpit, passing out quilts to the displaced — like himself — to bed down in the church. Sarah Morrison smiled at his side. He reached to take a quilt from her hands. Their eyes met and held. Inez tugged at me. I lifted her into my arms, my focus stuck to Chet and Miss Morrison. Her whispered words, his low chuckle. My heart lurched. Had I waited too long to admit even to myself my true feelings for Chet?

He turned his head, looked straight at me. I let my gaze fall from his, peered into Inez's small face. "Let's go home, sweetheart."

Bo drove the children and me home, dodging tree limbs and other debris strewn across the streets. At Jewel's house, a few shingles from the roof littered the yard. I thanked Bo, grateful for his help, his presence, but wanting him away, needing to be alone.

"I'll check in when I'm able," he said before motoring off.

Inside, I fumbled for candles and matches, finally acquiring enough light for us to mount the stairs without mishap. Exhaustion tugged at my limbs, but once the children were asleep beneath their blankets, I couldn't keep my mind still. Too many thoughts of Jewel and Bo. Of Louise and Chet. Of all I'd thought and seen and experienced in a few short hours that felt years long.

I cleaned the kitchen by candlelight, then curled on the sofa with one of Jewel's dime novels. Anything to distract me from a pair of dark eyes in a striking face — and the heart of compassion that beat beneath the broad chest. We'd been friends because of basketball. Because of Nannie and Blaze. I'd been the one to stop it there — at friendship. But now I wanted so much more.

A gentle tap startled me. Or had it been my imagination? I held my breath, listening. One of the children must have slipped out of bed to use the chamber pot. Or maybe the wind had blown a branch over rough ground.

I returned to my book, senses heightened. One sentence later, the plink of an object against glass gained my attention. I lit a larger candle and crossed to the foyer, cracking open the front door.

Soft footfalls over dead grass pulled my attention to the left. The flicker of candle-light caught Chet's face.

My heart skipped a beat. Had something happened to Jewel? To the baby? I sucked in a breath. He mounted the porch. "There's something I need to tell you."

"What is it?" I whispered, afraid of the answer, afraid of breaking the fragile connection between us.

"May I come in?"

My gaze swept over the yard, the street. I opened the door wide. "I'll put on some coffee."

I slipped into the kitchen, stirred the coals in the stove, and set the coffee pot to boil. If only I could read his face more clearly than in the dim light of a single flame. And yet I was glad he couldn't decipher mine. Desire to give in to my feelings for him swayed me like a sapling in a strong wind. And then I remembered I didn't have to hold myself upright.

Be near, Lord Jesus. My hope is built on nothing less.

The ground seemed to settle beneath my feet even though my heart pattered at a faster gait. *Boil, pot. Boil.*

I felt his presence, but refused to turn.

"I came tonight, Lula, because I thought you ought to know — and I didn't want you to hear it from anyone else."

Miss Morrison. The pounding in my chest rose into my ears. My hands trembled. Another moment of silence and I feared I'd fly apart. A deep breath. A slow turn.

His gaze met mine. "I've enlisted."

40

Chet

Lula's eyes squeezed shut. Then the hush between us stretched long and heavy, like one of Ma's quilts on washing day. The smother of it made me wonder if I'd misread everything, if she had cared for me at all.

"It won't matter much to you, I know," I mumbled.

Her eyes flashed to mine, as angry as the bubbling from the range behind her. The bitter smell of burnt coffee billowed into the room. I wrapped a towel around my hand and pulled the pot from burner to warming shelf as I searched for something to say.

How could I ask for the right to hold her — to love her — for the rest of my life? I'd forfeited any thought of that when I enlisted. I'd leave Dunn sooner than she would, and with no certainty of return. My jaw tightened. My fingers clenched and then flexed.

Even if I thought she loved me, I couldn't tie her to a dead man.

"Thank you for taking care of Ma. She's very grateful for your —"

A knock sounded, and Lula started for the door. I picked up the candle and followed, stopped short when the light in my hand fell on Mr. Morrison and Principal Gray.

Principal Gray's eyes locked on mine. My mouth went dry. Lula and I alone. In her house. At night. But this time, the witness wasn't Pastor Reynolds, willing to believe the best of us. This was Mr. Morrison, school board member. Father of the girl who'd taken up Miss Delancey's abandoned pursuit. The one batting her eyes and trying to help. Listening to my conversation with Ma and making sure word got to her father. And quick.

I stepped in front of Lula. "I can explain everything."

Principal Gray's gaze slid to the floor. He cleared his throat, pinched the crease in his hat. "We cannot have any appearance of impropriety among our teaching staff. You understand."

"But the children are upstairs," Lula whispered as her hands wrung in front of her.

"Miss Bowman, you are in breach of your teaching contract. You've been relieved of your duties. Please do not report to school again."

A tear slipped down Lula's pale cheek. Anger twisted inside me like the tower of cloud earlier that afternoon. Sarah Morrison had a powerful father and plenty of money. She didn't lack for admirers. So why, like Miss Delancey, had she set her sights on me for a husband? Why ruin my chance at happiness?

She'd done more than play havoc with my heart. She'd cost Lula her job. Not just this one, every one. Lula had already sacrificed that mathematics prize to take care of Jewel. Now, because of me, the rest of her dreams had been ground to dust, too.

I thrust the candle into Lula's hands, led Principal Gray and Mr. Morrison onto the porch, and shut the door behind us. "You can't do this. It's not right. There is nothing —"

"This isn't about you, Mr. Vaughn. Not yet." Mr. Morrison's finger wagged in my face. Then he jogged down the steps and walked away.

I gripped the porch railing, almost sure I could snap it in half. I'd been the one who compromised her reputation. Why shouldn't this be about me?

Principal Gray set his hat on his head. "I'm sorry, Chet." He glanced at the closed door. "For both of you." He left more slowly, as if weighted by the burden of what he'd been asked to do.

I slumped against the house. Then I paced across the porch twice, a low growl in my throat. Lula didn't deserve this. I had to explain, to apologize. But as my hand connected with the door knob, the bolt shifted and clicked into place and the light from the window vanished to black.

Principal Gray would not be moved. His hands were tied, he said, by the school board. But I knew he meant by Mr. Morrison.

Two days later, with electric service restored and much of the damage cleaned up, school resumed. I kept to my classroom, not wanting to cross any path that would remind me of Lula. Like I needed any reminders.

In the late afternoon, I stood in front of the shell of our house. With the help of a horse and wagon from the livery stable, my Tin Lizzie had been towed out of the wall. I walked around my auto, noting the dings and dents on the frame before trying to crank it to life. The engine sputtered and coughed, but eventually resurrected. If only my heart would do the same.

I steered it out of the yard and parked on the street. I'd drive it to Pastor Reynolds' house later, grateful for his offer of a place to stay for Ma and me until we could make other arrangements.

My stomach twisted as I climbed out of the car, set a foot on the running board, and rested my arms on the dimpled leather roof. All my life I'd believed that God could — and would — bring beauty from ashes. But since the day the telegram about Clay had arrived, the ashes had been piling higher than my faith.

After salvaging a few of our personal items, I motored through streets swept clean, only an occasional felled tree or boarded up window left as reminders of the power of the storm. The motorcar bounced into the grassy place between the parsonage and the church. With the engine silent, I prayed for Ma to be willing to consider a new type of living situation, like a room in a boardinghouse where there would be people around her. Where she'd have to remain engaged in life, no matter what happened to me. And she wouldn't need to worry over the little things to be maintained in a house.

The storm insurance would more than cover her expenses, especially in conjunction with my army pay.

I climbed from my car. Piano music bled through the walls and windows of the church. My heart twisted. Lula? I crept closer to the building, trying to place the tune, familiar and yet not quite right. Slower than usual, maybe? I pressed my ear to a smooth board, humming until the words and music connected in my head.

> The light in your eyes makes the bright
> stars grow pale,
> They're jealous as jealous can be;
> But one word or sign tells them all you are
> mine —

A crash of notes. I cringed, stepped backward. Then the music began again. More timid this time. Hesitant.

Then stronger. Louder. But not the same song as before.

A voice joined the chords, sure and strong. " 'On Christ the solid rock I stand, all other ground is sinking sand. All other ground is sinking sand.' "

I hung my head. Lula might have enough faith to believe that, but I'd sunk so far in the sand I expected it to close over my head and bury me at any moment.

There'd been no service for Clay. Not with the chaos of the tornado and my enlistment. A few days later, after a physical examination, I boarded the train for Kansas, like Pa had. I only hoped I'd acquit myself more honorably. Make Ma proud and honor Clay's short service. Blaze moped at the news. I didn't blame him, after the way I'd pushed him toward graduation and then abandoned him before it arrived. But at least he and Archie seemed to have found a mutual truce on the matter, for Blaze was still attending school every day.

Ma had taken my suggestion about the boardinghouse surprisingly well. So well it alarmed me. She settled into two rooms at Mrs. Morton's while I stayed the final few days with Pastor Reynolds and his family. I'd seen Lula only at church, her face drawn, her dresses hanging on a slimmer form. I didn't approach her, and she steered clear of me.

Once I arrived at Fort Riley, I didn't have time to think. I received my uniform, a blanket, even underwear, all government issue. A shaving kit and some hard tack. A rifle and bayonet, as well.

My waking hours belonged to the army.

417

And that was fine by me. Better to put those I'd left behind out of mind. Focus on the task at hand. Most days, that worked. Other times, like during guard duty or kitchen duty, my mind drifted home. I tried to focus those thoughts on Ma, but a pair of dark, serious eyes intruded far too often and stayed far too long. I'd come to Fort Riley hoping to escape all my feelings for Lula. I hadn't imagined they'd intensify.

My first seven-day pass came four weeks after my arrival. Clay hadn't used his to come home, and Ma had felt the slight. Besides, Ma's last letter had mentioned Lula was still in town. Could I find the courage to admit my love to her? If not, how would I find the strength to do what had to be done in the trenches?

I plunked down my money and boarded the train to Oklahoma.

41

Lula

"Why don't you sit down and play something? You're as unsettled as Davina tonight." Jewel cradled the squalling baby in her arms and swung her back and forth. I fought down a sob, wishing someone would attempt to soothe my irascible spirit. But no remedy would suffice.

I wandered the small room, adjusting knickknacks, picking lint from the rug, straightening the crocheted doilies that covered every surface. Five weeks since I'd been fired. Five weeks without a paycheck. At least Don and Janice had believed me instead of the school board. They'd each offered to help with the bills for a while, and Bo was providing money, as well.

But what was I to do now? I wouldn't be able to get another teaching job, so more schooling would do me no good. Bo would take on a family of six in the near future.

He didn't need a spinster sister-in-law added to that. Janice and Don had full households, as well. And Daddy — we all agreed not to tell Daddy. As the light of his life faded with each passing day, it seemed best to let him go in peace, believing I would return to the university and fulfill our dream. His dream.

At least Pastor Reynolds had kept me on as church pianist, in spite of the murmured dissent. But playing in front of the congregation had become a trial of my will again instead of a pleasure.

I trailed a finger across the top of Jewel's piano but couldn't settle at the keys. The curtains billowed out with the spring breeze and twilight bathed the room in a gentle glow. JC turned on the gramophone. The kids sang and danced, no doubt remembering times when their daddy had joined them. But Bo would make new memories with them now, help ease the pain of missing Davy. I prayed his quiet love would hold the same healing balm for Jewel.

My sister smiled at me from the sofa, but her eyes remained sad. "Chet leaves again in the morning, you know."

I plopped down beside her, rubbed the fuzz on Davina's head, and ignored her words.

"You never told him, did you?"

Fire burst into my cheeks as I glanced up at her, thankful for the music and the kids' commotion to cover our conversation. "Tell who what?"

"Chet. You let him go away to the army without telling him you cared."

A stray thread on the sofa caught my attention. I picked at it, tried to break it at the base. But it wouldn't budge. I'd given myself to Chet's game of basketball, to his kiss, to his mother's safety without thought of my own. In return, he gave me Fruity Lu. Unable to finish out the year of school. Unable to continue her education. He hadn't spoken to me since the day Mr. Morrison and Principal Gray had come to Jewel's house.

Davina's mewl turned to hiccups. I eased her out of Jewel's arms and cuddled my niece close, her head resting in the crook where my neck met my shoulder.

If only I'd let him back in the house. If only he'd later sought me out to apologize. "I guess he couldn't see how I felt —"

Jewel snorted, then giggled, then shook with laughter. "If I'd waited until Davy 'saw how I felt,' I'd still be a spinster waiting for him to propose."

My eyes stretched wide.

"Oh, Lula! I loved that man to distraction, but he wouldn't have recognized it unless I'd helped him along a bit."

My mouth dropped open. "You mean you flirted?"

Jewel shrugged, her eyes downcast. "Some might call it that, but I was never coy or evasive. I simply put myself in his path and let him know he had my heart. Not in words, you understand. In a look. A touch of the hand. A preference for his company over that of my girlfriends."

I poked my finger in Davina's mouth to quiet her. I'd assumed Davy had simply fallen for Jewel, declared his love, and she'd responded. This information turned everything on its head. "But you didn't do all that with Bo."

Her expression softened, almost as if warding off pain. "No, it was different with Bo. He knew my heart before I did." Pink scattered across her cheeks before her arm cradled my shoulders as gently as she'd cradled Davina. "Don't miss this, Lula. Not even for the satisfaction of saving your pride."

I'd seen Miss Morrison wave a letter he'd written her from camp a couple of weeks ago. Likely he'd seen her while he was home. The humiliation still stung. I had no job, no scholarship, no school money. If I demonstrated my feelings for him now, would he think my affections were tied to desperation? Would he once again try to do the honorable thing without attention to his heart? If a dutiful marriage was my most hopeful future, I'd take my chances on being alone.

I let Trula swing me in a circle to "Livery Stable Blues," losing myself in the music I'd once disdained. If these months had taught me anything it was that music — all music — fed my soul in a way nothing else did. Not even numbers. At least I'd always have that, even if I had nothing else.

A banging at the front door drew Jewel into the hall. I didn't think Bo'd get another pass for a week or so, but he had a way of sweet-talking his superior officers to get leave.

"Lula?" Jewel called. I ceased spinning, trying to catch my breath and still the dizziness, holding together the knot of hair at the nape of my neck that threatened to unfurl in a mass of tangles down my back.

Chet stepped into the room, clad in khaki, a wide-brimmed hat beneath one arm. I reached for the back of a chair.

"Come, children. We'll have some bread

423

and butter in the kitchen." Jewel shooed her brood away, leaving the room void of distraction, except for the scratch of the needle at the end of the recording.

My eyes followed Chet across the room as he silenced the noise. He looked different. Taller somehow. More serious, if possible.

He took my hand and led me to the sofa. My heart drummed behind my chest as the temperature in the room rose to midsummer. I wanted a fan, a sliver of ice, a glass of tea. His presence held me motionless and sent every thought fleeing from my head. I couldn't even recall Jewel's advice.

He cleared his throat, studied my fingers resting against his palm. "How are you, Lula?"

I wet my lips. "Fine. And you?" My voice squeaked a little. I winced.

The quiet *tick-tock* of the mantel clock filled the room. He cleared his throat again. "I came home on a seven-day pass." He looked at me as if needing an answer.

I swallowed, thrashed about in my mind for something to say. "That's nice."

His gaze returned to my hand, his expression squeezing and pinching. And then the realization hit: He was shipping out. His mother would be alone. It troubled him.

Louise and I had come to understand

each other as she sat listening to my reluctant performances, even before I realized who she was. Over the weeks Chet had been gone, I'd been dropping by the boardinghouse and escorting her to my practices at the church. It had seemed to assuage some of her loneliness, some of her fear. Likely Chet wanted to know if I'd continue to care for his mother. Which, of course, I would. Even if he couldn't return my feelings for him, I could soften his one regret.

I cradled his hand between both of mine. "You don't have to worry about your mother while you're gone. I'll watch out for her."

On Christ the solid rock I stand, all other ground is sinking sand.

That Rock would hold me firm, even if everything else my heart desired washed away in the storm.

42

Chet

My head jerked up. I stared at Lula as if seeing her for the first time. And perhaps I was. I'd come to offer her my heart. Haltingly. Fearfully. Instead, she'd seen my deepest need and met it, without reservation or condition.

Ma was right. I'd never find another girl like Lula. I could shut away my feelings for her until I returned, safe and sound, from the Western Front, or I could trust that God would hold us secure.

Her slender fingers still covered my hand, making no move to let go. I needed to see those strong hands in motion, hear what they would say to my heart. I cleared my throat. "Play for me once more?"

Her delicate eyebrows dipped as she frowned. But she rose, set herself at the piano, and ran through a quick chorus of something. It didn't matter. I simply needed her music to give me courage.

I stood at the piano, facing her, as her hands stilled. "I don't want to go," I said.

Her dark eyes glistened before her gaze slid to the floor near my feet and her hands rested in her lap. "I know. But you'll be fine. And so will your mother, and even Blaze. I'll keep after him until graduation." Her voice hitched on the final word.

My fingers found the soft skin beneath her chin. I guided her head up, willing her eyes to meet mine. "I'm not worried about all of them. I don't want to leave *you*."

Her lips parted in a gasp. The pools in her eyes expanded, overflowed. I pulled her to her feet, held her face between my hands, caught the trails of tears with my thumbs. "I'm sorry. I should have sought you out after . . . after Principal Gray came. I should have made them see it was all my fault. I told myself you'd never want to see me again. Can you forgive me for being a coward?"

Her head dipped forward. I pulled her closer, my face inches from hers. "I know I did this wrong the first time. I was thoughtless and frantic and just . . . dumb."

Her mouth curved in a slow grin as she leaned her cheek into my hand, then turned her face until her lips met my palm. I sucked in air but couldn't find my voice.

"I can't bear to see you leave, and yet you must go, mustn't you?" She brushed my cheek with her fingertips, sending bolts of electricity from my head to my toes.

I smoothed her silky hair away from her face, memorized the color of her eyes, the slope of her nose, the shape of her mouth. The smooth, round jaw. Dark eyebrows and hair against ivory skin. I dropped to one knee. "Could you, Lula? Would you marry me?"

Her hand covered her mouth. My heart sank. Had I done it wrong again? But then she looked at me, her eyes soft with understanding. "Oh, Chet. I never thought you'd ask again. Yes, I'll marry you!"

I locked her tight in my arms, her tears wetting the front of my uniform.

Clamoring whispers, loud hushes. I peered over Lula's shoulder. Jewel peeked into the room, Russell on her hip. Her eyebrows arched in question. I nudged Lula. She turned, flew from my side into the arms of her sister.

Moments later, the room teemed with people. Jewel and the children. Ma, hustling in behind them, folding Lula into her embrace. Even Blaze and Nannie, hands clasped, faces bright.

Those who loved us, who loved one another, all gathered around. Ma and I had lost both Pa and Clay, but oh, how much God had given to us in return.

The next morning, Lula and I stood on the train platform, a bit of a chill in the early April morning. Smoke puffed in small clouds from the stack on the train's engine. When the whistle blew, we would have to say good-bye.

Ma stood rigid, but calm, as if willing herself not to cry. Jewel tried to keep the children from darting onto the tracks. Nannie flitted from person to person, Blaze in tow, enjoying the drama, I supposed. And Lula clung to my hand, pressed close to my side.

I looked down at our intertwined fingers. "I'm sure someone will report this to Principal Gray," I said with mock severity. As if any more damage could be done. And yet, without all the adversity, maybe Lula and I wouldn't be standing like this at all. We'd still be separate, each pining for the thing we thought out of reach.

Lula glanced across the platform and tightened her grip.

Principal Gray strode toward us. "Chet. Miss Bowman." His gaze wandered to our clasped hands and he grinned. "We'll miss you, Chet. *I'll* miss you. But maybe we'll have the Huns put in their place in time for you to lead our basketball team next season."

"We can certainly pray so." I shook his hand.

He cleared his throat and turned his attention to Lula. "Miss Bowman, I'm glad you're here, too. I've talked to the school board and explained to them that I'm in a precarious position with so many men joining up. I need a full staff next year. A staff of good, experienced teachers. It took some talking, but they finally listened. And understood."

Lula lifted her chin. "What are you saying, Principal Gray? Are you offering me my job back?"

"Not exactly."

Lula seemed to shrivel. I wanted to slug the man. "Now look here —"

Principal Gray held up his hands and chuckled. "Hold your horses, son. I said I wasn't offering her *her* job back. Instead, I'm offering her yours."

"My job?" I swung my head toward Lula. Her mouth hung open. I chuckled. Who knew that by leaving I'd give her exactly what she'd wanted all along? At least in part.

"Yes, your job. Until you return from doing your duty."

Lula bit her lip and looked at me. I nodded. She dipped her head in Principal Gray's direction. "I'd be more than happy to step into Chet — Mr. Vaughn's place."

Principal Gray's eyebrows lowered playfully. "As long as you can assure us you will stick to the terms of your contract, of course."

Lula grinned and pressed her shoulder into mine. "As soon as my betrothed boards this train, there will be no other men in my life, Mr. Gray. Except my nephews, of course. And my brother-in-law to be. And Blaze Clifton, when he needs help with mathematics."

Principal Gray's laughter rang in the morning air. He slapped me on the shoulder. I joined the merriment.

"Miss Bowman, that is just the answer I'll give to anyone who questions your situation, for I would sorely hate to lose two good teachers at once."

"Thank you, sir." Lula rested her cheek against my arm as the train whistle ended the conversation.

Principal Gray shook my hand again and walked away. I hugged Ma, Jewel, and the children.

Blaze mumbled good-bye, hands in his pockets, eyes on the ground.

I clapped him on the shoulder. "I'm counting on you, Blaze."

He looked at me.

I leaned in. "I expect you'll keep an eye on Ma and Miss Bowman. And I'll see your diploma when I get back."

He grinned and saluted. "Yes, sir."

The iron horse behind us belched steam. I pulled Lula away from the others.

"Don't say good-bye," she whispered. "I can't bear it."

"I'll be back before you know it. Until then, I expect you'll hold your own."

She pressed her forehead to my chest, then raised her face to mine. I rubbed my thumb across her damp cheek.

"I love you, Chet Vaughn. Come home to me soon."

I leaned toward her, the wide, flat brim of my campaign hat shielding us from the view of the world.

EPILOGUE

Lula

The rubber soles of boys' shoes slid on the wood floor, providing high-pitched squeaks to balance out the bass-clef thud of the basketball on the ground. They took some getting used to, these new Converse All Stars. But Felix and the other boys insisted the canvas sneakers that rose over their ankles helped their game.

A whistle shrieked. The referee called a foul, declaring a free trial for goal. William, a new student, stepped to the free throw line. He rarely missed, often giving us an edge.

Play resumed. With little to do on the bench, my gaze roamed the room, and my heart swelled. Despite the fact that we were no longer promising to buy war bonds with the price of admission, or that a new gym would be built if the team delivered an undefeated season, the town of Dunn had embraced basketball like a lover back from war. The stands were packed, and the school board had been besieged with requests to see the plan for the new gymnasium, folks wanting it to be a structure that rivaled the best the state of Oklahoma currently had to offer.

Brian Giles smiled at me from the bleachers, Bitsy nestled beneath his arm, a small bulge showing at her belly. He'd been sent home with a limp in the summer of 1918, not long after Chet shipped out for Europe. He'd married Bitsy a month later, and when the school year began, he'd resumed coaching the girls' basketball team.

I'd tried to insist he take the boys' program instead, but he and Principal Gray wouldn't hear of it. *"You're the one the boys want,"* they both told me.

I leaned back against the wall and sighed at the sight of Bo and JC sitting together, both intent on the game and comfortable with each other. With a bit of cajoling, Bo had managed to stay at Fort Sill to train troops rather than march into France with them.

A flash of khaki in the crowd quickened my pulse and pulled me from my repose. Then I remembered Chet wouldn't come home in uniform. I leaned forward, elbows on my knees. His company would arrive in the States soon. He'd be cashed out and on his way home. *"I won't take the time to write,"* he'd told me. *"I just want to get on my way."*

My lips twitched in amusement as the boys executed the play Blaze had devised — a fake to the right wing while the left wing ran beneath the basket, took the ball, and shot.

Two more points. A comfortable lead.

Chet wanted to surprise me with the moment of his homecoming. But I had a surprise for him, too. A letter beneath my pillow at Jewel's house. From Professor Clayton. Assuring me there would be a place in post-graduate studies for both me and my husband.

So many dreams Chet and I had disclosed in letters. The small stipend left in Daddy's will for my wedding day gave us options we wouldn't otherwise have had. Dreams for us both that would have made Daddy smile — and that felt like the right answer to me, too. If only Chet would get home.

Gerald stood in the center of the court, opposite the other team's center, both of them with one hand behind their back. The ball flew into the air. Then the whistle, signaling them to jump. A grunt and a slap, the ball in Felix's hands once more.

The timekeeper put the whistle in his mouth, eyes on his timepiece. Another season almost over. I'd so wanted Chet to see them play at least once.

The referee signaled the end of the game. I rose from the bench, turned.

Nannie rushed across the court as the boys shook hands. "Blaze gets leave in two weeks!" She shook a paper in front of my face. I laughed, hugged her, and wished I was as sure when Chet would arrive.

The boys gathered round. I'd grown used to the after-game odor now. The smell of a job well done. A goal accomplished.

"I'm pleased with our season, boys, though I had hoped —"

Ten pairs of eyes stared over my head. I twisted. My heart leapt into my throat.

"Nice evening to take in a basketball game." Chet, hands in his pockets, rocking up on his toes, a grin stretched across his handsome face. I searched for any sign of illness, of injury, but he looked much as he had when he'd boarded the train all those months ago. Only the shadows under his eyes were new. I hoped they'd be cured by sleep.

Peace drifted down like a late-spring snow, cooling my soul. At least until Chet's hand captured mine.

"Aren't you happy to see me, Fruity Lu?"

The name that had once so riled me now brought a sweet thrill. He trailed his thumb across my cheek. Fire blazed a trail over my skin and through my heart, then smoldered back at me in his eyes.

A long-forgotten voice rose from my memory. *"Couldn't you find a man who would have you, Miss Bowman?"*

I smiled, rested my head on Chet's chest. Broader now. Stronger. His arms wrapped around me, pulled me close.

No, Mr. Graham. I couldn't find a man. But I came to find my hope in God, and He gave me someone exponentially greater than anything I'd ever imagined.

"Let's go home, Mr. Vaughn." I curled my hand around his arm and started for the door. "We have a wedding to plan."

A NOTE FROM THE AUTHOR

What a fun book to write! The kernel of this story started as bits of two stories, one from each of my grandmothers. One grandmother, upon taking a teaching job at a high school, was also put in charge of the girls' basketball team even though she knew little to nothing about basketball! (This is also my grandmother whose nickname was, indeed, Fruity Lu!) The other grandmother told me the story of the girls playing a game of basketball with pins in their shoes to stick the other team! Combine that history with a long line of teachers behind me, years of sitting on bleachers watching games, and a son who hopes to coach basketball, and a story appeared. Interestingly enough, another story thread also runs in my family: My youngest son is an accomplished pianist.

As with each book, there are many who have contributed to the final product. My amazing editors at Bethany House get tons of credit for seeing flaws in the story and characters that I couldn't see. Their suggestions make the story stronger every single time. And then there is the rest of the staff at Bethany House — art, marketing, and everyone in between. I am so very grateful for your time and attention to this project and your kindness to me.

As usual, I have had a team of pray-ers to get me through long days of researching, writing, and revising. Thank you, Jeff, Elizabeth, Aaron, Nathan, Ann, Don, Debra, Kirby, Dan, Jennifer, Dawn, Billy, Robin, Bill, Mary D., Leslie, Andrea, Jana, Becky B., Becky H., Cheryl, Cherryl, Jill, and Mary L. Your sacrifice of time on my behalf is a gift I am humbled to receive.

Thank you to Life Sentence: Mary De-Muth and Leslie Wilson. You continually encourage me to make my stories better. You are awesome editors!

To my kids, who put up with me and my frenzy of work — thank you! You are all amazing young adults. I love being your mom even more than being an author. And of course to my sweet husband, who supports and encourages and puts up with my craziness (and a dirty house and unimaginative dinners!). Every day I think I can't love you any more than I do, but then the next day, that love grows deeper.

Finally, as always, the glory goes to God and God alone. Without Him, I have nothing good in me to pour onto a page. I am so grateful for the work He started in me so many years ago and that He is faithful to see it through to completion. I continue to be humbled and amazed.

ABOUT THE AUTHOR

Anne Mateer has a passion for history and historical fiction, and her vacations often revolve around research trips in different parts of the country. She and her husband live near Dallas, Texas, and are the parents of three young adults.

For more information about Anne and her books, please visit her website and blog at www.annemateer.com.

The employees of Thorndike Press hope you have enjoyed this Large Print book. All our Thorndike, Wheeler, and Kennebec Large Print titles are designed for easy reading, and all our books are made to last. Other Thorndike Press Large Print books are available at your library, through selected bookstores, or directly from us.

For information about titles, please call:
   (800) 223-1244

or visit our Web site at:
   http://gale.cengage.com/thorndike

To share your comments, please write:
   Publisher
   Thorndike Press
   10 Water St., Suite 310
   Waterville, ME 04901